FRASER VALLEY REGIONAL LIBRARY

D0486522

A Touch
of Scarlet

Also by Eve Marie Mont

A Breath of Eyre

A Touch
of Scarlet

Eve Marie Mont

KENSINGTON PUBLISHING CORP.
www.kensingtonbooks.com

K TEEN BOOKS are published by

Kensington Publishing Corp.
119 West 40th Street
New York, NY 10018

Copyright © 2013 by Eve Marie Mont

All rights reserved. No part of this book may be reproduced in any form or by any means without the prior written consent of the Publisher, excepting brief quotes used in reviews.

All Kensington titles, imprints, and distributed lines are available at special quantity discounts for bulk purchases for sales promotion, premiums, fund-raising, and educational or institutional use.

Special book excerpts or customized printings can also be created to fit specific needs. For details, write or phone the office of the Kensington Special Sales Manager: Kensington Publishing Corp., 119 West 40th Street, New York, NY 10018. Attn. Special Sales Department. Phone: 1-800-221-2647.

Kensington and the K logo Reg. U.S. Pat. & TM Off.
K Teen is a trademark of Kensington Publishing Corp.

ISBN-13: 978-0-7582-6949-2
ISBN-10: 0-7582-6949-8

First Kensington Trade Paperback Printing: April 2013
10 9 8 7 6 5 4 3 2 1

Printed in the United States of America

For my mom and dad, lifelong teachers whose greatest lessons—tolerance, empathy, and kindness— were taught at home

ACKNOWLEDGMENTS

When I began writing *A Touch of Scarlet* back in 2011, I had no idea what a long and harrowing journey it was going to be. One reason is that the book is a sequel, and sequels are notoriously dastardly for authors. Another reason is that the book is inspired by *The Scarlet Letter,* a nineteenth-century novel about a woman scorned by her Puritanical society and forced to live in exile—not exactly crowd-pleasing material. Reading it in high school had been a chore; Hawthorne's writing is difficult, and the story itself is relentlessly dark. But Hester Prynne is the shining beacon throughout, a character known for her strength, integrity, passion, and resilience. I knew Hester was the perfect role model for Emma as she continues on her path to self-discovery.

In a way, I felt like a bit of an exile as I wrote the book. I neglected friends and family, shirked housework and other responsibilities. I often felt alone. But there were those who made the journey a little less lonely, those who read and provided feedback and support, those who loved me unconditionally and were there when I finally emerged from the writing cave.

Deep from my well of gratitude, I'd like to thank:

My editor, Martin Biro, for continuing to believe in me and for loving these characters almost as much as I do.

Vida Engstrand, publicist extraordinaire, and the entire team at Kensington/KTeen.

My friends and fellow writers in the Class of 2k12, particularly Kathryn Burak and Gina Rosati for beta reads, professional guidance, and all-around loveliness.

My local Philly writers' crew—Elisa Ludwig, Eugene Myers, Tiffany Schmidt, and Kate Walton—for friendship and camaraderie throughout this crazy adventure.

My students at Lower Moreland High School for surprising me every day with your maturity, intelligence, and kindness.

My friends and colleagues for providing early reads and much-needed moral support, especially Annie Boagni, Carol Burton-Haldeman, Barbara Kavanagh, Kimberly McGlonn-Nelson, Sandy Oechslin, and Ashley Seiver.

The Krauters, Hogans, and McLaughlins for cheering me on and bolstering me up. I couldn't ask for a more supportive family.

Erin and Anna, my wonderful nieces—I can't wait until you're old enough to read my books!

Mom, Dad, Phil, and Pete—for being there every step of the way and never losing your enthusiasm.

And last but not least, my husband, Ken, for your boundless patience and love. None of this would mean anything if I couldn't share it with you.

. . . somewhere between the real world and fairyland, where the Actual and the Imaginary may meet . . . Ghosts might enter here, without affrighting us.

—Nathaniel Hawthorne, *The Scarlet Letter*

CHAPTER 1

The Scarlet Letter was going to kill me.

Over the past week, I'd been trying to get through its 375 pages of densely packed text, and all I had gained for my efforts was a newfound hatred for nineteenth-century prose. Hawthorne never used seven words if twenty-seven were available. And so far, Hester and Dimmesdale's forbidden romance wasn't setting off any fireworks in my heart.

Not to mention, it was my birthday, the sky was a glorious blue, and I had the keys to the car. So why was I spending the day inside with dreary Nathaniel Hawthorne? Because I'd procrastinated and left my summer reading assignment for the very last minute. This was totally out of character for me. Then again, the entire summer had been out of character.

For one thing, I had a boyfriend. Admitting Gray Newman was my boyfriend still made me a little giddy. I'd always imagined my first boyfriend would be some sweaty-palmed thirteen-year-old, not this very grown-up guy with the hazel eyes and twice-broken nose. Over the past two months, we had seen each other almost every day, taking lazy drives to Salem and Yarmouth, window-shopping in Beacon Hill and Back Bay, hiking the trails at World's End, walking the beach at night. Always the beach at night. Being with Gray felt as natural as breathing. The knowledge that he was leaving tomorrow for Coast Guard training made me feel like someone was slowly carving out my insides with a dull knife.

For eight weeks, I wouldn't see him, wouldn't even be able to talk to him or e-mail. And after the training was over, we had no idea where they might send him. Best-case scenario was somewhere local like Cape Cod; worst case was some godforsaken part of the Bering Strait, one of most treacherous places in the world, particularly if you made your living rescuing people from frigid waters.

Resigned, I opened *The Scarlet Letter* and tried to resume reading:

> *Tomorrow would bring its own trial with it; so would the next day, and so would the next . . .*

This was hopeless. I flung the book on the coffee table.

And then I got the strange sense that someone was watching me. I glanced out the window and saw Gray's Jeep parked in the street. He was leaning against it in this casually sexy way, just waiting for me to notice him. We were kind of psychic this way that summer, deeply attuned to each other's presence.

I jumped from the sofa and ran outside, a smile bursting across my face. We hugged like we hadn't seen each other in weeks, and he spun me around in a circle before setting me gently down. Then he kissed me somewhat chastely given that we were standing in front of my house.

"You're early," I said.

"And you're beautiful. I couldn't wait another second."

"But I'm not ready."

"Then go and get changed. I can watch . . . I mean, wait." He cracked a sly smile.

"Very funny," I said. "Dad and Barbara are home."

"Oh, Barbara loves me," he said.

This was true. Over the summer, my stepmom Barbara had become Gray's third-biggest fan, behind me and my grandma. Gray was polite, good-looking, and attentive, *and* he was joining a branch of the military, a major plus in Barbara's book.

"Barbara may love you," I said, "but my dad worries you're going to steal my virginal innocence."

"Rightly so," he said, swooping in for another kiss.

I swatted him away. "Rein in those hormones, Mr. Coast Guard. It's going to be all discipline and self-denial for you from now on."

"Even more reason we should enjoy ourselves now."

I rolled my eyes, but my insides melted. The truth was, I had been thinking about sex a lot. I never thought I'd be ready after dating someone for only three months, but things moved quickly when you saw someone every day. And I did love Gray. But there was something so weighty and scary about that word that neither of us had said it yet.

I grabbed Gray's hand and led him inside the house. My dad was in the kitchen, going over finances. It had been a slow summer for him. Overfishing had led to dwindling numbers on stripers, cod, and flounder—my dad's livelihood—not to mention, the heat of deep summer tended to slow down everything with fins. Fortunately, Barbara's real estate venture was keeping us afloat. But my dad still fretted about money daily.

He barely looked up from his books to say hello. But Gray had been a familiar face this summer; my dad didn't stand on ceremony. Barbara compensated for my dad's chilliness. When she came out of the den-turned-office, she gave Gray a huge hug.

"Well, you're looking handsome, Mr. Coast Guard," she said, eyeing his crisp green shirt, khaki pants, and gray linen blazer. "Where are you two headed for the big birthday dinner?"

"Melville's," I said.

Barbara scrunched her nose in disdain. It was true Melville's would hardly qualify as fine dining, but it had sentimental value. I loved it for its greasy fried food served in red plastic baskets and the tacky whale murals that covered every square inch of wall. Melville's felt like home.

Knowing Gray was in good hands with Barbara, who could make small talk with a band of terrorists, I went upstairs to shower. I spritzed myself with perfume and put on a cotton floral dress that was as comfortable as it was pretty, then grabbed my espadrilles with the ankle laces, perfect for carrying when we went for our inevitable walk on the beach later.

When I went downstairs, I kissed my dad and Barbara good-bye. "Not too late, Emma," my dad warned as we headed out the door. "Gray's got an early start tomorrow. And you still have to finish that summer reading."

He tried to veil his misgivings with a smile, but it didn't work. I knew what he was really worried about. Guilt settled over my shoulders, but I shrugged it off. It was my birthday, and I wasn't going to let my dad's overprotectiveness ruin it.

At Melville's, Gray and I shared a seafood dinner, followed by a giant piece of Oreo cheesecake topped with seventeen candles. Gray even had the waiters come over and sing "Happy Birthday." I shook my head in mortification, but secretly I loved it.

When we came out of the restaurant a little after nine, the sun was already dipping out of sight, a sign that the days were getting shorter. The sky was awash with red and pink streaks, reminding me of an old fisherman's proverb.

"Red sky at night, sailor's delight," I said.

"Red sky at morn, sailors take warn," Gray said.

"That's a good omen, right?"

"Of course." He smiled reassuringly, but I felt a shadow of doubt descend. "Let's go to the lighthouse," Gray said, grabbing my hand as we crossed the street. "I want to give you your present there."

We drove to the lighthouse and parked along the beach road, tumbling out of the Jeep into a dusky violet night. The lighthouse sat on a crest of the beach a few hundred yards away. We held hands as we walked the dune path toward it. A bronze placard showed the image of a Labrador retriever named Rex who had guarded the lighthouse for fourteen years, greeting visitors, providing companionship for the keeper, and chasing off ghosts. This part of the Massachusetts Bay was known for being treacherous; there were dozens of tales of sailors and keepers who had lost their lives along this coast and still haunted the dunes where we stood.

And nine years ago, my mother had killed herself on her birthday by walking into the ocean.

I shivered, pushing away the memory of my mother as we walked out onto the beach. The surf was pounding on the sand, moaning and hissing like a living thing. Coming to the lighthouse had sounded romantic when Gray suggested it, but now that we were here, I felt edgy and sick. Trying to quell my unease, I turned to face Gray, who was pulling something from his pocket.

He gazed at me sweetly and handed me a small box. "I know you always wear your mother's dragonfly," he said nervously, "but I wanted you to have a part of me, too."

I opened the clamshell lid and lifted up a dog tag hanging from a silver chain. Gray always wore his uncle's dog tags, but I knew him well enough to know he'd never surrender those, not even to me. I brought the necklace closer and inspected the tag, etched with the small image of a scorpion.

"It's your zodiac sign," I said.

"Look at the other side."

I flipped it over and read the inscription out loud: "To Emma, the only antidote for my sting." Tears welled in my eyes before I could stop them.

"I'm wearing yours, too," he said, pulling his collar away

to reveal a dog tag he'd added to his chain, this one showing the profile of a woman with wings.

"The Virgo angel," I said.

"I was hoping you'd be my guardian angel while I'm away."

This made me lose it completely, and then I was sobbing and sniffling into his shirt in a completely undignified manner. Gray pulled me into a hug, and I melted into him, inhaling the comforting scent of his skin mixed with cologne and laundry detergent. Gray's particular smell had always reminded me of the ocean, which was fitting now that he had decided to spend the rest of his life on it.

"You okay?" he said after I'd wiped the last tears from my cheeks onto his sleeve.

I looked up at him, studying his downturned eyes and stubbled jaw. He cupped my face with his hands and brought his lips down on mine in that way that never failed to render me senseless. His hands followed the contours of my summer dress, pausing at my hips, then gripping my waist. My body lit up like a pinball machine.

Before I knew it, I was lying on the ground, my dress hitched up around my waist, with Gray's body shifting on top of mine—all rock-hard 170 pounds of him. I was so stunned by the intimacy of it that I barely felt the sand jabbing into my elbows or the cold breeze creeping up my bare legs.

I tore at his shirt, trying to undo the buttons with cold, nervous fingers, then traced the lines and curves of his stomach as he arched above me. Part of me wanted to go for it—to lose myself in this moment and not think about tomorrow. But the smallest reminder that a new day was coming—a day without Gray—paralyzed me.

He must have sensed my hesitation, because that quickly he was moving off me, and I was turning from him, overcome with emotion, adrenaline, and a shrieking sense of doom. My breath was thick in my throat, my face and hair soaked with sweat and sea air. Gray collapsed onto the sand behind me, wrapping his arms around me and hugging me so tightly it hurt.

"We don't have to do anything just because it's the last night," he said by my ear.

"I know."

"I don't want you to do anything you don't want to. Not ever."

I turned to face him now, coming apart at the sight of his eyes, filled with worry. "Believe me, Gray, I want to. It's just . . ."

"You don't have to explain," he said. "I want the moment to be right."

I burrowed into his embrace, and we lay like that for a small eternity. With my ear pressed against his chest, I waited until our heartbeats synchronized, then pulled away, not wanting to feel mine rush past his.

Finally, I propped myself up on an elbow, and he did the same, flashing me a sexy grin. "It was fun, though, right?" he said.

"Oh, yeah."

His grin faded slowly, his eyebrows knitting together. "I want it to be me," he said.

"What?"

"When the time is right, I want it to be me."

I laughed nervously. "What, you think I'm going to run off and have sex with the first guy that comes along?"

"No. It's just, we're going to be apart for a while, and the thought of some other guy being there for you when I can't be . . . it makes me sick."

"That's not going to happen."

"I'm just saying, don't do something with someone else because you miss me, you know? I want to be the first. Your first."

"Gray, you will be my first."

"Promise?" he said, gripping my hands, his face as vulnerable as a little boy's.

"Promise."

He collapsed onto his back, sighing in relief. I lay down next to him, one arm behind my head, the other resting on his chest as we stared at the stars.

"Hey, did you see that?" he asked a few minutes later, sitting up and pointing toward the sky. "That shooting star?"

I sat up and hugged my knees to my chest. "No, I missed it."

He leaned in and kissed me on the cheek. "I'm giving you my wish," he said. "Go ahead, Emma. Wish for something."

"I don't believe in wishes."

"Come on," he said. "The universe has to know what you want before it can give it to you."

"You really believe that?"

"Yeah, I do."

"All right, then," I said.

And I looked into his sad lovely eyes and made a wish I knew could never come true.

When I crept into the house a few minutes later, expecting to tiptoe quietly up to my room, I nearly knocked the lamp over when I saw my father sitting on the sofa in a dim pool of light. His hands were knotted tensely in front of him. I looked down at my body self-consciously. In my damp and crumpled dress, I felt like a cupcake whose frosting had melted.

"Do you know it's two in the morning, Emma?"

Truthfully, I didn't. I'd been thinking it was closer to midnight. "I'm sorry," I said. "We must have lost track of time."

"The one thing I asked of you was not to stay out too late," he said, his voice cold.

"I know, Dad, but I figured since this was my last night with Gray, and since it's my birthday—"

"Can you think of any reason I might be worried sick about you particularly because it *is* your birthday?"

Guilt washed over me like a toxic cloud. "Oh God, Dad, I'm sorry. I forgot."

"You forgot?" His face was incredulous. Because I hadn't really forgotten. Some things, you never do. "It seems like you've forgotten a lot this summer."

"What do you mean?"

He wrung his hands together, bracing for a fight. "Your relationship with Gray has taken over everything. I hardly remember seeing you."

"Dad, we were here all the time."

"But you weren't really here. You were always taking off somewhere to be on your own. And even when you were here, it was like you were on your own planet. You were so wrapped up in each other you couldn't see anything else."

"Well, what did you expect?" I said, anger burning through me. "Last summer, you told me I should stop moping around the house and do normal teenage things, and now that I'm doing that, you can't handle it."

"It's you I'm worried about not being able to handle things."

"Dad, I'm fine."

"No, you're not." He ran his hands through his hair. "What's going to happen when Gray leaves? How are you going to go back to school when you can barely go a day without seeing him? I don't like you being so . . . dependent on each other. I don't want you making yourself so vulnerable."

"But, Dad, if you love someone, it makes you vulnerable. You of all people should know that."

He closed his eyes and blew air out his cheeks. "I'm not going to tell you that you don't love Gray, because I'm sure you think you do. But, honey, you're seventeen years old. Gray's two years older than you. He's leaving for the Coast Guard tomorrow, and you're going to be stuck here, pining for him. Without knowing it, you're going to let yourself get in deeper and deeper until you don't even know which way is up. Believe me, I know what I'm talking about."

"Dad, you're wrong," I said, tears springing to my eyes.

"I see the way he looks at you. Like you're the sun and moon. But you can't be everything to him. It'll suck you dry."

"Dad, I'm not going to let that happen."

"I thought the same thing. I thought I was strong enough for your mother and me both. But I wasn't. I just wasn't." His voice trailed off, and he let his head fall into his hands.

All these years later, and my mother's suicide still haunted him. It still haunted me, too.

"Dad, I'm so sorry."

"I know you are," he said, wiping his cheeks, embarrassed. "I'm sorry, too. I didn't mean to ruin your birthday."

"You didn't. We're both just stressed out and tired."

"Yeah," he said. "Why don't we get some sleep and we'll talk about it in the morning?"

"Okay." I stood there, waiting for one of us to say something else.

"Good night," he finally said.

"Good night."

I headed upstairs, feeling sick to my stomach. Because the thing was, we wouldn't talk about it in the morning. We'd suppress it and resent each other later. This had been our pattern all summer.

And in a way, I knew my dad was right. Gray and I had been inseparable. I had neglected everything else this summer—my friends, my family, my schoolwork—to spend more time with him.

I crawled into bed and picked up my father's present to me—a journal with an embossed red leather cover. My grandma said it looked like *The Communist Manifesto*. I wrote the date at the top and filled the first page with thoughts about Gray leaving and me going back to school, about love and fear, expectations and change. Then I set the journal on my nightstand and tried to shut out the voices in my head that were warning me of loneliness, sadness, pain.

It took me forever to fall asleep.

In my dreams, I found myself walking on the beach. I was very small, dwarfed by the sea grass as I scrabbled over the dunes. The ocean looked immense, steely and wild with foam. Moonlight shone down on the breakers, creating a shimmering white light that pulled me closer.

And then I saw her. Standing in the surf, wearing a white nightgown that billowed like a sail. Her black hair whipped around her head like feathers on a captive bird.

"Mom!" I cried.

But she couldn't hear me. I tried to run after her, but my legs were stuck in the sand. My mother was already waist-deep in the water, and I knew what was about to happen.

I was eight years old, and my mother was about to kill herself.

And the child in me truly believed I could stop her.

With every ounce of my strength, I willed my legs out of the sand and began to run, crashing into the shallow surf behind her, the cold water hitting my legs like icy knives. I called her name again, but the roar of the waves drowned me out.

Panicked, I looked in all directions for any sign of her, but all I could see were whitecaps and inky blackness. She was already gone.

I shivered and gasped from the cold. A wave toppled overhead, submerging me. I felt so small. So helpless. Another wave battered me down. I plunged to the bottom, trying to dive under the tumult, but the waves kept careening over me, one after the other, flipping my body until I had no sense where I was.

Underwater, no sky, no idea which way was up.

Thinking was not possible. Instinct made me reach out for air, my lungs desperate for oxygen, and then I felt not air, but ice-cold flesh. Large hands grabbed me and hauled me out of the water. Air detonated in my lungs. I coughed and sputtered, collapsing onto the shore.

I heard my father say my name. "Emma, honey, wake up. Wake up!"

I sat up quickly and latched onto my father's arms. "It was Mom," I said. "I couldn't stop her. I couldn't—"

"Shh," my dad said, stroking my hair. "It was just a nightmare."

Just a nightmare. Three words meant to comfort me.

And yet, we both knew they weren't true.

CHAPTER 2

M y dad and I didn't talk much on the ride to Lockwood even though a thousand unspoken words hovered in the air. We drove down the main drive of campus, lined with scarlet oaks that would flame brilliant crimson in a few weeks. As the trees loomed overhead, I couldn't help but feel the oppressive weight of everyone's expectations and judgments weighing on my shoulders.

My dad parked in the visitor lot, and we hauled my bags and suitcases to the dorm. Girls thronged the hallways and music blared while parents made quick getaways. Lockwood girls didn't like their parents sticking around any longer than necessary, anxious to break out the booze for first-night celebrations.

Elise Fairchild watched the proceedings from a comfortable perch in the lounge. I was surprised to see her alone, unflanked by the rest of the Fearsome Four. If Elise was top dog around here, Amber Stone was her canine accessory, the Chihuahua in her Prada purse. And then there was Jess Barrister, a sleek Doberman with a lethal stare, and Chelsea Anderson, the least popular of the group and sort of their bait dog.

My dad and I walked past Elise, who barely acknowledged my presence, as we made our way to my room. Michelle was there already, unpacking her clothes while she bopped her head to her music. I threw my bags in a messy jumble on the floor so I could hug her.

"We haven't seen much of you this summer, Michelle," my dad said.

"Yeah, I've been taking extra classes," Michelle explained.

"See, Emma, some people have their priorities straight. I'll bet those summer classes are going to impress the MIT admissions counselors."

"Dad, she needed the extra credits because her old school didn't offer calculus."

"That's true," Michelle said, backing me up.

"I'm just saying, it wouldn't kill you to get a head start on your college planning," he said. "The binding of that SAT book I bought you hasn't even been cracked."

"Dad, some schools don't even care about SATs anymore. Hampshire College is SAT-optional."

"SAT-optional?" he said. "What is the world coming to?"

I rolled my eyes at Michelle, who seemed amused by our father-daughter sniping. My dad could be relentless about meeting responsibilities, but I knew he meant well.

"Well," he said, mercifully giving it a rest, "I should leave you to your unpacking. Have a great year, Michelle."

I followed my dad out into the hallway, where we both stood staring awkwardly at the floor.

"So, I guess this is it," he finally said.

"Yep."

"You know you can call anytime you want."

"I know."

"For any reason at all."

"I will, Dad."

Then he dipped his head to my level. "Are you sorry I told you? About Mom?"

I shook my head. "No, Dad. Don't ever think that. I'm glad I know."

"It's just, I worry about you. These nightmares you've been having . . ."

"Dad, it's okay," I said, grabbing his wrists. "You don't have to worry. I'm fine." I stood on my tiptoes and gave him a reassuring hug. Then he pulled away quickly and turned to go, not wanting me to notice that his eyes were misty.

When I got back in the room, Aerosmith's "Dream On" was blasting from the speakers. A suitcase lay open on the floor, and I smiled as I saw the piles of familiar red clothes. Michelle had a slightly unhealthy obsession with the color red. It had been her mother's favorite color, and after her mom died, Michelle had taken to wearing red almost exclusively.

"I've missed you," I said.

"I've missed you, too," she said. "I hardly recognize you. You're almost as brown as I am."

I laughed. Gray and I had spent so much time outside that my usually pale skin had turned a reddish brown, and my dark hair was burnished gold at the tips. I flopped down on my unmade bed and watched Michelle fill her dresser with clothes. I didn't feel like unpacking yet. Somehow it meant admitting that I was really back and that Gray was really gone.

I took out a photo Barbara had taken of Gray and me and set it on my dresser. Gray's arm was around me, and we were both wearing exaggerated smiles for Barbara's benefit. We looked goofy but happy.

"You miss him?" Michelle said.

"So much."

"Are you guys in *luvvv?*" she teased.

"I think we are."

"I knew it." She made the universal symbol for "Gag me!" and threw some rolled socks at me. "You're so in love you're actually glowing. Either that or you're pregnant."

"Impossible," I said.

"Oh, really?" she said, studying my face. "So you guys haven't . . . you know? Taken the plunge."

I blushed furiously and shook my head. "First of all, that's a horrible euphemism, but no, we haven't 'taken the plunge.' We thought about it. But it never seemed like the right time." I tossed the socks back at her. "What about you and Owen?"

"No," she said. "In fact . . ."

She let the silence hang over us until I couldn't stand it any longer. "What?"

She dropped the T-shirt she was folding and came to sit next to me on my bed. Her voice grew hushed even though there was no one else in the room. "Can I tell you something?"

"Of course."

"You have to promise not to tell anyone."

"Okay. But you're freaking me out here. What's going on?"

She took a deep breath and then she blurted out, "I cheated on Owen this summer."

My eyes popped wide. "You what?"

"Don't make me say it again."

"What do you mean, you cheated on him? With who? When?"

"Someone I met this summer."

"What? Just some random guy?"

"Something like that."

I could tell she was seeking my approval. "So you kissed another guy?"

She chewed her lip. "It was a little more than kissing," she said. "Well, a lot more." Now my eyes bugged from my skull. "Emma, I had to tell someone. It's been eating me up inside."

"Well, sure," I said.

For a few seconds, I just stared straight ahead of me, taking it all in. I could tell Michelle was waiting for me to say something that would absolve her from her guilt.

"You don't have to seem so shocked," Michelle said quietly, clearly disappointed by my reaction.

But I was shocked. I had always thought of Michelle and Owen as the perfect couple—they had kind of an "opposites attract" thing going. And Owen was a complete sweetheart and didn't deserve this.

"Look, I know you're good friends with Owen," she said, "but you can't tell him."

"I won't. But don't you think you should?"

"No. It'll only hurt him. Besides, it was a one-time thing. It's over."

"Are you sure? I mean, who is this guy? What's his name?"

She looked at the ground, unable to meet my eyes. "You don't know him. Besides, it's . . . complicated."

"Yeah, because you have a boyfriend."

"God, Emma. You're so judgmental. It happened, and I don't regret it. And if you could stop being Little Miss Perfect for a second, you might understand why."

She lurched off my bed and continued unpacking her suitcase, leaving me no choice but to do the same. But for some reason, the conversation had made me feel incredibly lonely. I suddenly felt like I was rooming with a stranger.

When the first day of classes rolled around, I was reminded of everything I hated about Lockwood. AP Bio was going to be my toughest course, as it would require fifty pages of reading a week and a dissection of a cat at the end of the year. Biology had always been taught by Ms. Brewster, the oldest and most crotchety member of Lockwood's staff, who was, therefore, likely to live forever. On the upside, she seemed to loathe Elise Fairchild almost as much as I did.

"Ms. Fairchild," she said when Elise showed up ten minutes late for class. "I understand that your father endows the school with enough money to fund a third world country, but you're still required to follow the most basic rules of the classroom, one of which is punctuality. I assume you have a compelling excuse?"

"Bad hair day?" Elise said, eliciting a few chuckles from the class. Then she went to take a seat, and I was surprised that she didn't sit with her friends. Amber and Chelsea were huddled together whispering on the other side of the room, and Jess Barrister was sitting by herself in the back.

I almost didn't recognize Jess. Last year, she had worn her chestnut hair long and sleek and had showcased an array of expensive tailored outfits that made her look like a Calvin Klein model. But now her hair was dyed black and cut in a chunky shag that partially obscured her face. She was sporting a stretchy black-and-white-striped shirt over black skinny jeans with black Converse high-tops. Michelle was staring at her, too, evidently as perplexed by the change as I was.

Ms. Brewster stared at Elise imperiously and said, "You'll have more than enough time to think of a real excuse this afternoon at detention."

My eyes went wide. Ms. Brewster's detentions were notorious for being two hours long and requiring a complete cleaning of the dissection closet, among other odious tasks. Moreover, she'd given a detention on the first day. To Elise Fairchild.

It was comforting to know there was at least one adult at Lockwood who refused to bow down to Princess Elise.

Unfortunately, this person was not our headmaster, Dr. Overbrook, who was teaching our AP American History class this year. Overbrook loved Elise, mostly because her father was on the school board and gave tons of money to the school. Unfortunately, Overbrook resented people like me and Michelle, who siphoned money away from the school in the form of scholarships. Last year we'd gotten caught up in a big scandal over a fire at the stables, and Overbrook had cobbled together some lame evidence that implicated Michelle in the fire. In a closed hearing before members of the Disciplinary Committee, Michelle and I testified against Elise, saying we had seen her smoking marijuana with her friends in the stables. As you can imagine, this went over really well with Overbrook and the school board. In the end, there wasn't enough evidence to find Michelle or Elise guilty of the fire, but the damage had been done to our reputations.

When I entered the classroom, Overbrook's large forehead gleamed in all its bald majesty, highlighting the strange purple birthmark shaped like Edvard Munch's *The Scream*. My stomach began to roil, whether from Overbrook's detestable face, Elise's presence, or the cafeteria's eggs Benedict, I wasn't sure.

"Greetings, young scholars," Overbrook said. His rasping voice had the effect of nails on a chalkboard. "I trust you've all completed your summer reading. In order to give you an opportunity to impart all that wisdom you've no doubt acquired, I'm going to give you a pop quiz." A wave of uneasiness swept the room. I wasn't too worried, as I'd done the reading back in June, but still, a pop quiz on the first day of school was mean-spirited, even for Overbrook.

He passed out the quizzes, and I quickly ran through the multiple-choice questions, which rehashed the conquest of Florida by the Spaniards, the history of Jamestown and Virginia, Pocahontas and John Smith, the *Mayflower* and Plymouth Colony.

After the quiz, Overbrook began his lecture on seventeenth-century Salem, informing us that we'd be spending extra time this fall focusing on Salem in honor of the three hundredth anniversary of the Salem Witch Trial acquittals. Apparently, our campus had been built on old plantation lands once owned by Thomas Danforth, the deputy governor who sentenced nineteen innocent people to hang during the Salem Witch Trials. Our main administrative building, Easty Hall, was named after Isaac Easty, the man responsible for reversing the court's judgment and restoring the good names of those condemned. In fact, Danforth himself later reversed his position and was believed to have run a sort of underground railroad for escaped witches, hiding them in caves that lay somewhere on this land.

"Mr. Gallagher will be directing a production of *The Crucible* at the end of October to commemorate the anniversary," Overbrook said. "I trust some of you will try out."

The mention of Mr. Gallagher's name sent nervous flutters through my stomach. I'd been infatuated with my English teacher ever since my first day at Lockwood two years ago. And even though I'd put that juvenile crush behind me last year, I had so many lingering feelings for him now—confusion, disappointment, and a tiny remnant of that old adoration.

I knew it was silly. I had the world's hottest Coast Guardian as my boyfriend. And Mr. Gallagher had basically hung us out to dry last year during the arson investigation. But as I walked into AP English and saw him at the front the classroom adjusting his glasses, I had a minor regressive episode. Despite everything, he was still handsome—lean and tall with a rugged face and wild dark hair. He looked like the hero of a Gothic novel. In fact, I'd made him exactly that in my dreams last year.

"Over the next few weeks," he began, "we will be immersing ourselves in Nathaniel Hawthorne's *The Scarlet Letter*, which I'm sure you all read diligently this summer." The class groaned, and Gallagher pretended to clutch a knife out of his chest. "Come on, people. *The Scarlet Letter* is the ultimate forbidden love story. Sex. Adultery. Secrets. I know the writing style is difficult, but what did you think of the story?"

The class fell into a treacherous silence that meant Gallagher was going to call on someone at random. "Ms. Stone," he said.

Amber, who had been flagrantly painting her nails, looked

up from her makeshift manicure and held the tiny wand in midair. "Huh?"

"I'd like your thoughts on *The Scarlet Letter*," he said. "Or Hester and Dimmesdale. Or anything non-manicure-related, perhaps."

The class giggled, and Amber squirmed uncomfortably in her seat. "The book is so long," she said. "And Hawthorne's writing is, like, so wordy. I don't mean to be rude, but it kind of seemed like a cheesy soap opera."

"You know, Amber," Gallagher said, "many critics agree with you, saying the book is no better than a Harlequin romance. But it deals with sexuality and sin in a way that was shocking to its nineteenth-century audience, and even to some modern ones. In fact, the book has been banned from school reading lists all over the country for being pornographic and obscene even though there's no actual sex in it."

"Too bad," Amber said under her breath, provoking more laughter, especially from Chelsea, who seemed programmed to admire everything Amber did. I caught sight of Jess Barrister glaring at Amber with what seemed like a fierce hatred. The chilling stare was nothing new, but the object of Jess's scorn was unexpected. I wondered if there had been trouble in Mean Girl Paradise.

Mr. Gallagher ran a hand through his thatch of dark hair, clearly disappointed by our lack of insight and enthusiasm. "Do Hester and Dimmesdale deserve the horrible fate that befalls them?"

"Well, what actually happens to them?" Amber said. "I mean, Hester has to wear a big letter *A* on her dress. Big deal. It doesn't seem all that tragic to me."

"Then you obviously haven't finished the book," Michelle said.

Amber and Chelsea turned around to give Michelle a brutal stare-down. "Michelle's right," Gallagher said. "The story gets more complex from here, and yet I think Hawthorne's point has less to do with the outward punishments people endure for their mistakes than with the inward burdens they carry. The scarlet letter becomes so much a part of Hester that even when she removes it, she can still feel its weight on her breast."

A few girls actually giggled when he said *breast*. It was going to be a long year.

Gallagher continued, undeterred. "So Hester is banished to the wilderness. Why is this important?"

The class stirred in their seats. Much as I hadn't enjoyed the book, I did think it explored some interesting themes. Fed up with our class's apathy, I decided to raise my hand. "The wilderness was associated with dark forces," I said. "The Puritans believed the devil lurked in the woods and that he tried to claim people's souls by making them sign his book. A mythology developed around these fears, and that's why it's significant that Hester is banished to the wilderness. She becomes the living embodiment of the dangers inherent when an individual breaks away from society's rules and expectations."

"Excellent," Gallagher said. "Yes, that's it exactly."

Elise turned and glowered at me.

The bell rang abruptly, and we all began frantically gathering our books, keenly aware that our lunch break was just moments away. "Before you run out on me," Gallagher said, raising his voice over the din, "auditions for *The Crucible* will be held next Monday at three-thirty in the assembly room of the Commons Building. The auditions are open, which means I've posted them at neighboring schools so we can solicit some young men to audition. If you know of anyone who might like to try out, please spread the word. I don't want a repeat of 2008 when we had to do a production of *Twelve Angry Women*."

A few of us laughed, but most of the girls were already out

in the hallway. I followed the crowd and waited while Michelle picked up a script from Gallagher's desk. Then we walked to the dining hall, making a beeline for the salad bar and grabbing a table by the windows where no one would bother us.

"So, you're thinking of trying out for *The Crucible*?" I said.

"Yeah," Michelle said. "I've always wanted to try acting. I think I might be good at it. What about you? You going to try out?"

"I don't think so," I said. "I've really got to focus on academics this year. Money's been tight, and my dad's counting on me to get a scholarship. We can't all be naturally brilliant like you."

"Ha," Michelle said. But she was being modest. Michelle was a math and science whiz, and I had no doubt she'd get a full ride to MIT. "Extracurriculars look good for scholarships, too," she said. "That's why I'm thinking of joining drama club. No one's going to give me a scholarship for horseback riding."

"Are you going to ride this year?" I said.

Michelle stared down at the condensation pooling around her soda. "No, I don't think so."

"Really?" Last year, riding had been Michelle's life. She had competed in the regional equestrian championship, coming in first place and beating out Elise. I couldn't believe she was thinking of giving it up, just like that.

She shrugged. "I already proved my point. I'm not going to give Elise a chance to beat me."

"Does Elise seem different to you this year?"

"Maybe a little," Michelle said.

"And how about Jess? Did you see her?"

"Jess Barrister?"

"Yeah. I almost didn't recognize her. She went from glam to goth in one summer."

"I know. But Amber's still in usual form," she said.

"Amber's an idiot. But I have to admit, I'm with her on *The Scarlet Letter*."

"You don't like it?"

"No, not really. It's a good story, but I don't like the characters. Chillingworth is vile. Pearl is freaky. And Dimmesdale is so weak. It drives me crazy that he just stands there on the scaffold and lets Hester take all the blame."

"But he's a minister. He would lose everything if he came forward. He wants to, but he knows he can't, and that's the tragedy of it."

"I guess."

"What about Hester?" she said. "You have to like Hester."

"I do, but I can't really relate to her. She's such a strong woman, but she frustrates me. I want her to shout, 'Hey, everyone, Dimmesdale is Pearl's father! Now can you all please get a life so I can go back to living mine?' I want her to ditch the preacher and leave that horrible, narrow-minded town for good."

"Now you see why I can relate?" Michelle said, and I laughed. "Hester's my girl."

After lunch, we went our separate ways, Michelle to AP Chemistry and me to French. One of the many mysteries of being in a coma last year was that I'd emerged from it almost entirely fluent in French, allowing me to bypass French III and go straight into French IV.

For our first class, Madame Favier told us to get into pairs to translate some Victor Hugo poems in preparation for reading *The Hunchback of Notre-Dame*. After everyone else had chosen partners, I was left with Jess Barrister by default.

"Hey," I said, opening our introductory proceedings with a bang. "You want to work together?"

"Fine," she said, her eyes fierce beneath layers of kohl eyeliner.

The first poem we had to translate was called "Demain, dès l'aube" or "Tomorrow, at Dawn," which Hugo had written after visiting the grave of his daughter, who had drowned in the Seine, pulled down by her own heavy skirts. I was translating the poem in my head when suddenly my throat constricted and my skin broke out in a sweat.

"Emma, ça va?" Madame Favier said, stopping by my desk.

"Oui, mais . . ." I was either going to faint or be sick. I lurched out of my seat and ran into the hallway, grabbing the wall to steady myself. I closed my eyes and tried to breathe.

Come on, Emma. Pull yourself together.

I stumbled down the hallway toward the bathroom, but the walls seemed to be closing in on me. I felt like I was slipping down a slope instead of walking. Finally I reached the bathroom and locked myself in a stall, sitting on the toilet and pressing my hands to my temples. Sweat prickled along my neck. It was bad enough that I constantly had nightmares about my mother's suicide. Now I had to relive it during my waking hours, too?

Feeling my heart rate slowly return to normal, I went to the sink and splashed some water on my face, catching sight of myself in the mirror. With each passing year, I looked more and more like my mother. Everyone said so. It was the reason my dad couldn't look at me sometimes. He couldn't help but see her, and in turn, see all the pain and anguish she'd caused him.

I splashed some more water on my face and opened my eyes. Through wet eyelashes, I saw my reflection ripple and change, so I was suddenly looking at myself as a little girl, the same little girl who had witnessed her mother walking into the ocean. The image only lasted a fraction of a second, but I staggered backward, feeling dizzy.

The next thing I remember was waking up with Jess Barrister's face above mine.

"Emma? Are you okay?" she said.

I shifted my head and saw baby blue tiles, metal pipes, the bottom of a porcelain sink. I was on the bathroom floor. "What are you doing here?" I said.

"You were gone a long time, and Madame asked me to check on you. Are you all right?"

I tried to sit up, feeling a wave of vertigo. "I'm okay. Just a little light-headed."

She rummaged around for something in her bag, then pulled out a piece of candy. "Jolly Rancher?"

It was an unexpected gesture coming from her, almost like a peace offering. I unwrapped the candy and popped it into my mouth, relishing the burst of sour apple on my tongue. The sugar gave me enough strength to stand and walk back to class with Jess's assistance. Madame asked if I was okay, and I assured her I was fine. But I felt shaky and faint for the rest of the period.

PE was the last class of the day, but Madame Favier wrote me a note excusing me. As I walked back to my room, I clutched my mother's dragonfly necklace, the only physical connection I still had to her. But it didn't provide the comfort it once had.

I wished I could talk to someone, my father especially. But he'd only worry about me. Or worse, make an appointment with the psychiatrist.

Gray would talk me through it, reassure me that I wasn't crazy. Automatically, I pulled out my cell phone, looking down at it like a drug addict staring at a fix. How had I forgotten? Gray was gone, and I couldn't talk to him for eight weeks.

Even though I knew it was pathetic, I dialed his number anyway and waited for his voice mail to pick up.

"Hey, this is Gray. Leave a message."

I waited for the beep and sat with the phone to my ear, wanting to say something just to feel like he was near. Feeling foolish, I tossed my phone on the bed and ripped a piece of paper from my notebook to write him a letter. I tried to tell him what had happened, but all that came out were mundane details about the first day of school—nothing real. I ended the letter with the most trite phrase of all: *I miss you.* It wasn't nearly enough to convey the hollow place his absence had left me with.

CHAPTER 3

The following Monday, Michelle convinced me to come with her to play auditions. We took the walking path to Old Campus, where the library, chapel, and Commons Building stood—all so strange to me now. It was here that I'd slipped into the fantasy world of *Jane Eyre* last year, where my brain had transformed our campus into the nineteenth-century estate of Thornfield. The giant oak tree in front of the Commons had been struck by lightning and was now split in two, twin branches struggling to grow in different directions from a burnt and scarred trunk. I wondered if the split would eventually kill it.

We entered the assembly room to see clusters of girls standing around reciting lines. Michelle froze, and I turned to see what had shaken her. Even with her back to us, there was no mistaking that enviable body and that perfect braid of hair, like a skein of corn silk down her back.

"God hates me," Michelle said.

"I thought you didn't believe in God," I said.

"That's why he hates me."

"Maybe she won't get a part," I said, but Michelle knew I was just trying to make her feel better. If experience had taught us anything, it was that Elise Fairchild always got what she wanted.

Michelle sighed and uncrumpled her script, looking nervous. "I'm going to run my lines one more time," she said irritably, crossing the room to rehearse in the corner.

I stood there aimlessly, my eyes falling on a guy sitting in front of an enormous sound system. He was pale with high cheekbones and almost black hair that hung over his eyes. Another guy came up behind him, and I smiled when I saw it was Owen. I felt a pang of guilt as I remembered what Michelle had told me. How could I look him in the eye and not say anything?

When Owen saw me, he jogged over and hugged me in that oddly formal way he did whenever Gray or Michelle were around. I understood why, but I wanted a real hug. When Owen hugged with abandon, there was nothing like it.

"I didn't know you were trying out!" he said.

"I'm not. I'm here for Michelle. Moral support. What about you?"

"Michelle told me they were desperate for guys, so I thought I might give it a try. How are you? I didn't see you much this summer."

"Yeah, well . . . you know."

"Yes, I know. You and Gray were attached at the hip."

"Like you can talk," I said, gesturing toward Michelle.

"Actually Michelle was busy with classes, and I spent a lot of time with the band, so we didn't see each other as much as I would have liked," he said. I willed my face to remain impassive. "Hey, speaking of the band, I want you to meet our lead singer."

He grabbed my hand and dragged me to the sound system, where the pale guy turned around and flipped the hair off his forehead, revealing piercing blue eyes lined in black eyeliner. I had actually met him once before, last year at the Braeburn bonfire. Up close, he was strikingly good-looking—almost pretty—but he seemed like he was trying his hardest to hide the fact.

"Emma, this is Flynn Markham. Flynn, this is my good friend, Emma Townsend." I extended my hand, and Flynn raised his absently. "Flynn's doing the music for the play," Owen said.

Flynn just nodded curtly and went back to making some adjustments on the sound board, his hair falling in an artful diagonal across his forehead. As he worked the knobs, a large tattoo shifted and warped along the inside of his arm. It looked like some form of calligraphy.

Before I could engage him in conversation, Mr. Gallagher moved to the microphone and announced that auditions were about to begin. His stage manager began corralling everyone toward the stage.

"I better go," Owen said.

"Break a leg," I said.

Owen smiled and went off, and Flynn continued ignoring me, so I found a folding chair up front where I'd have a better view.

Michelle was one of the first called to the stage. She got paired with some guy from Macomber High who had a lisp and an acne problem. Together they read a scene between Reverend Parris and his niece, Abigail, in which Parris comes upon his niece and daughter dancing naked in the woods. When the town finds out about the naked dancing, they suspect witchcraft. The lispy kid was perfect as the squirrely preacher out to save his own reputation, and Michelle was deliciously evil as the beautiful yet conniving Abigail.

Owen got paired with Elise to read a scene between John Proctor and his wife, Elizabeth, in which Elizabeth accuses John of having an affair with Abigail. Elise's angelic blond looks were well suited for the part of Elizabeth; she delivered the lines with just the right amount of self-righteous coolness. I had to admit, she and Owen had some real chemistry together onstage. For a moment, I saw Owen in a different light. Reading John Proctor's lines, he was no longer my fun-loving, goofy friend, but a guy with real presence and charisma.

The next morning before classes began, Michelle and I rushed over to Exeter Hall, where Gallagher had posted the cast list. Michelle did a victory dance when she saw that she'd been cast as Abigail. As I'd expected, Owen had been cast as Proctor, and Elise got the part of Elizabeth. We celebrated that night with a *Project Runway* marathon and buttered popcorn.

Over the next few weeks, I didn't see much of Michelle as she gave herself entirely to the play. I even saw her hanging out with Elise on occasion, running lines in the lounge or walking out of class together, chatting about a scene. Not only was this beyond weird given last year's events, but it made me feel left out, like I'd somehow lost my best friend.

I wrote Gray a letter almost every day, even if it was just a few sentences to let him know I was still alive. I hadn't gotten one back from him yet, but I knew he was busy. Instead of obsessing, I tried to throw myself into school, working on bio labs on photosynthesis and cell respiration, reading the first half of *The Hunchback of Notre-Dame,* and taking jogs through the woods behind campus.

I'd never been much of a runner, but I'd gone training with Gray a few times this summer and had kind of gotten addicted to the feeling. Those first few weeks of school, I needed to feel hard earth beneath my feet, to run until my calves throbbed just so I would feel a different kind of pain, something to assure me I could move forward without Gray by my side.

One gorgeous fall day in early October, I set off from the dorm on a run around campus. The first leg was all downhill as I passed Exeter and the dining hall and followed the path to the horse trails that skirted the stream and the woods. From there, I turned to slog up the hill toward Old Campus, past the chapel and the Commons Building. By the time I reached the dorms, I still hadn't hit my stride, so I decided to do another circuit.

When I reached the horse trail for the second time, instead of feeling that fabled runner's high, I felt only pain and breathlessness. I slowed my pace, hoping the stitch in my side would ease and my lungs would open up again, but it was no good. I stooped over to catch my breath.

As I walked it off, I wandered closer to the tree line that separated our campus from Braeburn Academy. A thick log bridge straddled the stream here. This was where Michelle and I had crossed to go to the Braeburn bonfire the night I'd been struck by lightning. The stream gurgled beneath the bridge, rippling over stones that had been shaped long ago by ancient glaciers. There was a feeling of timelessness to the spot, a sense that the rules of nature ceased to apply as soon as you crossed over.

I stepped onto the bridge now and crossed halfway, stopping to toss a pebble into the water. It sent ripples through the stream that radiated outward, leading my eye to something red on the opposite bank. A wild rosebush grew there, its branches overladen with blooms, some of them hanging so low they nearly touched the water. I made my way across to the other side and bent down to pluck a rose. Its fragrance was heady and rich and nearly overpowered my senses.

As I stuck the flower in my pocket, some strange force compelled me to move deeper into the woods. The forest was cooler here, protected by the canopy of trees, and the ground was covered in ferny overgrowth that cushioned my steps. I made my way through the brush, straying off the well-worn path and into more untamed wilderness, recalling the eerie history of this forest and imagining the spirits of the dead rising to haunt me.

The terrain became more rugged as I hiked uphill until I came to a clearing high above the stream, where piles of rock formed a lopsided pyramid. Clumps of scrubby trees grew haphazardly between them, forming a dense barrier.

Stepping closer, I spied something solid behind the choke of weeds. I knelt down and began scrabbling away at the vines and brambles until my palms pressed against something hard and cold. Like a fairy-tale heroine searching for a magic door, I felt my way across the ivy-covered slab until it gave way to an opening. Peering into the space, I immediately knew what I'd discovered. A witch cave.

Without thinking, I crept inside, just far enough to gauge its size. Maybe eight feet wide and ten feet long, at most. It was colder here in the cave and quieter, too, like the sounds of the forest had been swallowed up by the stone. Feeling a little claustrophobic, I shimmied out of the cave and investigated the area, finding two more caves, both of them nestled into the hillside behind thick foliage.

The caves were isolated and protected by natural camouflage, which must have been why Governor Danforth chose this place to hide the escaped witches. No one would find them here.

I wondered if there was any vestige of those witches now, some trace of their suffering that still lingered. This grim thought sent a panic through me, and suddenly I wanted to get out of the woods and back to the safe predictability of campus. But I couldn't remember how I'd gotten here.

As quickly as I could move without losing my footing, I scrabbled down the hillside until I was back on flat ground, then tried retracing my steps. But everything looked unfamiliar and hostile. The trees overhead seemed to bear down on me now, their limbs swaying as if to grab me.

Feeling suffocated, I quickened my pace, convinced that some evil presence was following me, just as the Puritans had believed. Thorns and brambles scratched my arms and legs, but I ignored the pain, desperate to escape. Finally, I found

the path that had been worn down by students traipsing between Lockwood and Braeburn. I knew where to go from
here, and I covered the ground quickly.

Momentarily, I saw the rosebush flanking the log bridge.

Just a few more feet to go—just cross over, and you're
home free.

I flew across the log, trying not to think of the water whoosh-
ing beneath my feet. When I reached the other side, I sank to
the ground in relief and laughed at myself. I had let my imagination get the best of me.

I took the rose out of my pocket just to convince myself it
was real, startled to see that it had already withered and
turned brown at the edges. My insides clenched as I thought
of the fates that befell girls in fairy tales who took things they
weren't supposed to take.

CHAPTER 4

Back in the safety of my room, I placed the sad and crumpled rose in a glass of water on my nightstand, hoping to revive it. Floating there in my room, the flower seemed like an enchanted rose, like the one trapped under glass in *Beauty and the Beast*. I still felt guilty, like I'd destroyed its beauty just by plucking it.

Feeling unnerved about the whole afternoon and the discovery of the witch caves, I took a long, hot shower, then turned on the hotpot to make myself some ramen noodles for dinner. I couldn't bear the thought of going to the dining hall alone.

I was watching the dry cake of noodles fall apart under a stream of boiling water when my phone rang. I glanced down at the display and smiled.

"Hey, you," I said, elated to hear Owen's voice.

"What are you doing right this minute?" he said.

"Making ramen noodles."

"So you're busy, then."

I laughed. "Terribly. Why? What's up?"

"Some friends are taking me out for an impromptu birthday celebration."

"I didn't know it was your birthday!"

"Well, it was actually yesterday," he said, "but I'm milking it for all it's worth. So what do you say? Are you in?"

"Of course I'm in. Who else is going?"

"Just Flynn and Jess so far."

"Jess?" I said.

"Jess Barrister. You know her, right? She goes to Lockwood."

"I know her. I just didn't know you did."

"Yeah, she's the drummer for our band."

"Jess Barrister is the drummer for your band?" I said.

"Yeah. What's so crazy about that?"

"I don't know, everything! If you'd known her last year, you would understand."

"Well, she's really cool. I think you'll like her."

"Okay," I said. "What about Michelle? Have you called her yet?"

There was a long pause. "She's going home for the weekend, isn't she?"

I hesitated a moment too long. "Oh yeah. I think she did say something about seeing Darlene. But I'm not sure. I barely see her anymore."

He paused again, and I wondered if I'd just caught Michelle in a lie. "No, me neither," he said. "So anyway, Flynn and I are coming to pick you guys up in an hour. Meet us in front of Easty."

I hung up and tried to ignore the sick feeling in my stomach as I changed out of my pajamas and into a T-shirt, hoodie, and jeans. Around six o'clock, I went outside. Jess was already there waiting.

"Hey," I said.

"Hey."

She handed me what was now her trademark symbol of goodwill: a Jolly Rancher. This one was watermelon flavored.

"Thanks," I said. "Do you know where we're going tonight?"

She twirled a strand of black hair through her fingers. "The Depot. It's this warehouse—well, really a dance club where Flynn DJs. We're gonna rehearse some songs, maybe get some Chinese food."

And that's how Jess, Flynn, Owen, and I ended up sitting on the floor of this shabby old warehouse/dance club on the old railway line. We passed around cartons of General Tso's chicken and sweet-and-sour shrimp and talked about music. Flynn kept dropping names of all these indie bands we had never heard of and scoffing at the bands we liked.

"What about Radiohead?" Jess asked.

"Sellouts," he said.

"How about Bob Dylan?" Owen asked.

"An incoherent hippie."

"Man, you're certifiable," Owen said.

"What about Coldplay or Snow Patrol?" I asked.

"Corporate whores."

I smirked. "So what you're saying is, a band can't be good if they actually sell their music?"

Owen and Jess laughed. "Once a band reaches a certain level of success," Flynn said, "they become tools of the industry. They keep churning out the same bland, inoffensive crap year after year."

"Hey, Flynn," Jess said. "How many hipsters does it take to change a lightbulb?"

"I don't know, how many?" he said, playing along.

"It's a really obscure number. You've probably never heard of it."

Owen howled with laughter, and Flynn just flipped his hair out of his eyes and scowled. I tried not to laugh, but it was hard not to.

After we finished eating, Jess and Flynn went up on the stage and started fooling around on the piano, Jess making up melodies and Flynn singing in exaggerated falsetto. I was thankful Owen and I had a few moments alone.

"So," he said, giving me a sympathetic pout, "how are you handling the whole long-distance thing?"

"Not well," I said. "I haven't heard from Gray since he left."

"Not even an e-mail?"

"No computers allowed. I've written him a few letters, but he doesn't have time to write back. I've just been going on faith that he still remembers me."

Owen rolled his eyes. "He more than remembers you, and you know it," he said. "You guys are so lucky."

"Why?"

"Because you found each other. I mean, I know there are lots of guys who want to hook up with a different girl every weekend, but that's not me. I'd love to have what you guys have."

"You have Michelle," I said. But the moment I said it, I knew it wasn't true. Not in the way Owen wanted it to be.

"Emma, you know Michelle," he said. "As much as anyone can know her. She's a mystery wrapped in an enigma wrapped in thorns so you can't try and unwrap her."

"Are things that bad?"

He shrugged and pursed his lips. "I don't know. At the beginning of the summer, things seemed okay, but then she started acting all distant and weird."

I nodded sympathetically. This close up, I saw that Owen had a tiny indentation at the tip of his nose. A crease had formed above his brow, and one of his dimples was showing, not from a smile this time, but from a frown. All these small hollow places gave his face a vulnerable, puppy-dog look that made me want to hug him.

I hated seeing Owen unhappy. It seemed against nature somehow. And I hated that Michelle had cheated on him, and I couldn't tell him about it. I felt like I was betraying them both.

"Hey," Flynn interrupted, "when are you two lovebirds going to get off your asses and join us onstage?"

"May I remind you," Owen said, "that Emma has a boyfriend? A big, buff Coast Guard boyfriend."

"Then she should stop flirting with you," Flynn said, flashing me a devious grin and flipping a chunk of dark hair out of his eyes. Maybe that hair was the reason he was perpetually in a bad mood. "Come on, man. We need a guitarist, pronto. What can you play, Emma?" he said, those ice blue eyes chilling me.

"I can't play anything," I said.

"Come on. Surely you can play the tambourine. Or the triangle."

Blood rushed to my cheeks. "I'm musically challenged," I joked.

"But she writes kick-ass poetry," Owen said. "She could help us with songwriting."

"Wonderful," Flynn said. "Our very own Yoko Ono."

Owen frowned. "Stop being a jerk, Flynn."

"Me?" Flynn said, all innocence. "I'm just trying to find out what makes Emma special. Can she sing?"

"No," I said.

"Come on, Emma, everyone can sing. Just put your lips together and—"

"Stop it, man," Owen said. "You're making her uncomfortable."

"Am I making you uncomfortable, Emma?" Flynn said, hopping off the stage and walking toward me. "I'm sorry. Allow me to apologize." He pulled a joint from one of his jeans pockets and lit it, then handed it to me.

"No, thanks," I said.

"You don't smoke?" I shook my head. "Well, we can take care of that."

"I don't care if you guys smoke," I said. "But I don't want to."

"How do you know if you've never tried? Come on. It might make you a little less . . . uptight."

"I'm not uptight," I said.

Flynn's eyes went unnaturally wide, and Jess laughed. "Maybe a little," she said. "Look, it's not a big deal if you don't want to. But it's not a big deal if you do. It's just a little pot."

I glanced at Owen for support, but he'd already taken the joint from Flynn. I watched as he inhaled slowly, holding his breath for a few seconds before exhaling. A plume of pungent, sweet smoke wafted toward me.

"I feel like I'm on an after-school special," I said, laughing.

"Believe me," Flynn said. "So do we."

Owen held the joint toward me, and I shook my head. Jess took a hit, then passed it back to Flynn. "Last chance," he said, gesturing to me one more time. "Suit yourself."

He took the last hit, gulping and swallowing the smoke like it was oxygen. "Okay, enough of this bullshit," he said. "Let's rehearse. Jess, see if you can keep up with us."

Owen grabbed his guitar from the corner, and Flynn sat down at the keyboards, pulling a small microphone in front of him. Jess went to sit behind the drum set, and I sat on the floor beneath them, a sober audience of one.

Flynn started the song off with some melancholy piano chords. After a few measures, Owen began strumming a chunky rhythm on his guitar while Jess did her best to provide a backbeat. When Flynn's vocals broke through the music, I felt an unexpected rush of emotion. I'd expected whiny, screaming emo vocals, not this full-bodied, visceral singing that could go from a throaty growl to a heartbreaking falsetto in a moment.

A few of the lyrics lodged in my brain: "In my dreams we are more than friends; the reason I never want my dreams to end," followed by a chorus that went: "Broken and battered is my heart, but it cannot be ripped apart. It will beat on, like this song. Like a boat against the throng."

The faster the tempo, the more frenzied Flynn's playing became until Jess realized her novice percussion skills weren't up to the task. Somewhere toward the crescendo, she threw her arms up and dropped her sticks to the ground, while Flynn collapsed onto the keys, making a jarring, discordant clamor that seemed a fitting end to this beautiful, schizophrenic song.

I didn't know whether to clap or holler or remain silently in awe. Flynn was really good. And for all his obnoxious swagger, he'd written a sentimental love song.

"That was . . . fantastic!" I said.

"I screwed up," Jess said.

"It didn't matter. It was so . . . raw. Full of emotion."

"You sound surprised," Flynn said.

"No," I said. "I've just never heard a song like that before."

"Because you listen to commercial crap," he said, putting us back on the solid ground of mutual animosity where we were both more comfortable.

"You really liked it?" Owen said.

"It was great. You guys sound amazing together. Do you have a band name yet?"

"Ice-9," Flynn said.

"I like that," I said. "Did you make it up?"

Flynn's glare went through me like a stab of cold metal. "It's from *Cat's Cradle*," he said. He might as well have added *dipshit* to the end of the sentence. Then he hoisted himself up on the edge of the stage and fumbled around in his backpack for a few minutes, pulling out a fifth of whiskey. "Anyone up for the finest Kentucky bourbon Massachusetts can sell?"

I had a headache and felt tired, and I didn't feel like playing another round of peer-pressure death match. "I hate to break up the fun," I said, "but I'm beat. I should probably get to bed."

"Already?" Jess said, and Flynn gave her a look like, *What did you expect?*

"I'll drop her off and come back," Owen said.

"No, Owen, that's okay," I said." It's your birthday. I can take the shuttle."

"No way am I making you wait for the shuttle," he said. "It'll take hours."

"You sure?" I said.

"Positive."

Flynn narrowed his gaze at me and said in a hypnotic voice, "Fly back to school, little Emma."

I rolled my eyes, trying to think of a stinging retort, but coming up empty-handed. I didn't know why I had let Flynn ruffle my feathers so much.

Owen put his hand lightly on the small of my back as we exited the club and escaped into the autumn air. I felt a rush of elation at being liberated from the uncomfortable tension of that warehouse and the constant appraisals of a guy who seemed to hate me for no reason at all.

"So what's Flynn's deal?" I asked Owen on the ride home. "Seems like he has a vendetta against the world."

"I know he comes off sort of rude," he said.

"Sort of?"

Owen smirked. "Not that it's an excuse, but he has a pretty crappy home life. His father's an asshole, and his mom's knocked out on prescription drugs half the time. Still, I don't know why he seemed to be taking it out on you tonight."

"Oh, so you noticed?" I said. I slumped in my seat, feeling uncomfortable about the whole evening.

"Don't worry about Flynn," he said. "I'm sure his attitude has nothing to do with you."

"It still sucks," I said. "I want to be able to hang out with you without getting verbally eviscerated every five minutes."

"I totally understand," he said, laughing. "We'll just have to hang out alone next time." There was a shy sweetness to his voice.

Owen parked his car in front of Easty Hall, and I turned

my head glumly, waiting for him to say something heartening.

"Are you okay?" he said.

"Yeah, I'm fine."

"You don't seem fine."

"I haven't been sleeping," I said.

"Is it Gray?"

I sighed. "I don't know. I think it's a lot of things. But don't worry. I'll be okay." I had the tremendous urge to lean my head on his shoulder. "Hey," I said, feeling suddenly shy around him. "We never even sang 'Happy Birthday.' "

"You can sing it to me now," he said, teasing.

"You really don't want to hear me sing."

"Actually, I'd like nothing more."

"Maybe someday. But for tonight, you'll have to be content with this. Happy birthday, Owen." And on some wild impulse, I kissed him on the cheek. His face broke into a smile that could have melted icebergs.

I jumped out of the car and ran all the way back to the dorm, feeling a surge of adrenaline that probably meant another sleepless night. Michelle still wasn't back when I let myself into the room. I felt a little guilty that I'd been hanging out with her boyfriend all evening, and that I'd been accused of flirting with him. I wondered why Michelle was pulling away from us both and why everybody seemed to be changing so much. A part of me wanted everything to go back to the way it had been—me and Michelle as allies against the evil Lockwood Empire, with Owen and Gray our two loyal boyfriends.

But another part of me wondered what would happen if I let myself change, too, if I stopped clinging to the past and opened myself up to whatever the future might hold.

CHAPTER 5

Over the next few weeks, I began running more frequently so I could get out of my room, but also so I could feel more connected to Gray. I'd imagine him beside me and have conversations with him in my head. The first few runs were painful, as my brain kept telling me I wasn't strong enough, that I should quit. But then Gray's voice would talk me through it until my conscious mind shut down and my subconscious took over. On those days, it was almost like I went into a trance. Miles would pass, and I couldn't even recall the run itself.

Sometimes I'd stop at the stream and think about going back up to the witch caves. I couldn't get over the sense that these woods were still alive with the ghosts of the condemned, and that their spirits were restless and lonely like me.

One rare afternoon when Michelle and I were both in our room doing homework, I decided to tell her about my discovery of the caves.

"What were they like?" she asked.

"Smaller than I expected and really dark. I can't imagine someone living in one for an entire winter. They were sort of eerie but cool. I'm thinking of hiking out there again," I said. "Would you come with me next time? So I don't wimp out."

"Emma, they weren't actual witches hiding out there," she said. "They were regular people who'd been falsely accused."

"I know. But still, I got this strange vibe when I was there. Almost like their ghosts were still trapped on that hill."

"Now you sound like Darlene."

I laughed. Michelle's Aunt Darlene was part dream interpreter, part voodoo practitioner, and all-around wise woman. She believed in the spirit world and claimed to communicate with the dead. Michelle discounted her beliefs as superstition, but last year when I'd been in the coma and had crossed over into the world of *Jane Eyre,* Darlene had helped me figure out what it all meant. She told me my dreams were a mystical pathway—a gift I'd been given by the spirit world so I could communicate with my mother.

"I'll take that as a compliment," I said. "I miss Darlene. We should go see her." Not only was Darlene incredibly insightful, but she owned her own bakery and plied us with homemade Haitian pastries and coconut drinks every time we went. "Have you been to see her lately?" I asked.

"No," Michelle said.

I hesitated about whether to ask the next question. "Then why did you tell Owen you were going home to see her the night of his birthday?"

She looked up from her book, clearly taken by surprise. "What?"

"Owen told me that's why you couldn't make it to the Depot to watch their band play."

She shut her book now, looking annoyed. "Well, for one thing, I took Owen out the night before on his actual birthday. Two, I can't stand Flynn. And three, I had to rehearse a scene with Elise."

"So why did you lie to Owen?"

"Because he doesn't like me hanging out with Elise," she said.

"Hmm, I wonder why."

"What's that supposed to mean?"

"Just that last year, you thought she was evil."

"Yeah, well, she's not as evil once you get to know her."

"Not as evil. A ringing endorsement."

"Really, Emma, haven't you noticed that she doesn't hang out with her old friends anymore? She actually seems sort of lonely."

"Oh God," I said. "Now you're feeling sorry for her? After everything she did to us?" I could feel the argument spiraling out of control, but I didn't know how to rein in my momentum. "You're defending Elise, lying to your boyfriend, and ignoring me."

"Ignoring you?" she said. "You ignored me all summer!"

That shut me up. Here I was getting jealous that Michelle was spending all her time with everyone but me. Yet all summer long, I'd chosen to spend time with Gray instead of her. And now I expected things to go back to the way they'd been? That wasn't fair.

"I'm sorry," I said. "You're right. I wasn't there for you this summer."

She sighed. "I'm sorry, too. It's not that I don't want to hang out with you anymore. It's just this play. I didn't realize it was going to be so all-consuming. Things will get better as soon as it's over, I promise. But right now, I really need to get some work done. I'm going to go to the library. I can't concentrate here."

"Meet back here for *Downton Abbey* tonight?" I said.

"Sure thing," she said. But I felt like she was humoring me.

As soon as she was gone, I wished I hadn't been so aggressive with her. But there was so little I understood about Michelle. Did she still love Owen? Was she still seeing that guy from the summer? Did she still want to go to MIT?

Maybe she didn't have the answers either. It seemed we

were both going through growing pains, trying to figure out how to roll with all the changes being thrown our way.

All I wanted was to see Gray, seemingly the only constant in my life. I couldn't wait to look into those hazel eyes that knew me so well, to fall into his arms where everything seemed to make sense.

When the weekend of his Coast Guard graduation finally arrived, I woke early, my limbs jangling with nerves. Owen was driving me to Gray's house that afternoon, and I was going to travel down with Gray's family to Cape May, where we'd spend the night in a hotel so we could make it to the ceremony by ten the next morning. I didn't love the idea of spending six hours in the car with Gray's family, but my dad wouldn't let me to drive all the way to New Jersey by myself.

Owen asked if I wanted to drive his Prius to the Newmans' house, and I jumped at the chance. When I sat down in the driver's seat, I had to adjust it a few inches forward so I could reach the pedals. "You got so tall this year," I said. "And I remained a midget."

"I like you short," he said. "It makes me feel manly." He beat his fists against his chest, Tarzan style.

"Oh jeez," I said, laughing.

I was mostly silent as we drove, trying to concentrate on the road and not think about Gray. Owen could tell I was nervous, so he tried to distract me by making up corny songs. For all his messing around, Owen had a beautiful voice. Not throaty and raw like Flynn's, but clean and pure.

"There was a short girl named Emma," he sang, "who had a major dilemma. She tried to write . . . a song about her height . . . but nothing else rhymes with Emma!" I was cracking up, trying my hardest not to drive off the road. "Hey," he joked, "be careful with Dolores!"

This only made me lose it more. "You named your car Dolores?"

"Don't diss Dolores," he said, patting the dashboard.

Owen dropped me off in front of the Newmans' house and I gave him a hug to thank him for the ride, feeling somewhat abandoned as he drove away.

Gray's mom, Simona, answered the door looking stunning as always with her strange combination of auburn hair and olive skin. "Emma," she said, pulling me into her warm embrace. But there was something sad in her expression when she looked at me, a pitying expression that made me uncomfortable.

The ride to Cape May was awkward. I was sitting in the backseat with Gray's sister, Anna, a precocious eight-year-old whom I adored. Simona made chitchat for the first hour, asking me about school, but then she seemed to run out of things to say. Gray's dad, never warm and fuzzy to begin with, was silent for most of the ride, so Anna and I ended up playing games on her iPhone. But I couldn't shake the feeling that something was wrong.

We checked into a hotel that night, and Simona came to our room to make sure Anna and I had everything we needed. She had ordered us a pepperoni pizza, so Anna and I camped out on one of the queen-sized beds and ate while we watched a Harry Potter marathon on TV.

"Who do you like better, Harry or Ron?" Anna asked me.

"Harry," I said. "What about you?"

She blushed. "Ron."

"Why?"

"Because he has red hair like me," she said. "Duh."

I laughed, and she nestled against me, looking sleepy. I cleared away the pizza box and paper plates and turned down the sheets on the other bed.

"It's nine o'clock, kiddo," I said. "Time for bed."

She immediately sat upright and pretended she wasn't tired. "Do I have to?"

"At least brush your teeth and get into your pj's."

Dutifully, she went into the bathroom and changed while I did the same. When she came out, she smiled and rubbed her finger along her teeth. "All clean," she said.

We crawled into our respective beds and I turned the volume down on the TV. Anna looked triumphant sitting in the middle of that enormous bed by herself, pulling the blankets up to her chin. "This is fun," she said. "Like a sleepover party."

"It is," I agreed.

"Want to play Truth or Dare?" she asked. I laughed because Gray and I used to play this all the time.

"How do you know about that game?" I said.

"Gray plays with me. Only, I just play Truth with him now because the last time I chose a Dare, he made me sing the Scooby-Doo song in front of Kyle Weaver."

"Who's Kyle Weaver?"

"A boy," she said, smiling coyly.

"Does he have red hair?" I asked.

"No, brown hair. And brown eyes, too. Girly eyes."

"Girly eyes?"

"Long lashes." Oh boy, Anna was in trouble already.

We played a few rounds of Truth or Dare during which I made Anna say tongue twisters while hanging upside down off the bed and she made me go into the hallway with toothpaste on my nose. For the final round, I chose Truth.

"Do you love Gray?" she asked. Without hesitation, I said yes, and she smiled. "Emma?" she said.

"Yeah?"

"I wish you were my sister."

"That's sweet," I said, getting up and giving her a kiss on the forehead. "I wish you were my sister, too."

"It's lonely without Gray. I wish I had somebody to talk to."

"Tell you what," I said. "I'm going to enter my number into your phone. Anytime you're feeling lonely or want to talk, you give me a call or text me a message. And I'll do the same." This seemed to please her because when she took her phone back, she pulled it to her chest and smiled.

Just before she fell asleep, she turned to me and said, "Emma?"

"Yeah?"

Our voices had that late-night hush to them, like no one else in the world existed.

"I love Kyle Weaver," she said, burying herself under her covers so I couldn't see her face. We were both fools for love.

The next morning, we arrived at the gates of the Coast Guard's training center around 9:30. After parking, we walked over to the parade field and found seats on the bleachers with the other parents and relatives. The sky was a clear lapis blue, and the sun kept me warm despite the chill in the air. We listened to a Coast Guard band play military marches while the recruits filed onto the field, a sea of white peaks and shirts over navy pants. I scanned the lawn for Gray, feeling my chest tighten, wondering if our connection was so strong he'd sense my presence.

And then I saw him—standing straight and tall, his face so stern and focused I almost didn't recognize him. His hat was pulled low over his eyes, casting half his face in shadow, but I knew it was him from the set of his jaw, from a certain way he had of standing. Watching him out there on that field awaiting this new mission was bittersweet. I felt a surge of emotions, the most overpowering of which was pride—pride at how far he'd come since last year when he'd been a broken boy haunted by his past. Now he was a committed Coast Guard recruit. And he was mine. The thought made me giddy.

I practically had to sit on my hands during the ceremony so I wouldn't accidentally rush the field and attack him. The recruits recited the Coast Guard oath and went through a highly choreographed drill with their guns. Then the instructors awarded various honors and awards. Gray was given an honor graduate ribbon, bestowed on the top 3 percent of his graduating company. He was also voted "Best Shipmate" by the guys in his company. Anna and I beamed with pride.

When the ceremony was over, we headed onto the field to congratulate him. I watched as he took off his hat and shook his father's hand. With his haunted eyes and close-cut scalp, he looked so vulnerable, like a warrior who'd finally come home from a long battle.

I hung back a little to let Gray's family congratulate him first, but even so, I was expecting some eye contact, some sign that Gray was as impatient to see me as I was to see him. But he didn't even look at me until he had hugged everyone else, until I was standing right in front of him, giving him no other choice.

"Hi," I said brightly, trying to disguise my concern.

"Emma," he said. His voice was heavy with some emotion.

I flung my arms around him, expecting him to pull me tight in his grasp, maybe sweep me off the ground and spin me like he'd done so many times before. He hugged me back, but it was cool and distant, a consolation prize of a hug.

I wanted to tell him how much I'd missed him, but Simona started talking about lunch plans, and we all began walking toward the car, and there wasn't any time. Or privacy. I couldn't exactly tell Gray I loved him with his entire family standing by.

We piled into the car and went to an elegant beachfront restaurant that looked like something out of *The Great Gatsby*. It had immense white columns and a wraparound porch with black-and-white-striped awnings. A pianist was playing jazz songs in the lobby, complementing the mood. In fact, everything was perfect. Except that Gray and I were barely speaking. When the waitstaff held chairs out for us, Gray took the chair opposite me instead of beside me. As we looked over the menus, he and his dad got embroiled in some conversation, leaving me smiling uncomfortably at Simona while Anna wandered the front porch.

The ride home was even more uncomfortable, as Gray and I were sitting in the back with Anna wedged between us. He still hadn't looked me in the eye. And all of our conversation had been of the most bland, innocuous variety, the kind usually reserved for the dentist or hairdresser.

When we reached my house, Simona and Mr. Newman decided to go in and say a quick hello to my parents. Finally, I would get a chance to be alone with Gray. Anna was hanging outside with us, but I drew her aside and asked if she could go in with the grown-ups. "For me," I said. "As a favor. I want to tell Gray something important."

I winked at her, and she totally got it, winking back and heading inside. The air was cold, and the sky was brilliantly clear and punctured with stars. "So," I said, teasingly, "we're finally alone."

The old Gray would have raised an eyebrow and grabbed me around the waist, stunning me with a passionate kiss. But when he turned to me, his eyes lowered, and for just a moment, I thought he was going to cry.

"Emma, I have to talk to you," he said. Oh God. Suddenly, it all seemed wrong, like I'd imagined everything, like I was just some foolish girl who had let herself believe in true love. "Come with me. To the beach."

The surf was rough that night. I could hear distant flags snapping against their poles. The wind whipped fiercely across the sand, flinging it at our ankles.

"Gray, what's wrong?" I asked when I couldn't take the suspense any longer.

He shook his head, casting his eyes to the ground. "I can hardly look at you."

"Just what every girl wants to hear," I said, trying for a joke.

"I mean, it's hard for me to look at you and tell you this."

"Tell me what?"

He finally met my eyes, and there was such sadness and regret in them that I would have done almost anything to comfort him. "Emma," he said. "These past eight weeks have been the most difficult of my life. You have no idea what it's been like without you."

"I have some idea," I said.

He took my hands in his, and for a moment, my hopes soared. This wasn't going to be calamitous after all. Here we were, back at our favorite stretch of beach, the beach where we'd almost made love this summer. There was the lighthouse in the distance, its beacon flashing steady and true. "These last few weeks I met guys from all walks of life," he said. "And each of them felt the same calling I did. They each wanted to be part of something bigger than themselves, to give up their pasts and forge ahead on this dangerous path, this . . ." He stumbled on his words, seeming overcome with emotion.

"Gray, you sound like a spokesman for the Coast Guard," I said. "This is me, remember? Just tell me what you want to say."

He gazed out at the water, which hammered onto the sand and then hissed its way in retreat. "I finally figured out what I want to do with my life. What I'm meant to do."

"I know, Gray," I said. "I think it's wonderful."

"The thing is," he said, "those plans can't include you."

My heart lurched into my throat. "What do you mean?" I said.

"Because I'm leaving."

"I know you're leaving. I've always known that. But I don't mind waiting—"

"That's just it, Emma," he said, gripping my hands tightly. "I can't ask you to do that for me. You're seventeen. I don't want you waiting around for me while I go off on assignment."

"Why? Where are they sending you?"

"It's not where they're sending me. It's where I'm choosing to go. I'm going to train to become a rescue swimmer," he said. "I leave for St. Petersburg next week."

Florida. That wasn't so bad. At least it wasn't Alaska. "So we'll just have to spend every second together before you go," I said.

"Emma, you don't understand. St. Petersburg is just my first boat station. I'm on the waiting list for the Airman Program."

"Airman Program?"

"Rescue swimmers have to be trained in basic aircraft knowledge. If I get accepted there, that's sixteen weeks."

"That's only . . . four months."

"But that's just the beginning. When I'm finished the Airman Program, I enter AST School in North Carolina to become a rescue swimmer. It's one of the most intense training programs in the military. That's another four months. Followed by EMT training. We're talking about a year that I'll be away from you."

My legs wobbled, and my spine felt like it was dissolving. Because I knew where all this was going. I think I'd known it from the moment Simona opened the door yesterday. "I'll wait as long as it takes," I said.

"Emma, I can't let you put everything on hold for me while I go away for a year, maybe even more. You should be enjoying life and school and having fun. Not writing letters to some guy who doesn't even have the time to write back."

Oh God. All those letters I'd sent. All the stupid words I'd written, pouring my heart out to a guy who'd been waiting to break up with me. *Idiot!*

"So it was the letters," I said, my voice growing defensive. "They scared you off."

"No, Emma, the letters were beautiful. They kept me going. It's just, I can't hold you back anymore. Being with me . . . it's not good for you."

"How can you say that?" I said, hating the desperation in my voice.

"Because I need to do this alone."

"Why?" I pleaded. A cold wind ripped through us, like it was trying to separate us by force. "You don't have to give me up."

"I do, though. I can't be with you and do this," he said, gesturing at his uniform. "Each one takes too much out of me, and you deserve more than I can give right now. All my life, I've never had a purpose, and now I do. And I want it more than I've ever wanted anything." Silence hung between us as I took in his implication: He wanted this more than he wanted me.

"So you're breaking up with me?" I said. "Because that's what it sounds like. I just want to be sure." My voice had grown clinical and detached. Self-protective.

Gray turned toward the water and ran a hand across his scalp. "That sounds so brutal," he said. "But I have to, Emma. Don't you see?"

No, I didn't see. I swayed a little, and Gray gripped me by the shoulders to steady me. Everything was starting to go numb, like I was raising some sort of force field around myself to protect me from further damage. Releasing myself from his grip, I staggered backward and began walking away, not toward the house, but toward the ocean.

"Emma!" he called after me, following my footsteps and grabbing my arm.

"Let go of me," I said calmly, dispassionately. I was in control. I felt nothing.

"Emma, listen. I want you to understand. It's not that I don't love you—"

Love. There was that lethal word, those four letters filled with dynamite. I didn't want to hear them now. "Gray, stop. Nothing you say right now is going to make this any better."

"But you mean so much to me!"

I laughed in his face. "What do I mean to you?" His brow furrowed. "Seriously. Was I just the girl who had to heal you so you could move on with your real life? A temporary refueling station for your soul?"

"Emma—"

"God, Gray, if you say my name like that one more time, I'm going to kill you." He flinched. He didn't understand what I meant because he couldn't hear the pity in his voice, the absolute smugness I heard. He really thought he was doing this for my own good. "Just leave me alone, Gray. Just leave like you want to anyway."

"I can't leave. Not with you so angry."

"I think you'll manage," I said. He was pleading with me now, tugging my arms, trying to get me to look at him. "I mean, what did you expect? Did you think I was just going to roll with it?"

"No, but I want you to understand why I'm doing this. You saved me, Emma. In more ways than one. And I don't know if I'm strong enough to keep going without you. But I have to try."

I folded my arms across my chest, shivering in the wind. "So go off, Gray, and do your civic duty. Prove whatever it is you have to prove to yourself. But don't use me as some memory you can come back to when you're feeling lonely. I'm not going to stand here and tell you everything's okay or that I understand, because I don't. I'm not going to give you my blessing so you can leave with a free conscience." I didn't know where all this anger was coming from, but it was like someone else was speaking through me, someone much tougher and more sure of herself than I was.

I could feel Gray's eyes on me. He was waiting for me to turn around, relent, hug him and wish him well. Whatever. It wasn't going to happen. I refused to be that girl. Part of me knew that by leaving things like this, Gray could very well leave, and I might not see him again for six months. Maybe longer. But I couldn't give an inch or I'd crumble. "Goodbye, Gray," I said, without looking at him.

There was a long silence, and finally, he said, "I'm so sorry, Emma. For everything."

I stayed there shivering on the beach, waiting until I felt my heart return to its usual place, until I was certain Gray had gone because I could no longer feel his pitying eyes on my back. I couldn't go back to the house and face him and his family. Or my own.

So I stayed until the clouds obscured the stars, until the tide turned out to sea, until the cold of night hit me full force and my father came to the beach to fetch me. Putting an arm around me, he guided me back to the house without saying a word, knowing that no words could help.

CHAPTER 6

That first day back at Lockwood, the rose lay in the glass on my nightstand, completely dead. Fitting.

Owen called my cell a few times, but I couldn't bear to talk to him. Someone knocked on my door around dinnertime, maybe Jess, but I didn't get out of bed to see. When Michelle got back from rehearsal that night, she took one look at me and knew.

"Oh God, Emma. Is it Gray?" she said.

All I could do was nod.

For the first time in weeks, things felt normal between us. Michelle made me tea and Pop-Tarts, our usual comfort snack, but I couldn't eat. I lay in bed feeling drugged. All the butterflies that had ever fluttered in my stomach seemed to have died and rotted inside me.

I dragged myself to class each day and went through the motions, sleepwalking through my waking hours, then coming home to sleep some more. Sleep relieved me for a little while, but then I'd wake and remember, only to feel pain rip through me fresh and raw as ever. Owen kept calling and leaving sympathetic messages—Michelle must have told him what had happened—but I couldn't face him. For some reason, I felt ashamed, as if I'd somehow brought this upon myself.

On Thursday, I got a text from Anna that said: **Gray's gone. I miss him already.**

I wrote back to her: **Me too.**

We texted back and forth a few times, and she asked me if something bad had happened between me and Gray since he'd seemed sad while he was home. I told her we'd had a misunderstanding, but that everything was okay. I'm not sure she believed me. Then she wrote: **Truth. Do you still love him?**

Feeling sick at heart, I slowly typed, **Yes.**

The following weekend marked the opening of *The Crucible*. Out of guilt for being so pathetic and mopey all week, I took the shuttle into town and bought some cheap bouquets of roses at the grocery store—a dozen red roses for Michelle, and a dozen yellow for Owen. Then I changed into a black sweater and jeans and wrapped Michelle's red scarf around my neck to keep me warm.

It was cold and blustery as I made my way to the Commons. Other students passed me by as if I were a ghost—a real one, not a Halloween specter in a white sheet. Before my mom had died, Halloween had been our favorite holiday. She used to make my costumes from scratch, telling me stories about her Celtic ancestors who celebrated Samhain, the night the doorway between the living and the dead was at its widest and the spirit world could commune with the living. If you had lost a loved one, you were supposed to set a place for them at the dinner table in their honor. I regretted that my father and I had never enacted this simple ritual for my mom.

A low peal of thunder rumbled overhead. I shivered as the leaves swarmed around my feet, seeming possessed. When I reached the Commons Building, parents and students were congregating outside the doors of the auditorium, talking and browsing through their playbills. Feeling conspicuous on my own, I entered the auditorium and found a seat.

Lights flickered momentarily, and everyone converged into the room. As soon as the house went dark and the curtains parted, I allowed myself to be transported, losing myself in Arthur Miller's ingenious dialogue and the strong performances. Michelle ceased being Michelle, transforming into the villainous Abigail, a girl so desperate for John Proctor's love that she sticks a large needle into her belly and claims that John Proctor's wife, Elizabeth, sent her spirit out to stab her. When officials come to arrest Elizabeth for witchery, she denies the charge, but the constable finds a poppet with a needle in its belly and accuses Elizabeth of using it as a voodoo doll.

I watched with tears in my eyes as John Proctor clung to his wife, who nobly walked toward her doom. Flynn's haunting score punctuated the final scene, in which the innocent victims walk the scaffold and three nooses descend from the ceiling. Then the music halted abruptly as the theater went black.

A few seconds of silence ensued before the audience erupted into applause. After the lights rose and the actors took their bows, I scooped up the bouquets of flowers and jostled my way to the stage. When Michelle and Owen finally emerged from backstage, along with Elise and the others, it seemed that some magical transformation had taken place. Michelle and Elise were smiling at each other, Owen was rubbing Elise's shoulders and telling her what a great job she'd done, and Gallagher was beaming and congratulating the entire cast and crew. They were surrounded by a field of energy I had no part of.

I slunk up to Michelle, hoping to avoid Elise. "Emma, you're alive!" she said when she saw me. "My hermit roommate has come to celebrate with us!"

"Hey," I said, handing her the flowers. "Congratulations! You were wonderful."

"Aw, thanks, Em. That was sweet."

Elise glared at me from a few feet away, and I wished I could teleport myself back to my room. I felt so raw and vulnerable, and Elise was the last thing I needed.

Or maybe the second to last, because Flynn Markham suddenly appeared beside me and passed me a flask. "Here," he said, handing it over. "I think you need this more than I do. I heard about the big breakup."

Great. Everyone knew I'd been dumped. "No thanks," I said, falling under the scrutiny of his steely eyes. He'd lined them in a deep violet color tonight, so they looked fierce and alien, almost reptilian. He shrugged his shoulders and took a swig from his flask.

"Where's Owen?" I asked.

"Over there. In that sea of girls."

I glanced over and saw that Owen was, indeed, surrounded by a circle of girls, most of them still in their Puritan "witch" costumes. I muttered a halfhearted thanks to Flynn, then maneuvered my way through the bodies to get to Owen, handing him his bouquet.

"You didn't have to get me anything," he said, giving me one of his patented hugs. He leaned into my neck and whispered, "I'm so sorry about Gray." I wanted to melt into his arms and cry. When he pulled away, he said, "We're having a cast party in the gardens out back. You're totally staying."

"But I'm not part of the cast."

"So what? You're my honorary guest. Flynn's DJing, and Gallagher ordered a ton of pizzas."

"I don't know if I'm feeling up to it," I said. "I was planning on wallowing back in my room."

"You've done enough wallowing for today, I'm sure. You're staying."

A few moments later, we headed out to the gardens. The trees had been strung with lights, and the pathways were filled with students, talking and laughing and drinking spiked punch. Punk music with a driving rhythm came crackling out of the speakers, courtesy of Flynn. It was drizzling lightly, but nobody seemed to mind. Michelle had disappeared, but Owen wouldn't leave my side. It was like he felt obligated to stay and make sure I had a decent time. I was starting to feel a little better, but I was freezing since I'd forgotten to wear a coat. Owen offered to get his from inside.

Together, we went into the warmth of the Commons Building and wandered down the darkened hallway, trying to find our way back to the auditorium. All the lights were off except the emergency lights, which cast only a dim glow along the floors. Once inside the auditorium, we went up to the stage and Owen flicked on some stage lights. I sat down on the edge of the stage to wait for him as he found his coat. When he came back out, he joined me on the floor, scooting close enough that I could smell his cologne, woodsy and sweet.

"So how are you doing?" he said. "Still thinking about Gray?"

"What else?"

"It sucks," he said. "I really thought you guys had something."

"Yeah, well, I'm beginning to think nothing good ever lasts."

"If it makes you feel any better, I think it's over between Michelle and me, too."

"What?"

"I think we're through."

"Really? Why?" I said, trying to keep my voice even.

"I can just feel it coming," he said. "The only thing I can't figure out is why she hasn't done it already."

I bit my lip. "Maybe you're just imagining things."

"I don't think so," he said. "I just wish I knew what I did wrong."

"I'm sure it's nothing you've done."

He gave me a sidelong glance. "Has she said something to you?"

Blood rushed to my cheeks. "No," I said, a little too emphatically. "Honestly, Owen, we barely speak anymore."

"If you know anything, Emma, please tell me. I feel like a tool just waiting around for her to cut me loose."

He turned to look at me, and a curl of brown hair flopped onto his forehead. Without thinking, I reached over and pushed it out of his eyes. When my fingers grazed his temple, a surge of energy thrummed through my arm. For the first time that hellish week, I felt a spark of life again.

"Whatever happens," I said, "it's not you. You're wonderful."

He gave me a half smile, but he looked so sad, and I wanted him not to be sad anymore. And because I wanted to tell him the truth about Michelle but couldn't, and because I was feeling sorry for myself, and mostly, because he wasn't Gray, I leaned over and kissed him on the cheek. He turned his head slightly, surprised, and then we were really kissing, his lips on my lips, his hand gripping the back of my neck.

The kiss only lasted three or four seconds, but in that span I noticed his lips were thinner than Gray's, but warm and dry and strong. And even though I knew this wasn't right, my body responded to the kiss until a moment later when I felt him pull away. My eyes fluttered open to see his boyish face gazing at me in surprise.

"Oh my God." A voice sliced through the silence. I didn't have to turn around to see who it was. Her voice was almost as familiar as my own.

Owen jumped to his feet. "Michelle, it's not what you think—"

For some reason, I wanted to laugh. People always said such clichéd things when they were caught in the act. *It's not what you think. . . . I can explain. . . . It's not you, it's me. . . .*

But Michelle didn't wait for an explanation. She took off out the side door in a rage. Owen just glanced back at me with a heartbreaking expression and then followed after her.

I slumped back down on the stage, overcome by a mind-blowing, bone-numbing fatigue. The voodoo doll used in the play was lying about two feet in front of me. I leaned over and swiped it, holding the doll in my lap. It provided a strange comfort.

Finally, I shoved myself off the stage and walked back toward the party to face up to what I'd done. As I walked through the hallway, I had the strange sensation of someone following me. A chill ran up my back like a cold finger. Shivering, I quickened my pace, almost breaking into a run by the time I reached the back door.

When I opened it, I stopped cold on the threshold. No music was playing, and everyone in the garden was staring at me. Michelle and Owen weren't there, but Elise was, standing sentinel at the front of the group, her eyes boring into me with disgust.

My instinct told me to turn and go the other way, but that seemed too cowardly. And then Elise began to laugh. "So Little Miss Perfect ain't so perfect after all," she said. "I mean, really, Emma. We all know you're on the rebound, but going after your roommate's boyfriend? That's low, even for you."

Everyone had gathered behind her, and I got the surreal feeling that it was happening to someone else, that if I pinched myself, I'd snap out of this living nightmare and realize that nothing from the last week had actually happened: Gray was still my boyfriend, Owen was still a friend I'd never kissed, and Michelle was still a friend I'd never betrayed.

And because I wasn't prepared for this sort of attack, because I refused to believe that Michelle could have set me up like this, I just stood there, shocked into silence.

"What kind of person would do that to her best friend?" Elise said.

"A bitch," said another.

"What a slut."

The stream of epithets continued. When I'd finally summoned the strength to move, I descended the stairs and passed through the mob as they continued to taunt me and stare, then I set off toward the stables, hoping to find Michelle and Owen there.

About halfway down the path, the sky opened and a cold rain descended. It wasn't until I reached the bottom of the hill that I remembered the stables had burned down and a sterile new equestrian center now stood in its place. The barn where Michelle and Owen and I had forged our friendship last year was gone.

Lightning lit up the sky, followed by a low rumble of thunder. Perversely I went to stand in the same spot where I'd been struck by lightning last year, wondering if God would be audacious enough to strike the same place, and person, twice.

But this was sheet lightning, the kind that lights up the entire sky rather than descending as a scary cloud-to-ground bolt. I walked past the equestrian center and toward the stream, feeling that strange compulsion again to cross over the log bridge and into the woods. Lightning flickered sporadically, illuminating the rosebush on the opposite bank, its red blooms still brilliant even in late October.

Before I knew it, I was over the bridge and running like my life depended on it. Branches and twigs snapped below me as I trudged through the brush, moving deeper into the woods with every step. The faster I ran, the more numb I became to the elements. The rain barely seemed to touch my skin, and the storm grew distant and muffled, like something from a dream. Some mysterious momentum kept moving me forward until I burst into a clearing and onto Braeburn's playing fields.

Except the bleachers and the track and the white chalk outlines were all gone. And the sky was bright and clear, lit with a peach glow as if dawn was already approaching. The atmosphere around me seemed to change suddenly—the rain stopped, the air stilled. And while the rest of the world seemed to pause, my body hummed, like it was surging with electricity. Every one of my senses tingled.

I walked across the field, trancelike, until I reached the hill where the bleachers usually sat. From just beyond the hill came a murmuring, the sounds of many voices mingling and growing more animated. Curious, I clambered up the slick hillside, nearly toppling over when I reached the top.

Standing before me was a crowd of people all dressed in black and staring at something on the platform beyond them. Their faces were shrouded by white caps and broad-brimmed hats. It looked as though someone had assembled the cast of *The Crucible* here on the lawn. But their figures were blurry, as if I was viewing them through a piece of cloth.

"At the very least," I heard a woman say, "they should have put the brand of a hot iron on her forehead to mark her. Little will she care what they put upon the bodice of her gown. She may cover it with a scarf, and so walk the streets as brave as ever!"

I flushed when I felt Michelle's scarf around my neck, wondering if they were talking about me.

But then another voice said, "Let her cover the mark as she will. The pang of it will be always in her heart."

I recognized the line. It was from *The Scarlet Letter*.

Surely this was some kind of joke. The cast of *The Crucible* had assembled here to play a practical joke, to teach me a lesson.

I scanned the crowd to see who had spoken those words— Elise? Michelle?—yet their forms were vague and shadowy, almost interchangeable. Like faces from a nightmare.

But if this was a nightmare, then that meant it was happening again, that I had somehow lapsed into sleep and been transported into a dream.

Trying to get a grip on things, I squeezed through the crowd toward the scaffold so I could get a better look. And there stood a woman I could only presume was Hester Prynne. While I couldn't see the details of her face, her skin glowed beneath lustrous brown hair, and a scarlet letter embroidered with gold thread gleamed from her chest. Despite the fact that she stood on a scaffold holding an illegitimate baby in her arms, her expression was not humiliated at all, but proud and defiant. Almost regal.

I stood on my tiptoes trying to peer over the crowd when a voice behind me said, "I pray you, who is this woman, and why is she here set up to public shame?"

I almost answered until I saw who had asked the question. He was an older man, hunched over and wearing a multi-colored Native American garment as a disguise. This was Chillingworth, Hester's husband—thought dead at sea, now returned to find his wife a harlot. I also knew that in his zeal to uncover his wife's lover, he would destroy three lives, one being his own.

I wanted to hit him in the chest, yell at him, warn him of the devastation he was going to cause if he insisted on taking revenge, but it was as if someone had lodged a wad of cotton in my throat. No matter how hard I tried to speak, nothing came out.

"You haven't heard of Hester Prynne?" a woman said.

"I am a stranger," Chillingworth lied, "and have been a wanderer, sorely against my will. Will you tell me of Hester Prynne's—of this woman's offenses, and what has brought her to this scaffold?"

The woman told Chillingworth the story he already knew of a learned man who had married Hester, though she was half his age. He had sent her ahead to America while he tended to his business affairs in Europe, but after two years, everyone assumed he had drowned at sea. Hester, thinking the same, had taken a lover and conceived a child.

"And who may be the father?" Chillingworth asked.

"She refuses to say," the woman said.

Chillingworth frowned. "It irks me that the partner of her iniquity should not, at least, stand on the scaffold by her side. But he will be known. He will be known." A horror twisted across his features like a snake gliding across them.

I heard someone cough behind me and turned to see a young man whose face was shadowed by a pointed black hat. Though I couldn't see him clearly, he was wearing the garments of a minister and could only be the Reverend Dimmesdale. The crowd parted for him as he approached the scaffold and stood beneath the spot where Hester and the baby were.

"Hester Prynne," he said, his voice quavering. "Please speak out the name of your fellow-sinner and fellow-sufferer. Be not silent from any mistaken pity and tenderness for him, for believe me, Hester, though he were to step down from a high place and stand there beside you on that pedestal of shame, better were it so than to hide a guilty heart through life. What can your silence do for him, except tempt him to add hypocrisy to sin?"

A few months ago I had read these lines, and they had not moved me. But hearing them spoken from Dimmesdale's lips made my heart ache for him. I suddenly realized that Michelle had been right—Dimmesdale wanted to confess, but he didn't have the strength. I almost wished I could do it for him and spare him all the years of torture and heartache that would follow this night. But again, my voice failed me.

Hester shook her head. "Never!" she said, looking straight into his eyes, defiant once more.

"She will not speak," Dimmesdale said, turning to the crowd with his hand upon his heart. "Wondrous strength and generosity of a woman's heart. She will not speak."

The baby Hester was holding began to cry, and still the crowd stared on. I watched for some time as well, amazed that everyone could stand idly by while the baby wailed. Were they monsters, these Puritans?

While I couldn't speak, I could move. I rushed up to the scaffold and took my place next to Hester. No one in the crowd seemed to see me. I knew Hester's punishment was to stand here for three hours holding Pearl. If I couldn't free her, at least I could lighten her load. I placed my arms underneath the baby, and while neither mother nor child registered my presence, Hester closed her eyes and seemed to fall into a sort of trance.

This was the moment that made the townspeople most livid. Instead of looking cowed and remorseful, Hester seemed to accept her punishment gracefully, and her face was utterly serene. I knew from reading the book that she was thinking of her childhood now, recalling simpler and happier times in order to get through this ordeal.

I tried to do the same myself, recalling pleasant moments from my past—Gray and me playing in the backyard as children, our mothers watching us from the deck. My father bouncing me on his knee at church, looking down at me with adoration. Gray's hand around mine as we walked the beach this summer and promised to be there for each other always.

Shutting my eyes tightly, I imagined Gray and me out on the open sea, reunited under a star-flung sky. I wanted my reality back, not this horrible Puritan nightmare.

As I stood there channeling thoughts of Gray, my temples began to throb painfully. Lights danced before my closed eyelids, and a ringing in my ears drowned out the sounds of the townspeople. My body began to sway.

I doubled over, wishing I was free, wishing I was anywhere but here—wishing until the pain and ringing subsided, until the lights stopped dancing and the world before my eyelids went suddenly black.

CHAPTER 7

Vague memories trickled over me. I tried to ignore them, reluctant to wake and face the terror of what had happened to me. But I couldn't ignore the ache in my back.

As I sat up, pain ripped through my body, and the events of the previous night came back in a jarring wave: the cast party, the kiss with Owen, all of those accusing stares and spiteful judgments out in the garden. And then of course, the run through the woods and the nightmare that followed with Hester, Dimmesdale, and Chillingworth. But where was I now?

I whipped my head around and studied the terrain. Oh God. I was lying on the soccer field of Braeburn's campus by the bleachers, my clothes soaked from last night's rain. Thankfully, it was too early for runners to be out on the track, but I knew I needed to get out of there and back on campus soon. I thought about calling Owen to see if he could drive me back to Lockwood, but a plausible explanation for why I was there seemed to require more strength and creativity than I was feeling at the moment. Feeling achy and disoriented, I stood up and stretched, then jogged across the field and back into the woods.

The air was frigid, so I broke into a run, thankful to feel the blood pumping through my limbs. It was November first, not yet winter, but cold enough to freeze the edges of the stream. When I reached the log bridge, I had the sensation that I was crossing from one world into another, from my unsettling dreams to an even more frightening reality.

I continued up the hill to the Commons garden where everything had gone wrong last night. Signs of the cast party lay strewn about—empty soda cans, paper plates, crumpled napkins. I braved my way past the scene of my public shaming and came to the path that led back to Easty Hall and the dorms.

Fortunately, the campus was dead; I didn't spot another soul on my walk. I let myself into the dorm and walked upstairs, temporarily relishing the warm blast of heat from the ancient radiators. I was so relieved when I entered my room and saw Michelle in her bed. She began stirring when she heard the door close.

"Michelle," I whispered, terrified of what she might say.

She was rubbing sleep out of her eyes, trying to sit up. "Emma, I don't want to talk to you right now. Just leave it."

"I know, but Michelle, I wanted to say I'm sorry. I don't know what came over me last night." I sounded as pathetic as Owen had.

"I can't trust a word you say," she said. "I'm only here because the sofa in the lounge was giving me a crick in my neck. But I'd rather sleep in the parking lot than listen to your excuses right now."

She turned toward the wall and slunk down into her covers, effectively shutting me up. I sat on my bed feeling useless and awful until I heard Michelle's breathing slow down, signaling that she'd fallen back asleep. I took a quick shower and changed, then went out to the lounge to call Owen.

He answered a little groggily.

"Owen, it's me. Sorry to call so early, but I had to know if you were okay."

"Me? I'm fine. Are you okay? I couldn't find you last night."

"I've been better," I said. "What happened with Michelle?"

He sighed, and I could tell he was sitting up in his bed. "It was awful. I followed her back to the dorm, and we got into a huge fight. Then she started crying and ranting, and I could barely understand a word she was saying. It took me forever to get her to calm down enough to talk to me. She's really hurt, Emma."

"I know," I said.

"I tried to explain that, you know, the kiss—it didn't mean anything. That you were just feeling sad about Gray, and I was trying to comfort you."

"Did it work?"

"Does that ever work?" he said. "We decided we need some time away from each other. Shit, Emma, this has all gotten so screwed up."

"I'm so sorry, Owen."

He was quiet for a long time, then he said softly, "That is the reason you kissed me, right? Because you missed Gray?"

Words froze in my throat. *Why did I kiss Owen?*

My emotions had been so raw and unpredictable lately. I felt like there was someone else inside me making me do things I wouldn't ordinarily do. "Yeah," I said, finally. "I was just upset. I'm sorry I put you in the middle of it."

Silence radiated across the phone lines as I waited for him to go on, to say something comforting. As always, Owen didn't disappoint. "You're going to get over him," he said. "I know it feels like you won't, but you will. You're stronger than this. You're going to be okay."

Something in the tone of his voice undid me, and the tears started coming. But I didn't want Owen to know I was crying. "You're right," I said. "I'm going to be fine."

When we hung up, fatigue descended over me like a drug. I went back to the room and tried to sleep, but I couldn't stop thinking about what had happened last night.

Who were those characters I had seen? Figments of my

imagination? Ghosts lingering in a parallel universe, caught between my world and their own?

Why was this happening again?

Was it because I'd stood at the place where I'd been struck by lightning last year? Maybe I shouldn't have tempted fate.

But I couldn't help myself. It was like some sort of electricity, some unseen current, still ran through that place, attracting me to it like lightning to a lightning rod.

I grabbed my copy of *The Scarlet Letter* from my nightstand and flipped through its pages until I found the passage I was looking for:

> There is a fatality, a feeling so irresistible and inevitable that it has the force of doom, which almost invariably compels human beings to linger around and haunt, ghostlike, the spot where some great and marked event has given the color to their lifetime.

In my dreams, my mother haunted the beach where she killed herself. Was that what was happening to me? Was I drawn to the place where lightning had forked my life into two branches, just like it had that oak tree?

And would the split eventually kill me, too?

CHAPTER 8

I walked listlessly to Exeter Hall on Monday morning, feeling a knot in my stomach the size of a grenade. Michelle gave me the cold shoulder in Bio class, the actual "pretending I can't hear you" freeze-out. As immature as this was, the reality of my best friend and lab partner blatantly ignoring me as I repeatedly called her name sent me into a brain-curdling panic.

We were starting a new lab that day, and Michelle chose to work with Elise instead of me. I suppose some mystical bonding rites had taken place during play rehearsals, or maybe she was just trying to get back at me, but I still couldn't believe that my former best friend, not to mention Elise's former archnemesis, was now consorting with the very devil who had sought to ruin us last year.

"You can work with me," Jess said, an angel in black eyeliner.

I moved over to Jess's lab table and stared at the backs of Michelle and Elise, who last year had pretty much been the physical embodiments of good and evil in my world. It was like we were living in some alternate universe, a bizarro backward world in which everything was turned inside out.

This sickening exhibition of friendship continued in History as Overbrook droned on about how Thomas Jefferson was our country's finest and most noble president. I caught Michelle rolling her eyes at Elise. Last year I would have been the recipient of that sarcastic eye roll. And last year Michelle would have challenged Overbrook. Jefferson might have been a fine president, but he was also one of history's most flagrant hypocrites, writing that all men were created equal while he avidly defended slavery, even suppressing the newly freed country of Haiti because he feared a successful revolution in that country might inspire American slaves to revolt as well.

I only knew about this because Michelle's family was from Haiti; she had taught me all about her country's history last year. I kept waiting for her to say something, to counter Overbrook's jingoistic propaganda with her own brand of pragmatic politics, but she remained silent. I guess it was safer that way. She hadn't had an easy time of things last year, but still, I missed the days of her fiery rebuttals in the classrooms, missed our afternoons hanging out at the stables talking about school or music or boys. Life had changed irrevocably, and I found myself desperate to return to the past when everything had seemed so much simpler.

When we got to AP English, Gallagher began his unit on *The Awakening*. The class had moved beyond *The Scarlet Letter*, but I hadn't. Hester and Dimmesdale's story still burned in my brain, and now I seemed to be living my own version of it.

Glares and whispers followed me as I left English class and made my way to the dining hall alone. There is no place more hellish to a teenage girl in poor social standing than a high school cafeteria. Girls sit in packs like wolves waiting for something they can sink their teeth into.

I didn't know why I'd gone to the dining hall at all—I had amassed an impressive stockpile of microwaveable foods for just such an occasion. But I wasn't going to run away or let myself be cast out of society just for kissing a boy. I thought back to the way Hester had stood before that crowd for three hours, looking proud and defiant. I could do that, too.

But as soon I set foot in the dining hall, my bravado waned fast. Michelle was sitting with Elise. Amber and Chelsea were at another table, gossiping. I was relieved to see Jess at a corner table, reading by herself. I speed-walked past the glares of my classmates and took a seat across from her. She looked up from her lettuce wrap, surprised.

"Is it okay if I sit here?" I asked.

"Yeah, sure," she said. I set my tray down across from her, took a seat, and looked down at my meatball sub, hardly hungry. "So it's your turn for the social pariah treatment this week?" she said.

"Apparently."

"Because you kissed your roommate's boyfriend?"

"Ugh, you heard?"

"Everyone's heard. That's pretty high on the list of high school don'ts."

"Yeah, I'm aware. I just . . ."

"Didn't think you'd get caught?"

I glanced up at her, defensive. "No, it's not that. It's more complicated than that."

"Always is."

"No, seriously, you don't understand. Michelle . . ." I fell silent, realizing I couldn't tell Jess that Michelle had cheated on Owen this summer.

"Michelle what?" Jess said.

"Nothing."

"I'm not judging you," she said. "It's not like Michelle and Owen were couple of the year. I saw it coming for a while."

"Saw what coming?"

"Their breakup. I knew it was over . . . before it really was."

"How did you know?"

"Michelle used to hang out with us during band rehearsals

at the beginning of the summer. I could see her gradually pulling away from him, but she just didn't have the heart to tell him."

"Did she tell you that?" I asked, feeling hurt that Michelle had never confided any of this to me over the summer. Then again, I hadn't really given her the chance.

"Well"—Jess shrugged—"Not exactly. I just picked up on the signs."

"But if she didn't want to be with him anymore, then why is she so angry with me?"

"It's the principle of it," she said. "You don't kiss your best friend's boyfriend. Period."

She was absolutely right. It didn't matter if things were almost over between them. I had betrayed Michelle's trust and violated our friendship.

"God, I feel horrible. I wish there was something I could do. I hate not being able to talk to her."

"I hear you," Jess said.

"And now it's like she's become best friends with Elise just to spite me. I can't believe it. No offense. I know Elise is your friend."

"*Was* my friend."

"You guys had a falling-out?"

She took a deep breath. "You could say that."

"I thought something must have happened," I said. "You all used to have your little clique of cool, and this year . . . well, I don't see you guys together anymore."

She studied my face, perhaps wondering if she could confide in me. "Look, I know what people used to say about us. The Fearsome Four and all that. I know sometimes we acted like bitches."

"Sometimes?"

She smirked. "I'd been sick of it for a long time, but I didn't know how to get myself out. It was like I was a member of some twisted teenage mafia. And then Elise's sixteenth birthday party gave me the out I was looking for. We all got pretty drunk and something really ugly happened—I'm not going to go into it right now—suffice it to say, we all said things we regretted. And then we went our separate ways. End of story."

So that was why Elise didn't have her posse around her anymore. Maybe that's why she seemed hell-bent on befriending Michelle.

"Do you miss her?" I said.

"Who?"

"Elise."

Jess gave me a momentary *let's drop it* look, but said, "Elise and I have been friends since third grade. So yeah, sometimes I miss her, but . . ."

"But what?"

"Was there ever someone who knew you really well, but she only knew you in this one particular way, so you were afraid to show her this other side of you because you worried how she might take it?" I nodded ruefully, thinking of my dad and how much I worried about not remaining the perfect little girl he wanted me to be. "That's how it was with me and Elise. Around her I always felt like I was in second place before we even started. So eventually I stopped trying, even when I wanted to. We got trapped in these roles we played, and it was like we prevented each other from growing up. Once we stopped being friends, I could finally move on and be myself."

"So that explains the new clothes, new hair . . ."

"New me. But strangely, this is more me than I ever was before."

I took a bite of my sandwich, unsure what to say, but grateful that she had trusted me enough to share something so personal.

When we got to PE later that day, I felt angry when I saw Elise. Angry for Jess. Angry for myself. Elise's villainization of me for kissing Owen wasn't fair. My punishment didn't fit my crime. I was sick of all the slut-shaming that went on around this place, particularly as kissing a guy, even if it was my roommate's boyfriend, didn't exactly qualify as slutty behavior.

Since it was drizzling outside, Ms. Loughlin had us playing floor hockey indoors. Before the opening whistle, I stood across from Elise at the centerline. She glared at me with an intensity that only solidified my hatred for her. "You're going down," she hissed.

The whistle blew, and I slapped the puck. Jess picked up my pass and dribbled it down court, making our first goal. We returned to the centerline, and this time Elise got the puck first. She sailed down the court and scored a goal for her team. The game went back and forth like this for twenty minutes until our teams were tied. Elise was my permanent shadow on the court. At one point, I almost scored the tie-breaking goal, but Elise stuck out her leg, sending me sprawling onto the floor. From the laughter that ensued, you would have thought we were a class of socially challenged third graders. Jess came to my rescue and helped me stand up.

As I was brushing myself off, Elise strode over and said, "Told ya you were going down."

And that was it. Something snapped inside me.

I headed back up the court, my leg aching, adrenaline surging through my body. When the whistle blew, I seized the puck and dribbled it down the court. When I saw that Elise had left the corner of the goal open, I prepared to take a shot. For a fraction of a second, I stared at the open goal as Elise moved in for the block. But as I drew my arms back, I shifted my aim ever so slightly and smacked the puck. I watched in fascination as it sailed through the air, seeming to hover in slow motion right before it connected with Elise's exquisite cheekbone.

The whistle screeched, and Elise crumpled to the floor. Ms.

Loughlin came running onto the court to make sure she was okay. When Elise finally drew her head up, her hand clutching her cheek, she glared at me and said, "You bitch!"

I was breathing heavily from exertion, but I managed to say, "Whoops, sorry."

"Did you hear that?" Elise said to Loughlin. "She did it on purpose!"

"Girls, that's enough," Loughlin said.

"I think I have a concussion," Elise said.

Loughlin bent down and examined her face. "The worst you'll have is a black eye."

"A black eye?" Elise said. "But I can't! We're having dinner with the Hilfigers this weekend."

A few girls chuckled, including Amber and Chelsea. I tried my hardest not to smile.

"It was an accident," Loughlin said. "Now, everyone to the locker rooms."

"It was no accident," Elise snarled.

But Loughlin was already shooing everyone off the court. Elise glared at me from the ground and finally got up and stalked to the locker room. I hesitated, wondering whether I could retrieve my clothes later in the day. But then Ms. Loughlin asked to speak with me privately.

I jogged over to her, and at first she regarded me with teacherly disapproval, but then her face softened, almost like she was semi-amused by what I'd done.

"What's going on with you two?" she asked.

I was still out of breath from that last run down the court. "I'm sorry," I said. "I know I shouldn't have. But it's like . . . everything built up inside me, and I just . . . snapped."

"Listen, Emma," she said. "You're a good kid. I hate to see you giving in to your anger like this. You're better than that." She put a hand on my shoulder.

I knew she meant well; so many grown-ups did. But I wasn't sure she was right. Was I really better than that? Why did I always have to take the high road? It had felt good to let go of my anger and smack that puck in Elise's face. Whenever I did the so-called right thing, I ended up feeling like a doormat, stepped on and abused.

And since the night of the cast party, something had begun inside me. An unraveling. A loosening that made it feel as though parts of me were coming unhinged, but that this loss of control was exactly what I needed. It was freeing and terrifying at the same time, the way I imagined hang gliding would be—exhilarating until that moment when you realized there was nothing standing between you and the hard earth below.

I skipped several classes that week. School had become far too heinous to attend on a regular basis. And the next weekend, I bombed the PSAT. I knew I was blowing it even as I filled in the tiny bubbles on the Scantron, but there was no way I could sit still for three hours focusing on theoretical multiple choice questions when my real life was falling apart at the seams.

Thanksgiving came and went without incident. Unlike Elise, we didn't have any glamorous plans to sail to Nantucket to dine with fashion designers and millionaires. We had a quiet meal in which Barbara cooked the turkey into shoe leather, Grandma got a little silly on old-fashioneds, my dad complained about finances, and I sat as silently as possible, hoping no one would pay me any attention.

By dessert, my father had gotten around to his requisite college badgering, and just to appease him, I rattled off a list of colleges I was planning to apply to: Boston College, Wellesley, Mount Holyoke, Amherst. Given my performance in school lately, I might have been aiming a little high. I got a stomachache thinking about what my dad's reaction would be once my PSAT scores arrived.

The next morning, I went for a run on the beach, trying to take out all my stress and anxiety on the sand. I ran all the way to the lighthouse, sprinting the last two hundred feet or so, then stopping so suddenly I thought my heart might give out. I doubled over to catch my breath, heaving in bursts of cold air that burned my lungs.

I peered up at the lighthouse and watched its steady beam, wondering if there was some sailor out in the sea right now watching it, too, thinking of a loved one he'd left on shore. Of course, this made me think of Gray, and a fresh wave of pain ripped through me.

It had taken Gray an entire year to fall in love with me and only two months to fall out of it. But me? I couldn't seem to let him go. I wondered if I'd ever stop loving him.

I wanted to scream at the unfairness of it, pull my hair out, smash something hard against the ground. I latched onto the scorpion necklace.

To Emma, the only antidote for my sting.

What a crock!

Impulsively, I yanked the necklace off and chucked it into the ocean. I stood there for several minutes staring angrily at the waves, watching them churn and break into foam. When the roaring became too maddening, I started for home. I'd only taken a few steps when a glint of light on the sand caught my eye. I leaned down to inspect it and laughed bitterly. It was Gray's scorpion pendant.

I had tried to get rid of it, but like a sick joke, the sucker had washed back to me. Some uneasy, superstitious feeling made me refasten the dog tag around my neck. I knew Gray had meant the scorpion to be my touchstone, my lifeline to him. But now it felt like a burden I had to wear, a stinging reminder of the love I no longer had.

CHAPTER 9

As soon as we got back from Thanksgiving break, the teachers went into high gear in preparation for midterms. When Elise walked into Bio, I noticed a small red scar under her right eye where the hockey puck had hit her. I felt a tiny smidgen of guilt mixed with a good deal of satisfaction.

But when Elise sat next to Michelle, my momentary feeling of victory faded, and I only felt depressed. I hated that Michelle was falling for Elise's charms and that I couldn't do a thing to stop it. And even though I didn't trust Elise's motives, I couldn't believe that Michelle's judgment had lapsed so severely as to allow her to befriend someone who wanted to destroy her.

Toward the end of the day, I sat in French class, taking out my anger on a piece of loose-leaf. We were translating the last chapter of *The Hunchback of Notre-Dame,* in which excavators find Quasimodo's dead body embracing Esmeralda's skeleton. It was both morbid and heartbreaking.

At the end of class, Madame cleared her throat. "Mademoiselles, j'ai un annonce special," she began to say in French. I'd sort of taken to tuning Madame Favier out, but when I heard the words *Paris* and *école,* my ears sprang to attention.

Apparently, our sister school in Paris was sponsoring a full scholarship of tuition, room, and board for an entire year for an incoming Lockwood senior with a stellar academic record and a desire to study French literature. A letter of interest was due before winter break, followed by transcripts and letters of recommendation in January.

Everything fell away—the chattering of the students, the sound of Jess cracking her gum, the buzz of the fluorescent lights overhead—as I realized this was exactly what I needed. To make a clean break from this place. To cut my ties with all these bad memories and venture out on some exciting new journey in a foreign city. And what's more, to study French literature. I wanted—no, I needed—this scholarship.

My biggest competition would be Elise. Not that she needed the money, but once she found out I was interested, she'd apply just to spite me. I got a sudden image in my head of Elise striding down the Champs Élysées wearing a striped boat-neck top with black wide-leg trousers and a beret. She'd stop at a little café where everyone knew her name and where the proprietor, Phillipe, always reserved her favorite table.

Non, non, ce table est reservé pour Elise! Mon petite ange! Ugh.

Maybe the Admissions Committee would sympathize with the fact that I'd never been to Paris before. Maybe between now and March, I could brush up on French literature and impress them with my vast knowledge of Camus and Sartre, my stunning command of French naturalism and existentialism. Maybe Elise's head would spontaneously combust in Biology.

I was still daydreaming about it as I left class and headed toward the gymnasium. "Hello?" I heard behind me. "Terre à Emma!"

I turned to see Jess struggling to catch up with me. "Hey," I said. "Now you're mocking me in French?"

"Mais oui," she said. "You're thinking of applying for that scholarship, aren't you?"

"Definitely," I said. "Aren't you?"

She shook her head. "I have no desire to rub shoulders with a bunch of snotty Gallic prep school kids. Everyone chain-smoking and quoting Baudelaire all the time? No, thank you."

I laughed. "Well, I'm in love with the idea. I'm going to type up my letter of interest and get it to Favier this afternoon. I'm not taking any chances on this one."

"You shouldn't," she said. "Elise will be gunning for it."

"Don't remind me. I feel like no matter where I turn, she's always there."

Jess was nodding; she knew exactly what I was talking about. "Hey, what are you doing this weekend?" she said.

"I'll have to check my calendar," I said. "My social life is a whirlwind of activity." Jess grinned. "Why? Did you have something in mind?"

"Want to get out of this place? Like, go into Waverly or something? I've been meaning to get my roots touched up."

I studied the crown of her head and saw that her natural brown hair was indeed growing in. "I would love that," I said.

She glanced over at my hair, her brows knitting together. "You know, I think you ought to do something with your hair, too."

"What's wrong with my hair?"

"Nothing. You just need a change. A symbolic break."

"A break from what?"

"More like who?" she said, wagging her eyebrows knowingly. "This weekend, I'm taking you to Salon Axis. And we're going thrift shopping for some new clothes." I looked at her skeptically. "You're going to forget about Gray, and we're going to set you up with someone new. Now that Owen and Michelle have broken up, maybe you could—"

"Don't even say it," I said. "Way too complicated. Even if I thought of Owen as more than a friend—which I don't—it would never work. There's too much history there. And of course, there's Michelle."

"Why are you going out of your way to protect Michelle's feelings when she won't even talk to you?" she said.

I shrugged and shook my head, but she had a point. "How about you and Flynn?" I said. "You two have that love-hate thing going."

She laughed a little too loudly. "Flynn? Are you serious?"

"What? You guys seem to flirt a lot."

"It's not flirting," she said. "I assure you."

"Okay, okay."

She laughed again like the idea was absurd. As much as I disliked Flynn, he was easy on the eyes, and he had that whole rebel-without-a-cause vibe that was pretty much catnip to girls my age. If he wasn't such an asshat, I might have had a thing for him myself.

That Saturday, as planned, Jess and I stood waiting in front of Easty Hall for the highly unreliable shuttle. With any luck, by this time next year I'd be driving my dad's Volvo, which I'd have to wash and scrub within an inch of its life to get out the fish smell. The car was a boat—long, bulky, and pumpkin orange. But I didn't care. As a senior with wheels, I would no longer be a prisoner at Lockwood. I could take off every weekend, drive anywhere in the country. Briefly, I allowed myself to entertain the fantasy of visiting Gray in North Carolina before my stupid subconscious realized the error.

"Terre à Emma," Jess said.

"Huh?"

"You were off in the clouds again. Please tell me you weren't thinking of a certain muscular Coast Guardian."

"No," I said. "But it would help if you wouldn't remind me how muscular he is."

"Fair enough," she said.

"I was just thinking what it would be like to have a car next year. All the cool stuff we'd be able to do."

"Hello," she said. "You're not going to be here, remember? You're going to be in Paris, eating chocolate croissants and drinking too much wine and maybe developing a fashion sense."

I scoffed and rolled my eyes, conjuring up the image of Elise in pinstripes again, Parisian Barbie.

The shuttle finally arrived and took us into Waverly Falls, an old mill town turned eco-friendly shopping mecca and the only place within a ten-mile radius where a Lockwood student could buy somewhat fashionable clothes, a decent cup of coffee, and a meal that wasn't patty or finger-shaped.

We started our tour at Vintage, where it became clear that Jess was an expert at thrift-store shopping and I . . . well, wasn't. As I strolled through the rows of tightly packed jeans and halter tops and wedge shoes, I realized Jess was right: I had no fashion sense. It wasn't that my clothes were hideous or outdated, just that I dressed to disappear. Fade into the woodwork. Lots of beige and gray and black. On that particular day, I was wearing a black turtleneck over a gray skirt with black tights and black boots. I might as well have been a Puritan.

Jess encouraged me to choose clothing for more frivolous reasons, say, just because I liked the color or the material felt good in my hands. After several failed outfits, I tried on a halter dress in a blue textured knit with a pattern of opposing diagonal stripes that met at a vertical line down the center, in effect splitting me in two. With my black tights, the dress looked both playful and sexy, sort of rock star.

When I emerged from the dressing room, Jess raised her eyebrows admiringly. "That's a hot dress," she said. "But you know what it needs?" She ran back into the store and came back with a pair of Mary Jane heels in glitter red.

"Really?" I said. "*Wizard of Oz* shoes?"

"Trust me. Put 'em on." And so I did, to Jess's enthusiastic approval. "Oooh, devil in a blue dress, yes!" she said.

I stared at myself in the mirror. I had to admit, Jess had a certain flair for styling an outfit. And the dress, while a bit out of my comfort zone, looked like me. Or at least the "me" that had been emerging lately. I went back into the dressing room and changed into my normal clothes, feeling that temporary thrill of transformation dissipate, like all the air deflating from a balloon.

Afterward, we strolled through Waverly Falls, making our way across the covered bridge to the other side of town where the falls were. Salon Axis was on the opposite side of the train tracks.

Jess knew all the employees there and introduced me to a tiny stylist named Tilda. "You're in good hands," she told me, then said to Tilda, "Don't let her wimp out!" just before I got dragged out of sight.

I sat in Tilda's chair and she gathered my hair into her hands, studying it. I suddenly felt self-conscious about my lack of style. "So," she said with a heavy Italian accent, "what would you like?"

I wasn't sure. I hadn't really thought it through. "Maybe we could just do a consultation today and I could come back another day for the cut?"

Her eyes met mine in the mirror, issuing a challenge. "No, you should cut it. Get rid of this dead stuff that's weighing you down."

I glanced around nervously, my eyes falling on a woman at the far end of the salon. She had chin-length black hair, straight and shiny, with a widow's peak. But a chunk of her hair was ice blue. It made her look like a comic book hero, spunky and fearless.

"How'd she do that?" I asked.

Tilda glanced over. "The blue streak? Her hair's been double processed, stripped of its real color, then the blue added on top."

I watched as the girl shook out her hair, that streak of blue fanning out and settling back into place like magic. "I want to do that."

Tilda's eyes bulged. "With your hair this long, it won't work."

"So cut it," I said. "Up to my shoulders. And I want to do red instead of blue. A red streak on the right side."

"Are you sure?"

"I'm sure. And can you put some layers in the front so it'll fall like that?"

Tilda nodded, a satisfied smile on her lips.

An hour later, I sat under one of those finishing helmets with foil wrapped around the chunk of hair, wishing I could turn back time. Jess came over to keep me company. "I'm dying!" she said, glancing up from her magazine. "I can't believe you did this."

Neither could I. And I was getting that regretful feeling in the pit of my stomach, that pang people must get when they wake up to find a tattoo on their body. Only my stripe wasn't permanent; at least, that's what I told myself. Finally, Tilda took me back to the sink to remove the foil and wash off the extra dye.

When I sat back down in the chair, I couldn't see the stripe since my hair was so wet. But as Tilda dried it, the cut revealed itself as a sleek asymmetrical bob, and the streak emerged like a lick of flame. Tilda called it vermilion red, and it was anything but subtle. And so far in my life, I'd been all about subtle.

"Oh my God!" Jess squealed.

"Is that a good or bad squeal?" I asked.

"Are you kidding? It looks amazing!" Tilda nodded solemnly. "With that hair, your new dress is gonna look amazing."

After thanking and tipping Tilda, we headed back to the shuttle stop. I paused when I caught sight of my reflection in the glass. It was me and yet not me. Bold and vibrant. Light and carefree. It made me feel stronger and more alive.

As we crossed the bridge to the other side of town, it wasn't the broken Emma passing through; it was this new girl, and some foreign energy radiated from her, so powerfully that even a stranger might have recognized it as something close to audacious.

CHAPTER 10

It's surprisingly easy to avoid someone, even if you share a room. Michelle and I continued our standoff over the next few weeks, but I was growing impatient. Yes, I had kissed her boyfriend, but Michelle had cheated on him, too. I knew two wrongs didn't make a right, but it wasn't as black and white as Michelle liked to believe. I couldn't understand why she wanted to cut me out of her life so completely without even trying to resolve our differences.

To make matters worse, Overbrook asked me to stop by his office after school one day. In front of the entire class. The girls *ooohed* dramatically, hoping I was in trouble, which I probably was. I felt like I was about eight years old, getting reprimanded for fighting at recess. I reminded myself that my number one priority was to win that scholarship to Paris so I wouldn't have to deal with any of this nonsense next year.

At the end of the day, I walked to Easty Hall with an ache in my gut. When parents come down the main drive to campus, Easty Hall is the first building they see—a long, low building of dull gray stone with leaded casement windows and four commanding gables that give the impression that the building disapproves of you.

My footsteps echoed across the wooden floors as I walked

to Overbrook's office. I found him sitting at his desk, red pen in hand, his eyes tracing over someone's essay.

"Ms. Townsend, please sit," he said, barely looking up from the paper and gesturing to the small, uncomfortable chair across from him. The stack of papers in front of him was held down with a snow globe paperweight. Inside the snow globe was a tiny miniature of Lockwood. When he caught me studying it, he picked it up and shook it.

"It's lovely, isn't it?" he said, watching fake snow float down on his miniature school. "A gift from an old friend who knows Lockwood is my home. My sanctuary." I nodded politely and waited for him to get to his point. "Ms. Townsend, I've always considered you a bright, sensible girl, but your behavior of late suggests that you may be straying a bit and losing sight of your future."

"What do you mean, sir?"

"You seem distracted in class, your average has decreased several points, and your attendance has been spotty. When I see a student heading down a treacherous path as you are, I feel compelled to step in. I am here to help you, after all. You do believe that, don't you, Ms. Townsend?"

"Yes, sir," I lied.

"Your reputation is vital if you want to succeed in college and in life. Grades will only take you so far. Teacher recommendations, honors and accolades—these are what will set you apart when it comes time to apply to colleges." He cleared his throat with a phlegmy gurgle. "It has come to my attention that you're vying for the scholarship to attend our sister school in Paris next year. A very prestigious program. It would do wonders for your transcript."

"Yes, sir?"

"I want you to keep in mind that even though your grades in French are very strong, you can be rejected for many reasons. And you're up against some very stiff competition." As if he needed to remind me. "The application will require a letter of recommendation from me, which I would be happy to write, provided you are able to keep your behavior . . . well, more in keeping with the core values of a Lockwood student."

"And what are those?" I said, hearing a note of insolence creep into my voice.

"Why, you must know them, Ms. Townsend," he said. "They're part of the Lockwood code. Leadership. Academics. Respect. Discipline." I didn't bother to tell him that our core values spelled out the word LARD. "If you aim to exemplify these values in everything you do, you may find yourself in Paris this time next year. But you must make certain you get yourself back on the right path, is that clear?"

"Yes, sir," I said, feeling my insides go cold. Because right now, nothing in my life seemed very clear.

I fled from his office and out of the building, taking shelter against the cold stone wall. I felt breathless and a little dizzy. I wasn't used to being scolded by teachers. I was the good kid. The A student. Not the truant. The discipline case.

I walked back to the dorm, feeling sick to my stomach. Maybe a good run would clear my head and get me back on "the right path," as Overbrook had said.

After suiting up in leggings and a sweatshirt, I set off down the hill past the equestrian center and headed up toward Old Campus and the Commons. By the time I reached the top of the hill, I felt winded and light-headed. That runner's high kept eluding me. I was determined to keep going until I found it.

When I came to the woods for the second time, I hit my stride. My body was moving almost robotically, and my mind had achieved that blissful, trancelike state.

Suddenly, I heard a trilling coming from across the stream. At first I thought it was a bird, but as I listened more intently, it sounded like a child's humming.

Mesmerized by the song, I crossed the log bridge and saw

a flash of red dart ahead of me. The scarlet flash was like a beacon, calling me forward, so I followed it until I came to a pebbly area by the water's edge. A little girl in a red dress and a white cap was skipping along the stones. She seemed oblivious to my presence at first, but when she saw me, a smile leaped across her face like she'd been waiting for me. Her clothing was old-fashioned, yet there was something familiar about her face, like maybe she was one of the teacher's daughters who had gotten into the wardrobe closet for *The Crucible.*

I approached to ask who she was and what she was doing here, but every time I got too close, she squealed in delight and ran in the opposite direction. The sun seemed to follow her as she did, a roving spotlight that danced with her across the ground.

I followed her even as she tried to evade me, and our game continued until she tired and sat down on the bank. She leaned over the stream to spy her reflection in the water, and protectively, I ran to grab her and keep her from falling in. Briefly, I saw our two reflections, one slightly larger than the other, but otherwise, almost mirror images. Before I could observe any further, she pulled out of my grasp and went running back up the bank, leaving only my reflection in the stream.

When she came to the rosebush, she leaned over and plucked a flower, then scampered off through the woods. Curious. The roses in the Commons garden had died already. How did this rosebush still have blooms in the middle of December? What strange enchantment was it that allowed these roses to bloom past their prime?

Before I could wonder very long, I realized I'd lost the little girl. I broke into a run after her. Wintry branches blurred into streaks of brown and black as I ran faster and faster, losing all sense of time.

When I reached the clearing at Braeburn, the little girl

danced into the sunlight of the broad expanse of lawn. She stopped to grab two sticks and some leaves from the ground, then attached the leaves to the sticks so they looked like arms and legs. She placed a black leaf on top of one of the sticks to make a hat. On the other stick, she pierced a red rose petal onto a small branch in the center. Then she waved her puppets back and forth, making them dance like marionettes.

Manipulating her little voice into the deep bellow of a man, she said dramatically, "You will leave this town at once, Hester Prynne, never to return. Your name shall be black in the village, and all will know you for a harlot by the scarlet letter on your breast."

I took a step back at the sound of Hester's name. The little girl looked at me, and I knew suddenly who she must be. "What's your name?" I asked.

"I am Pearl," she answered, meeting my eyes. Pearl was Hester Prynne's daughter. Only she was no longer an infant, but a girl of seven or eight.

I blew air through my cheeks, letting the truth wash over me. Somehow, it had happened again. I had involuntarily traveled into *The Scarlet Letter,* only this time I was able to speak.

Pearl continued her dialogue. "Woman, you are a sinner!" she said in the same booming male voice. "It is because of your mistakes that we must transfer the child to other hands." The words were so carefully chosen I thought she must be recreating some scene she had actually witnessed.

She staked the puppet of the man into the ground and began animating the other puppet, the one with the rose petal in the center. In a high-pitched, female voice, she said, "God gave me the child! She is my happiness. She is my torture. You shall not take her! I will die first!"

Pearl then began hurling stones at this puppet with a vicious intensity. I was watching in horror until a woman appeared behind her, grabbing Pearl's arms to still them. But

Pearl struggled out of her grasp, manic with anger and aggression. She stared at me with a directness that chilled me.

An oily voice seeped into my consciousness. "What naughty elf is this?"

I looked at Pearl to see if this was her mimicry, but instead found myself face-to-face with Chillingworth. He seemed to have aged immeasurably since I'd last seen him, like he was slowly decomposing above the grave. Amusingly, with his bony limbs and his head topped by a narrow black hat, he resembled Pearl's makeshift puppet.

He walked by me as if I were invisible, ripping Pearl's puppet from the ground.

"A very strange child!" Chillingworth said. "She talks to imaginary voices and has no friends but the sticks and leaves. Yes, a strange and lonely child. It is easy to see you in her, Hester Prynne. Would it be possible, do you think, to analyze that child's nature, and, from it, give a shrewd guess at the father?"

"Nay," Hester said. "A knowledge of men's hearts would be needful to complete the solution of that problem. And you know nothing of the heart; only vengeance."

"Do you know me so little, Hester Prynne?" he said. "Even if I wanted vengeance, what could I do better than to let you live with this burning shame upon your bosom?" He laid his forefinger on the scarlet letter, which seemed to scorch Hester's breast. "Hester," he said, "I gave my best years to feed the hungry dream of knowledge. What business did I have to attach myself to youth and beauty like your own? How could I have deluded myself with the idea that my intellectual gifts might veil physical deformity in a young girl's fantasy? Nay, from the moment we came down the old church steps together, I might have foreseen that scarlet letter blazing at the end of our path."

"I was honest with you," Hester said. "I felt no love, nor pretended any."

"True," he replied. "It was my folly."

"But I have greatly wronged you," she murmured.

"We have wronged each other," he said. "Therefore, I seek no vengeance, plot no evil against you. But, Hester, the man lives who has wronged us both! Who is he?"

"Please don't ask me!" Hester said, looking firmly into his face. "You will never know."

"Never?" he said. "Hester, know that I shall seek this man, as I have sought truth in books. I shall see him tremble. Sooner or later, he will be mine!" Hester broke down crying, and I felt helpless to do anything for her. "Just as you protect him now, you must also protect me," he said. "Tell no one of my identity. Under the guise of a physician, I will seek him out and ruin him. You may weep for him now, but you and yours, Hester, belong to me. My home is where you are, and where he is." His eyes blazed and a twisted smile warped his face.

"Why do you smile?" Hester said. "Have you enticed me into a bond that will prove the ruin of my soul?"

"Not your soul," he said. "No, not yours."

With one last glance at Hester and Pearl, Chillingworth left the clearing and ascended the hill toward the scaffold.

"I do not like that man," Pearl said.

"Then we shall not tarry near him," Hester said. "Come." She took Pearl's hand and led her toward the wood.

"Wait, Mother," Pearl said, remembering me.

"What is it, child?"

"We must wait for the girl."

"What girl is this?"

"I do not know," she said.

I called out my name.

"It is Emma," Pearl repeated. "She walks behind us now."

"Foolish child," Hester said. "Perhaps Chillingworth is right. There is witchcraft in you yet."

I followed behind them at a distance, but Pearl kept turning around to make sure I was still there. We hadn't walked very long when I realized where we were headed. We were climbing a rather steep hill, and the terrain was growing rockier, the foliage denser. And then I saw the familiar sight—boulders piled in formation, as if they'd been placed there by mankind instead of nature. Here were the witch caves I'd discovered months ago.

Hester and Pearl disappeared behind the overgrowth, and I ran after them until I'd reached the entrance to one of the caves. Weeds obscured whatever lay beyond. Ripping off the mass of tangled vines revealed a small wooden door, painted red.

I knocked once, then pushed the door open, surprised when it gave way to a tiny cottage within.

"Emma is with us now," Pearl told her mother when I came in. "See? The door just opened."

"Peace, child. That is only the wind," Hester said. "Now stop imagining ghosts and get ready for bed."

"Mother . . . ," Pearl began to say, but I held my finger to my lips, not wanting her to upset Hester. I glanced around, noticing a small living area with chairs and a table, a woven rug on the ground, ashes in the hearth, and a thatched area covered with blankets. Hester sat at the table and began to work on a piece of embroidery. I had forgotten this was how Hester made a living—sewing and doing embroidery for the very townspeople who had banished her.

I sat down on the thatched area, the closest thing to a bed, and watched Hester sew. Pearl took off her dress and put on a white nightgown. Without the brilliant red dress and cap, she looked even younger than before.

"Mother," she said. "There is a girl here, even if you can't see her."

"Hush, and cease these fancies," Hester said. "The girl is in your head."

"That doesn't mean she is not real," argued Pearl.

Hester sighed, exasperated. Then she set down her sewing and lifted Pearl from off the floor, placing her on her lap. "Where do you come up with such stories?"

"It is not a story," Pearl said. "Emma is real. She belongs here."

I felt a tremor in my stomach at her words. What did she mean?

Pearl giggled when she saw my reaction and grabbed her rose from the floor, plucking off its petals and tossing them at me, one by one. Then she began humming the playful melody that had lured me across the bridge, only now it sounded dark and foreboding.

Hearing it gave me an eerie chill, and I backed toward the door, anxious to leave.

"She is leaving now, Mother," Pearl said.

"Who?"

"Emma."

"Pearl, I told you—"

But Hester stopped mid-sentence. Her eyes grew wide as if she were seeing me for the first time. Pearl came to stand by her side, and the two of them stared at me like I was a ghost.

Looking directly into their eyes, I realized why Pearl had looked so familiar to me, why my reflection in the water had merged so seamlessly with hers. Because Pearl was me. And now that I could see her face clearly, so was Hester. They were reflections of me at different stages of my life—Pearl, my little girl self, and Hester, my future self.

An icy chill enshrouded me. Without thinking, I tore out of the cottage and began running, back down the hill and through the forest until I reached the place I knew so well— the bridge that lay across the boundary between these two worlds. I flew across it faster than I'd ever dared and didn't stop until I was safely back at the dorm, wondering how long I'd been gone and if anyone had even missed me.

CHAPTER 11

It was dusk, and once again my room was empty. I had to talk to someone about what had just happened. And while that someone probably should have been my father, I didn't want to worry him or bring on the inevitable doctor's appointment, even if I was beginning to wonder if I might not be crazy after all.

I tried to rationalize what had happened. Maybe I'd run too long and had gotten dehydrated. Or my runner's high had made me hallucinate. Maybe I just needed sleep.

Maybe everything would make sense in the morning.

Only, when I woke and saw Michelle lying in bed with her back to me, nothing made any more sense. Later that day once Michelle had left for the afternoon, I called Owen. I hadn't planned on telling him about my bizarre experience in the woods, but as soon as I heard his voice, I knew I had to confide in someone.

Owen had believed me last year when I'd told him about my travels into *Jane Eyre*. At the very least, he'd hear me out and wouldn't rush me off to the nearest psych ward.

When I finished telling him my story, he said, "Jeez, Emma! You sleepwalked to Braeburn?"

"Not exactly," I said. "Because I wasn't really asleep. It happened when I was running. I fell into a sort of trance, and then suddenly I was across the log bridge and in this other world."

"So it's kind of like you were dreaming while awake?"

"Sort of."

"Were you lucid?" he asked. "I mean, did you know you were dreaming?"

"Vaguely," I said. "I knew I was conversing with fictional characters, but I couldn't shake myself out of the fantasy."

"It sounds like some form of narcolepsy," he said.

"Isn't that where you fall asleep at unexpected times?"

"Not necessarily. I heard of this woman who fell asleep every time she laughed. The trigger is different for everyone. In your case, it seems to have something to do with running. Your body's moving, but your mind goes on autopilot. It's kind of how dolphins sleep."

"Dolphins?"

"Yeah, half of their brain shuts down to let them rest, and the other half stays active and alert so they don't get eaten by predators. They never stop swimming even while they're sleeping."

"So what you're saying is, I'm part sea mammal?"

He made a few dolphin clicks and squeaks. "Did you understand that?"

"You are so mean," I said, laughing.

"Here's what I recommend," he said. "A day away from Lockwood. Let's go to Boston this weekend. We'll see the Christmas decorations, maybe go ice-skating."

"Ice-skating?"

"Yeah, it'll be fun."

I agreed that maybe I should get away from a place that was so stressful it was causing me to sleepwalk or hallucinate, or both.

On Saturday morning, I dressed warmly in a soft, chunky-knit sweater and wool skirt with boots and waited for Owen to pick me up in front of Easty Hall. When he got out of the car, I saw that he was wearing jeans and a plaid shirt under a blue V-neck sweater, the shirttail hanging out so he looked sort of disheveled in an intentional way. Instead of his usual jokey T-shirts and dirty jeans, Owen looked like he had dressed for a date. It was then that I realized, so had I.

Owen drove us into Boston, where we did some sightseeing and Christmas shopping and bookstore browsing. We stopped for lunch at a Revolution-era tavern that touted the best lobster roll in Boston. All biases aside, I had to admit it was better than Melville's greasy version.

After lunch, we went to an ice-skating rink in Roxbury since the local ponds weren't frozen yet. Owen was a good skater, having played ice hockey as a kid. I was anything but graceful as I wobbled around the rink, but Owen grabbed my hand whenever I was about to fall.

Despite some near collisions with the wall, the cold air and exercise made me feel better, and Owen's presence reassured me that I wasn't as alone as I felt.

As we were getting back into his car he said, "Hey, aren't we close to Darlene's bakery?"

"Aunt Darlene?" I said.

"Yeah. I could go for some of those pumpkin fritters right now. And some hot coffee."

"I don't know," I said. "I'd feel weird going to see her when I'm not even talking to Michelle."

Owen persisted. "Darlene's not like that, and you know it. Come on. Let's pay her a visit. Besides, she might have some advice about your dreams."

I gave him a suspicious glance. "Was this your intention all along?"

Owen smiled sheepishly and blushed. He was always looking out for me.

We drove to Darlene's neighborhood and parked on a side street. Bec d'Or was an adorable French-Haitian bakery whose specialty was the namesake golden pastry in the shape of a bird's beak. When we entered, the bakery was mostly empty except for a middle-aged couple sitting in the back.

As soon as Darlene saw us, she came out from behind the counter and extended her arms. "Oh, Emma, how are you, child?" She gave me a rib-breaking hug, then moved on to Owen. "And look at you," she said, clicking her tongue and shaking her head. "Boy, you get more handsome every day. Doesn't he, Emma? What was Michelle thinking giving up this pretty young thing?"

I laughed, feeling embarrassed for Owen. "I guess Michelle told you about the breakup?" Owen said.

Darlene frowned. "I knew something wasn't right the last time I saw her. Sometimes I know a shadow's falling on her before she does."

I wondered if Michelle had told Darlene about me kissing Owen. It seemed unlikely given how friendly she was being to us. "Are you too busy to talk?" I asked.

"Never too busy for you, child. You two sit down there, and let me make you some cremas. And I got a batch of those fritters you love, Owen. They're just about to come out of the oven. Sit and take a load off."

We sat as instructed, and Owen fidgeted with his shirt sleeve. Darlene was right. Owen was looking really cute these days. The lines of his face were becoming more angular, less boyish. Until he smiled, of course, and his dimples broke the illusion.

Darlene came back out of the kitchen a few minutes later and brought us our coconut cremas and an entire platter of fritters with a selection of other pastries thrown in. She pulled a chair up to our table and sat with her legs spread, elbows on her knees, hands clasped in front of her.

"So tell me what you've been up to lately," she said. "I haven't seen you both in ages."

Owen and I looked at each other self-consciously. Briefly, we caught her up on school and asked her how the bakery was doing. But she seemed to sense we hadn't come for small talk.

"Is there something that's bothering you?" Darlene said.

I hesitated, unsure how to explain what had been going on.

"Actually," Owen said, "Emma's been having those dreams again."

"You still chasing after something in your dream world?" Darlene said. "Tell Darlene what's going on."

I explained to her how I'd gone running a few times and had crossed the log bridge, only to find myself moving as if in a trance and waking up in the woods.

"Well," she said, "you're not the first person to go wandering in your sleep. I heard of a well-respected businessman who got out of his bed every night and broke into his neighbor's houses to steal from them, only he'd wake up the next morning with no idea how all that loot got in his house." She laughed heartily, but I must have looked a little scared because she reached across the table and took my hands in hers, rubbing them in a consoling way.

"I remember everything," I told her. And then I started babbling, trying to explain about running across the bridge and hearing lines from *The Scarlet Letter* and meeting Hester and Pearl and noticing they both looked just like me.

"And what did this woman, this Hester, say to you?" Darlene asked.

"I don't know," I said. "I got scared and ran away."

"Why did you get scared?"

"Because the look she gave me was so . . . penetrating, like she could see into my soul."

Darlene paused and studied my face. "Darlin', dreams are the place where your subconscious works out its problems. And what it sounds like to me is your soul is doing some stretching."

"Stretching?"

She smiled. "The Haitian people believe you have two

parts to your soul—le ti-bon-ange, or your little angel, and le gros-bon-ange, your big angel. Now, the little angel is like your shadow soul. It's only visible in dreams or visions, and it helps you communicate with the spirits or the loa, kind of like your conscience. But the big angel is your fate soul, the one that determines your destiny or prophesies your future. That's the soul that makes you *you*."

"So what you're saying is that in my dreams, I'm meeting the two halves of my soul?"

"Not exactly," she said. "Most people are too literal to understand the loa. It's more like you're at the crossroads of your own spiritual growth. When a person communicates with the two parts of her soul, it's a metaphor for transformation, metamorphosis. Understand?"

"I guess so," I said. "Then how come only the little girl could hear me at first?"

"Because the woman represents the part of yourself you're still becoming. Your future self."

"But I'm nothing like Hester," I said.

"Are you sure?" she said. "Maybe that's why you ran from her. Maybe you're not ready to face your future."

I frowned as I acknowledged Darlene had hit on the truth.

"But it's not dangerous, right?" Owen said. "She doesn't have to worry about this?"

"So long as no one buries her alive," Darlene said, laughing. My stomach lurched.

"You're joking, right?" Owen said.

"Well, it is a form of dark magic in Haiti. Certain voodoo priests use potions to put people into trancelike states, and then they bury them alive. When they release their victims from the grave, they steal their ti-bon-ange, thus depriving them of free will and conscience. That's how zombies are created."

"Zombies are real?" I said.

"Mind you, I've never seen one myself. But I've seen plenty

of folks wandering around like they don't have a conscience, that's for sure." She laughed again, but I was feeling anything but cheery. Darlene grabbed my hand again. "Darlin', you need to take control of your dreams just like you do everything else in life. There are voluntary trances in which the person is an active seeker of truth, and then there are possession trances, in which a person is controlled by the spirits. It sounds like you're searching for something out there in the woods, maybe for some truth about yourself. I don't think the spirits are controlling you."

"But how do I make sure they don't?"

"Whenever you notice something unusual, something you know comes from your dream world, just remind yourself that it's only a dream and that you're in control. And don't let your body go wandering. I'm going to give you a technique to make sure it doesn't. Think about riding a stationary bicycle. If you close your eyes, it feels like you're moving, right? But you don't actually go anywhere. And yet you still get all the benefits of exercise. It's the same with your dreams. Once you realize you're in a dream state, you can control what happens. So the next time, I want you to create a mirror image of yourself, and send that version out into the dream, letting your body remain where it is. That way no harm can come to you. The dream will still be illuminating, but much less dangerous."

"So you don't think I'm going to become a zombie?" I said.

She laughed. "You could never become a zombie, Emma. There's too much strength in that ti-bon-ange of yours. Now, I'm sorry to do this to you after scaring you silly, but I need to get back behind that counter. The afternoon rush is starting."

"Oh, I'm sorry," I said, noticing the line of customers that had formed. "Thank you so much, Darlene, for taking the time to talk to us."

"Any time," she said. "And I mean that."

She packed us a bag full of snacks and pastries. Just as we were about to leave, she came out from behind the counter and grabbed my shoulders. "And, honey, don't give up on my Michelle, you hear?"

"What?" I said. Somehow we had avoided talking about Michelle during the entire visit.

"Michelle's in a dark place right now, dealing with some heavy things. I know she's gone cold on you, but don't turn your back on her. She's a soul friend, and you don't meet many of them in a lifetime."

I nodded, holding back tears and wondering whether Michelle's dark place was as lonely as mine.

CHAPTER 12

I lost my mother and stopped believing in Santa Claus in the same year. Needless to say, Christmas had not been my favorite holiday for a long time. This Christmas in particular, my family seemed painfully aware of the people who were missing in our lives, and we tried desperately to compensate. Barbara was pulling trays of burnt cookies out of the oven like her life depended on it, Grandma was setting a new world record for old-fashioneds consumed in one night, and my dad had gone on a decorating binge the likes of which I hadn't seen in ten years.

I wore my hair in a stubby ponytail for the first few days I was home, afraid of what everyone would say about my red streak. I'd gotten a few catty comments about it at school, but nothing so far to make me regret doing it. But my father was a traditionalist; New England practicality was in his bones. Anything newfangled or nonconformist smacked of trouble and rebellion, traits that didn't fly well in our stodgy blue-collar town.

On Christmas morning, I wore one of the six Santa hats my father had bought at the Dollar Store while we exchanged presents. For church, I swapped my Santa hat for a knit beret that I didn't take off for the rest of the day. When I came downstairs to help prepare for dinner, Barbara was manning the stove, my dad was washing lettuce at the sink, and my grandma was getting a head start on her drinking. I tried to be helpful and unobtrusive by setting the table, but as soon as I came into the kitchen, Barbara asked me to remove my beret for dinner.

"But I'll have hat hair," I said.

"It's only family," Barbara said. "No one will mind."

My grandma, who seemed to have a sixth sense about these things, said, "Let her wear it. That rule about hats at the dinner table is outdated. Besides, it makes her look Parisian."

"Speaking of which," I said, trying to change the subject, "I've applied for a scholarship to our sister school in Paris. If I'm accepted, I'll get to spend my senior year in Paris. The scholarship would pay for everything—airfare, room and board, tuition."

"Paris?" my dad said. "Why would you want to go to Paris for your last year of high school?"

My grandmother and I looked at my dad as if he'd just announced he was a robot. Which I sometimes suspected he was. Even Barbara said, "John, what girl wouldn't want to go to Paris?"

"I only meant, don't you want to stay and graduate with your friends?"

"I'd be back by May, in time to graduate with everyone else."

"I don't mean to interrupt," Barbara said, "but dinner's almost ready. And, Emma, dear, I really would appreciate it if you'd take off the hat."

Resigned, I slid the beret off my head and shook out my hair. My father and Barbara gasped, and Grandma raised an eyebrow.

"Emma, what have you done?" Barbara asked. As if I'd shaved my head bald.

"It's only temporary," I said.

My dad sighed. "You mean, for Christmas?" he said. "It'll wash out?"

"It'll grow out," I said.

He shook his head at me like he no longer knew who I was. Grandma was trying to squelch a grin, so she slung back the rest of her drink, possibly a diversionary tactic. "Emma, would you do me the honors?" she said, shaking her glass back and forth so the ice clinked up the sides.

"Elspeth, you've had enough whiskey for three people," Barbara said.

"And you wear enough hair spray for ten, but you don't hear me complaining." *Uh-oh.* The night was quickly getting away from us, a runaway train with a cargo of dysfunction.

Barbara's face went rigid. "Everybody, go into the dining room," she said in her pretending-everything's-fine voice. "I'm going to bring dinner in. And I hope it's not cold."

It would not have mattered if dinner was scalding, lukewarm, or frozen; we were all choking on bitterness anyway.

"What about your college applications?" my dad said, launching right back into our debate. Christmas cheer, be damned. "How are you going to take care of those?"

"They do have a postal service in France," I said, my sarcastic streak activated. "And most applications are online these days."

"But what's the point? You're trying to get into a good college. Paris can only distract you."

"Dad, it'll look good on my transcript. Only one girl from my school will be chosen. And I'm thinking about majoring in French in college."

"French?" my father said, as if I'd told him I was majoring in badminton or palm reading.

Then I thought of another tactic. "I've looked into the curriculum. It focuses on French literature, but we have all these choices of electives, too. Opera, Gothic architecture, even

French cooking. Jacques Pepin did a special seminar last year."

"Jacques Pepin!" Barbara said.

"Before I even think about letting you go," my dad said, ignoring the undeniable draw of Jacques Pepin, "we need to address another issue. I didn't want to bring this up, especially on Christmas, but . . . your PSAT scores arrived."

Oh God. "Yeah," I said. "About that. I had a really bad day."

"It seems you've been having a lot of those," he said. "Dr. Overbrook called and said you've been skipping an excessive number of classes, too."

My stomach dropped. "I wouldn't say excessive," I said. I could feel myself losing the battle, so I began putting up the defensive shield I wore when I didn't want to face things head-on.

"Cutting classes? Bombing tests? What's going on with you, Emma?"

"I don't know!" I said. "Maybe I'm going crazy like Mom. Maybe your worst fears are coming true." The words came spilling out of me before I had time to consider their impact. My mouth was like a defective grenade launcher.

No one said anything until the weight of our silence grew too unbearable. "I probably won't get the scholarship anyway," I said in a whisper, backtracking like a spineless worm. My father looked across at me, his eyes full of disappointment and regret. "May I be excused? I'm not hungry."

Barbara threw up her hands and sighed, and my father nodded stoically like his head bore the weight of the world.

I got up and went out the front door, then let the tears come. I felt so alone. I missed my mother. Somehow I felt like she would understand me. She would be excited for me. Dropping my head into my hands, I squeezed my temples hard.

I walked around my neighborhood for about an hour, trying to shake off my blues. When I got back to the house, the Christmas tree lights were still on, twinkling through the window and casting everything in a warm yellow light. It looked so warm and cozy, like I was staring into someone else's house. Because lately I felt like a stranger in my own home.

All was quiet when I went inside. My dad and Barbara must have gone to bed early. I wandered into the den and found my grandmother camped out on the sofa, watching *It's a Wonderful Life*. I sat down beside her, turning to give her a hangdog frown.

"I'm sorry," I said.

"For what?"

"For ruining Christmas."

"Don't take all the credit," she said, giving me a sly smile.

"God, Grandma, I'm such a mess. My boyfriend dumped me. My best friend hates me. And my dad thinks I'm a disappointment."

"No, he doesn't, Emma. He just doesn't remember what it's like to grow up. He's been an old man since he was a teenager."

"What do you mean?"

She pulled her afghan up around her shoulders, shivering a little. "Since the time your mother brought him home to meet me, I knew he was too serious for his own good. His father died when he was very young, so he always felt the need to be the responsible one. He practically raised his sister and he had to work at the docks as a teenager to help pay the bills. He never really had an adolescence."

I'd heard the stories about my dad's childhood, but I'd never understood the implications. I'd been too busy feeling sorry for myself.

"I know I've been a jerk to him," I said. "And to Barbara. I don't know what's going on with me. I feel so angry all the time. Like something's eating away at me, trying to gnaw its way out. I get scared sometimes, thinking I might be getting sick like Mom. Because I feel like I'm being split into two, and one part is the real me, the person I am deep inside, and the other is, like, the ghost of the old me, the one everyone else still wants me to be. Does that make me sound bipolar?"

She laughed. "That doesn't make you sound bipolar, honey. That makes you sound human. It means you're growing up, and that's not such a bad thing. It scares your dad because he still wants to see you as his little girl, but he'll come around eventually. Just give him time. And give yourself time, too. Don't be so desperate to grow up that you forget to have fun. Take risks. Make mistakes."

I grabbed her hand and smiled. "Don't worry, Grandma," I said. "I'm making plenty of those."

By New Year's Eve, things had quieted down in the Townsend residence. My dad was taking Barbara to a fancy event at a Boston hotel, where they were spending the night. Jess and Flynn were going to some raucous party in Jamaica Plain, and in my current mood, I just couldn't deal with that.

I was a little surprised when Owen opted to spend New Year's with me and my grandma instead of going to the party. Hull's Cove wasn't exactly a hotbed of holiday excitement. We were lucky to score a couple of noisemakers and some champagne from my grandmother. We hung out early in the evening and ordered takeout Chinese, then watched some terrible musical performances on a countdown show. By eleven o'clock, we shut off the TV and turned on the stereo, blasting oldies as loud as my grandma could take it. Owen was entertaining us with sing-alongs of Sam Cooke and Otis Redding, Elvis and Nancy Sinatra, the last accompanied by a cheesy sixties dance complete with Austin Powers mojo.

My grandma laughed harder than she had in a while, and by midnight, we were all feeling giddy and celebratory. We flipped the TV back on momentarily to watch the ball descend, then grabbed some pots and pans and whatever other acoustic household items we could find and went outside to shake up our sleepy little town. My grandmother stood on the front stoop smoking a cigarette—she wasn't really a smoker, but holidays were an exception.

Afterward, Owen said he should probably head home to avoid the post-party traffic.

"Why don't you stay the night?" my grandma said. "There will be some crazy drivers out there tonight, and I hate to think of you driving all the way home so late."

Owen looked at me for approval. "It's fine by me," I said, "if you think Dad won't kill us."

"I'll take the heat," Grandma said. "I'll tell him it was my idea."

We both gave her a kiss on each cheek, and Grandma just laughed and headed inside.

Owen and I strolled up to the beach to see if anything was going on there. A few kids were setting off homemade fireworks, and in the distance we could see a larger display exploding from a pier somewhere off the coast.

It was a clear night, very cold. We hadn't thought to grab jackets before running out, so Owen wrapped an arm around me as we walked up the beach toward the fireworks.

Even though my back was to it, I could see the lighthouse beam in my peripheral vision, could feel its presence looming over me, reminding me of who wasn't here. A stab of pain pierced through me, so unexpected and unwelcome that I stopped moving. I pulled out of Owen's arm.

"Are you okay?" he said.

"Yeah, I'm fine."

I tucked my hair behind my ears, but the wind kept lifting it up again and into my face. Owen moved to stand in front of me and smoothed my hair over my ears and held it there. "There. Now I can see your face. And I can tell you're not fine."

I tried to smile. Here stood Owen, so sweet and patient and endearing that I wanted to grab him and pull him close. But not in the way he wanted me to. In fact, I felt guilty for even thinking it.

"You miss Gray," he said, reading my mind.

I nodded guiltily. "It drives me crazy that I do. I mean, he broke up with me, like, two months ago and I'm still pining away like some pathetic loser."

"You know what would help you get over him?" he said.

"What?"

"Kissing me." My mouth dropped, and Owen released my hair and laughed. "You know I'm only joking," he said. "But you did kind of throw yourself at me the night of the cast party."

"I did not!" I said, with mock indignation.

"It's okay, I don't mind. But admit it," he said. "You wanted me. If only for a second."

I laughed and met his eyes, surprised by the boldness I saw there. "Where did this come from?" I said. "This cocky, surfer-boy attitude?"

"Why? Do you like it?"

"I don't know. Maybe."

His stared at me, eyes questioning, lips partially open like he was about to say something. Something serious that might change everything. But then *they* appeared—the secret weapons that always disarmed me—two dimples and a smile that lit up his face like the fireworks behind his head.

"Come on," he said, laughing. "Let's get you back to the house. You're freezing."

We walked briskly, trying to keep the blood flowing, but my mind was stuck on that moment on the beach.

Why couldn't I like Owen? He was the most loyal friend I had, and I knew how he felt about me. He was adorable, funny, even sexy in a goofy way. And I *had* kissed him that night. But that was right after Gray had broken up with me when I was an emotional train wreck. The kiss had been an accident, a moment of weakness.

We got back to the house to find my grandmother asleep on the sofa in the living room. I didn't want to wake her, so I covered her with a blanket and led Owen upstairs to my parents' bedroom. I made the bed and laid out some towels for him. It was strange to think about him sleeping just a room away from me.

"Are you tired?" he asked.

"Yeah," I lied, lingering in the doorway and forcing a yawn. "You need anything?"

"Nope. It's like a fine hotel here. Queen-sized bed all to myself, cable TV, what more could I ask for?"

"A mint on your pillow?" I suggested.

He laughed. "Good night, Emma."

"Night, Owen."

As I was changing into my pajamas, I heard Owen go into the bathroom. I wondered briefly what Owen slept in. A T-shirt and boxers? Just boxers? Nothing at all? I laughed at myself and crawled into bed, my ears trained for every sound in the hall. After a few minutes, I heard the toilet flush and the faucet come on, followed by footsteps padding into my parents' room, and then the door closing behind him.

It took me forever to fall asleep as my mind tried to release itself from the hold Gray had over it. I imagined what it might be like to date someone else, to fall in love again, or at least fall in like. Develop a crush. Kiss someone new, like Owen had said. How freeing that would be! And that was the funniest part of all—I was free now, free to kiss whomever I wanted, love whomever I chose. But was love with someone else even a choice?

The next morning, I woke earlier than expected, given that I hadn't slept more than a few hours. It was just ten o'clock when I got out of the shower, so I headed downstairs to make coffee. Grandma had beaten me to it and was sitting at the table reading a book, waiting for the coffee to brew.

"Morning," she said.

"Morning," I mumbled, shuffling over to the cabinet and grabbing the largest mug I could find.

"Owen still sleeping?" she said.

"I don't know. We didn't sleep in the same room, remember?"

"I like him," she said. "He makes you laugh. And you need to laugh more."

I nodded, smiling to myself. "He's a good guy."

"He likes you, too."

"Yeah, I know." There was the guilt again, the unspoken accusation. I always felt like I was leading Owen on just by being his friend. "Want breakfast?"

"If you're cooking," she said.

I grabbed bacon and eggs and a loaf of bread from the fridge and put a skillet on the stove. Grandma poured us coffee and popped bread in the toaster while I whisked up some eggs and cheese for a giant omelet. While the skillet was heating up, I tuned the radio to the jazz station, and my grandma and I navigated around each other in the kitchen as it filled with the aromas of fresh-brewed coffee, melting cheese, and sizzling bacon.

Just as the bacon began puckering in the pan, the doorbell rang.

"I'll get it," Grandma said, setting a giant platter of toast onto the table.

Vaguely I heard voices coming from the living room and assumed one of our neighbors must have stopped by. I was removing several bacon slices from the skillet with a spatula and bobbing my head to "Take Five" when my grandma returned to the kitchen wearing a strange saucer-eyed expression.

Behind her was the last person I'd expected to see while

standing in my pajamas shimmying to Dave Brubeck on New Year's Day.

"Hi Emma," he said.

I stopped dancing, but I was still precariously balancing those slices of bacon in the air while I stared in disbelief at the boy I'd been obsessing over. He looked different than he had at his graduation. He was wearing civilian clothes, trim and clean-cut in a lavender oxford-cloth shirt and jeans. His hair was very short, his face thinner, more angular, so all the glorious planes of it were visible. Those lovely downturned eyes were staring back at me with an emotion I couldn't place, but whatever it was, it made my heart tighten and my face flush.

I don't know how much time passed while we stood staring at each other like idiots, but my grandmother had the presence of mind to say something before I burned the rest of the bacon.

"You're just in time for breakfast," she said. "Have a seat. You probably don't get to eat like this in the Coast Guard."

"No, ma'am," he said. "It smells like heaven."

I was still quietly sputtering for breath, but I managed to get all the bacon on a plate without dropping it. "Coffee?" I asked him.

"I'd love some, thanks." His eyes sparkled when he answered.

Taking a deep breath, I poured him a cup of coffee and set some cream and sugar in front of him, then sat down next to my grandma across from Gray. He hadn't taken his eyes off me since he'd entered the kitchen, and now he was pouring cream into his mug and smiling at me. I felt like I'd entered some twilight zone. Whatever breach of time and space had occurred, I didn't want anything to break the spell.

"So," Grandma said, "what have you been doing? Out saving the world?"

"I'm afraid it's not that glamorous," he said. "I mostly get mess duties and deck work until I get through 'A' School. But I just got some really good news. I got into an Airman Program months earlier than expected. I head to Clearwater tomorrow to start training."

"That's great," I said. "Congratulations!"

"It's a little premature to get excited," he said. "I have four months in Florida and then another four months in North Carolina for rescue swimmer cert, and I've heard that's the really tough part. Less than half the class graduates. Sometimes it's only one or two students."

"You'll definitely graduate," I said. "I have no doubt." He gazed at me with a smile full of so much mixed emotion— gratitude, regret, maybe even love—that I wanted to cry. I couldn't believe he was actually sitting here in my kitchen. And he seemed so at ease, so content just to talk and drink coffee with us that I wondered just what life had been like for him over the past two months.

Even with the weight he'd lost, he was so beautiful and vital-looking, even more so now that he'd regained his self-confidence, that coolness he'd always possessed until he'd broken down last spring. This was Gray Newman again, the boy I'd fallen in love with, not the martyr who had broken up with me on the beach in October. I wondered what had happened between then and now to account for the change. Perhaps he had found his purpose, that elusive thing he'd been searching for. My heart soared, wondering what this could mean for the future of him and me.

It turned out Owen slept in boxers and a T-shirt. At least that's what he was wearing when he came into the kitchen a minute later.

"Hey," he said, his eyes looking sleepy but surprised. He hadn't been expecting Gray. And from Gray's reaction, Gray certainly hadn't been expecting Owen.

"Hey," I said, a little too enthusiastically. This was all too weird. I glanced over at Gray and saw, to my horror, that he was misconstruing everything. His eyes had lost that dancing quality, and his mouth was rigid. I chose this inappropriate moment to find his clenched jaw unnervingly sexy.

"How you doing, man?" Owen asked good-naturedly. "You back from training already?"

"Just on a break," Gray said. His voice was ice. "I leave to-morrow. In fact, I should get going. I've got packing to do."

"But you only just got here," I said.

The expression on his face decimated me. All the joy and love and sparkle were gone, replaced in an instant with bit-terness and jealousy. "Thanks for the coffee," he said to my grandma.

My grandmother stood up, hoping to dissuade him. "Are you sure you can't stay? Emma made a delicious omelet."

"I'm not hungry," he said.

Owen moved out of Gray's way as he stalked toward the door.

"Gray, wait!" I said, following him outside.

He stopped abruptly, and I almost ran into him from be-hind. Slowly, he turned around, meeting my eyes with a look of betrayal. "What, Emma?"

"Nothing's going on with Owen."

"You warned me you weren't going to wait around for me. I guess I just hoped it might take you a little longer."

"What are you talking about?"

"You really expect me to think nothing's going on between you and Owen? When he parades into your kitchen in his boxer shorts?"

"Owen and I are *friends*."

"Friends." He spat the word. "We were friends once, too."

"It's not the same."

"God, Emma. Owen?"

"What do you mean?"

"He's always had a thing for you," he said, the vein in his

forehead throbbing. "It's so obvious. And of course, he just waited in the wings till I was gone so he could swoop in."

"It's not like that!" I said, feeling defensive of Owen and confused and suddenly very angry. "He was with Michelle last year, if you recall, and they only split up a few months ago."

"Oh, they split up?" he said. "Very convenient. That was right around the time we split up."

"Gray, you're being ridiculous."

He chewed the inside of his lip like he always did when he was nervous or frustrated. "I can't help it," he said. "The sight of him in your house . . . it makes me crazy."

I really couldn't take the jealous boyfriend act, not from a guy who wasn't my boyfriend anymore. "You left, you know," I said. "And Owen stuck around. He's the one who consoled me after *you* broke my heart."

He gave me a disbelieving look, which quickly trans-formed into a menacing glare. "That's noble of him, Emma," he said. "So noble, it makes me want to smash his face in!"

"Gray!" I shouted, hoping Owen wasn't listening at the front door. "What the hell has happened to you?"

He took an enormous breath and started pacing by the side of his Jeep. What *did* he expect? That he could come back, say he changed his mind, and put everything back the way it was? And even if that was what he wanted, he was leaving tomorrow anyway. He couldn't follow through on any of his promises. The unfairness of it all tore through me, and suddenly I wanted to hurt him the way he had hurt me.

"Owen's never tried anything with me. In fact, he pushed me away when I kissed him."

"When you what?"

I braced myself. "A week after you broke up with me, I tried to kiss him. Owen knew I was rebounding, and he did the right thing. He stopped us. You should be thanking him, not trying to smash him to a bloody pulp like some macho dickhead. This isn't you, Gray."

"Oh, and like that red stripe in your hair is really you." My hand went reflexively to my head, trying to erase the crimson stripe. "Who are you trying to be, Emma? You think this makes you look tough? This isn't you, either."

"How do you even know who I am anymore? You gave up on me, and now you're acting all offended that I would even talk to another guy. Isn't that what you wanted? Isn't that why you broke up with me, for my own good? Why are you here, Gray? What do you want from me?"

He shook his head violently, like it was taking all of his restraint not to punch his arm through the windshield of his Jeep. "I want you!" he said. "Isn't it obvious?" His face collapsed, and the anger dissolved until all that was left were his sad hazel eyes misted with tears. "But I lost my chance. I can see that now."

I shook my head, too. This wasn't going to work. It couldn't work. He was too angry and bitter, and I was too confused. I couldn't let him string me along for another four months here, five months there, until a year had passed and I realized I had stopped living entirely, just waiting for him to come to his senses and return to me. I reached around to the back of my neck and unclasped his scorpion necklace.

"Here," I said. "I can't wear this anymore." The last thing I could be for him now was the antidote to his sting.

He stared at the necklace as if it were a poison dart. "Emma—" His voice caught at the end.

"Just take it, will you?"

Very solemnly, he took the necklace from me, his hand lingering over mine for a few seconds. Even amidst this battle of wills, I could feel the sparks of attraction flickering between us. I pulled my hand away, leaving the necklace dangling from his fingertips.

I looked at his neck. "Where are your dog tags?" I asked.

Slowly, he pulled his necklace out of his pocket. My face fell. "You don't wear them anymore?" I said.

"I do," he said. "It's just, I'm superstitious. Whenever I'm flying somewhere, I put them on, and once I've arrived safely, I take them off. I know that probably sounds stupid, thinking a necklace could protect me."

I closed my eyes and tried not to cry. "It doesn't sound stupid at all," I whispered. For years, I'd been clinging to my mother's necklace for just the same reasons.

"Do you want me to stop wearing your Virgo angel?" he asked with an earnestness that made me soften.

How could I ask that of him after what he'd just told me? I shook my head, blinking back tears. Then I took the necklace from him and unclasped it, drawing the two sides over his shoulders. While I fastened it behind his neck, his lips brushed my forehead, feather light. I had to fight the urge not to lift my lips to meet his. I could have melted into his arms just then, forgotten everything. But in my heart, I knew I had to let him go. If I clung too tightly, I'd ruin us both.

When I felt his fingers thread through my hair, examining the red streak perhaps to see if he could grow to love it, I pulled away and ran to the house, stifling tears. Inside awaited a pair of arms to comfort me, but they would never be the right ones.

CHAPTER 13

When we returned from winter break, the campus was covered in a few inches of snow, but it wasn't the powdery kind that made everything look soft and pure; it was the kind mixed with frozen rain that stung as it landed on your face, that melted initially and then froze over, creating a layer of ice beneath the new snowfall, making for a treacherous walk to class.

When I walked into Bio that first day back, the buzz of some scandal was palpable, like electricity flying around the room, causing everything in its path to stand on end. I had grown so used to being the fount of all scorn that I assumed this most recent scandal had something to do with me.

When I looked at Jess, her face was a mask, but her eyes were simmering with rage.

"What's wrong?" I said.

She slammed down a piece of paper in front of me. It was scrawled with one word: *Dyke.*

Jess's face had gone blank, like someone had given her an injection of a numbing drug.

Before I could ask her anything else, Elise began striding over. When she saw we were looking at a piece of paper, she swiped it from Jess's hands. "Who wrote this?" she said.

"Oh, like you don't know," I said.

"Emma," Jess said, trying to rein me in. But I was furious. I took the note and tore it in half, throwing it back at Elise. The rest of the class had fallen silent, watching us. And then, Brewster got wind of the situation and began making her way over to our table. I gestured for Elise to get rid of the note, but Brewster had already spotted it.

"What did you just put in your pocket, Ms. Fairchild?" Ms. Brewster said.

"Just a piece of paper," Elise replied.

"What?" Brewster said.

"You know, material made from pulp and plant fibers, most often used to write things on?" Elise was trying to defuse the situation, but her comment only made Brewster more livid.

"Is that supposed to be funny?" she said. "Give it to me."

"Really, it's nothing," Elise said.

"I am asking you one more time to hand over the note, or I'll be seeing you in detention this afternoon." Elise clenched her lips but still didn't produce the note. "Perhaps another tactic," Brewster said. "For example, a phone call to the scholarship committee for that French school you're so keen on attending." Elise remained unmoved but I could see she was losing her composure. "Yes, we teachers talk in the faculty room," Brewster said. "And I know what you want most, Ms. Fairchild, is to get away from this place. But one phone call from me, and Paris will be nothing more than a pipe dream."

Elise's face collapsed, and she pulled the two halves of paper reluctantly from her jeans pocket and handed them over. Brewster reconstructed the note and read it to herself. "Is this intended for me, Ms. Fairchild?"

"No, Miss Brewster," Elise said. "It has nothing to do with you."

Brewster slammed her hand against the table. "I'm so fed up with your smug, self-important attitude. You think just because your father is on the school board that you can get away with anything. I am not a person to be trifled with, and until you learn proper respect, you'll be spending every afternoon in the dissection closet."

I suddenly had the strong sense that Elise had not written the note. And as much as I couldn't believe what I was about to do, I heard myself saying, "Wait a minute, Ms. Brewster."

"Yes, Ms. Townsend?" Brewster said, her eyes narrowing in on me now. "And before you say anything, I know that you are on that scholarship list as well."

"I know," I said, "but Elise didn't write the note. And it's not about you. She was telling the truth."

"So the note is yours then," she said.

"No," I insisted. "But it's not Elise's either."

"Then whose is it?"

"I don't know."

"Well, who was it intended for?"

"I don't *know*," I said with a little too much attitude.

"Well, Ms. Fairchild," Brewster said, looking at Elise, "it looks like Ms. Townsend will be joining you in the dissection closet today. I'm sure you two will find much to talk about. Now, everyone back to your seats, this instant!"

She strode back to the front of the room, and Jess let her head fall into her hands.

"You shouldn't have done that," Elise whispered to me, glaring because I'd stuck up for her.

I glared right back at her. Michelle was staring at us all, looking like she was in agony. But why? Because her new BFF had gotten detention?

After class, I tried to talk to Jess on the way to History, but she said she felt sick and began running back to the dorm. I didn't blame her. The gossip mill was wound tighter than I'd ever seen it.

But the story gradually unfolded as the day wore on.

Apparently, Jess had come out to her parents over winter

break, and her mother had flipped out. Convinced that some-one at Lockwood had corrupted her daughter, Mrs. Barrister had called the school. Overbrook, in his zeal to appease an-other wealthy Lockwood parent, brought in Jess's roommate for questioning, and since Chelsea had about as much discre-tion as a car alarm, she told everyone what she'd learned. That Jess was gay, and that she'd had a lesbian relationship with another girl on campus.

I didn't know what to believe.

In History, Overbrook was giving a lecture on westward expansion, telling us about the Donner party, a group of American pioneers who got snowbound in the Sierra Nevada Mountains and had to resort to cannibalism, surviving on the bodies of those who had died of starvation or illness. I gazed out the window watching the snow fall, wondering how many inches would accumulate and just how long it would take before all of us on campus succumbed to a simi-lar fate and turned on each other, taking advantage of each other's misfortunes to ensure our own survival.

In English, Gallagher began our unit on the transcenden-talists, beginning with Emerson's essay "Self-Reliance." As I listened to Gallagher read, certain passages rang out to me so clearly:

For nonconformity the world whips you with its displea-sure. . . . To be great is to be misunderstood. . . . No man can violate his nature. . . . Now we are a mob, yet we must go alone.

Gallagher followed the reading with his lecture. "Surely, Hawthorne had read these words before writing *The Scarlet Letter*. In fact, Hester would have made a good transcenden-talist, as she took this calling to heart—to rise above the mob and find the strength within, or as Thoreau would later say, to march to the beat of a different drummer."

He gave a satisfied smile, and I glanced back at the empty chair where Jess should have been. I wished she had heard all of this. Michelle caught my eye briefly and gave me a cryptic look before turning around and scribbling something in her notebook.

When the day finally ended, I reported to Ms. Brewster, who unlocked the dissection room door for our detention. I was dreading the thought of spending two hours in a closet with cat guts and carcinogenic chemicals, not to mention Elise Fairchild. When she showed up, Ms. Brewster instructed us to organize the lab equipment chronologically by the month it would be used and then label each drawer and shelf by hand.

After she left, Elise took out a giant thermos of coffee and sat drinking it while I eyed her enviously from my perch on the cabinet. Then she had the gall to pull a magazine from her bag and start flipping through it while I opened new bags of scalpels and placed them into drawers.

"Aren't you going to help?" I asked.

"I wasn't planning on it," she said. "Are you going to narc on me and tell Brewster?"

"No. In fact, I'm surprised you didn't call Daddy. Doesn't he usually get you out of detentions? Must be nice having a father on the school board."

"If you haven't noticed, that's why Brewster hates me," she said. "So no, it's not as nice as you think. And you're an idiot for defending me and getting on Brewster's shit list. Now she's not going to let you go to Paris either."

"First of all, I wasn't defending you. I was defending Jess," I said. "And secondly, we all know who's getting the scholarship to Paris."

"Yeah, no thanks to you. If you hadn't ripped up that note and made such a scene, Brewster never would have had a clue."

"Why did you come over to us in the first place?" I said. "Why suddenly pretend to be Jess's friend again?"

"I've never stopped being Jess's friend," she said. "She stopped being mine."

"Oh, sure."

"Look, I don't care if you believe me or not, but I've known about Jess being gay for a while, and when I tried to confront her about it, she shut me out. But I never told Amber or Chelsea. I never betrayed her."

"Spin it however you want, Elise, but don't pretend you actually care about Jess. Or about Michelle. With you, there's always an ulterior motive."

"Oh, like you're any better!" she said. "Where do you get off acting like friend of the year? You kissed Owen. Or have you forgotten about that? Is that what you do now? Steal other people's boyfriends?"

I got to my feet, rage shooting through every limb. "You don't know anything, Elise!"

"Yeah, well, I know you stole Gray from me last year. Then you went after Michelle's boyfriend. So who's the bitch?"

I had no words. I stood staring at her, realizing that from her point of view, she was absolutely right. I had taken Gray from her. I had kissed Owen. Elise and Michelle had every reason to mistrust me.

"Look," I said. "I made a mistake with Owen. But I care about Michelle. And you can't blame me for doubting your motives after the way you treated us last year."

She puffed out her chest. "If you care so much about Michelle, why haven't you tried to talk to her? At least I tried with Jess. You live in the same room with Michelle, and you let her push you away. Why don't you fight for anything?"

"What are you talking about?"

"You. You stand there like you're some victim in all of

this, when you should be begging Michelle for forgiveness. Last year, you would have fought harder. What's changed? It's like with the scholarship to Paris. I mean, you want it, don't you? But in your mind, you've already given it to me. You've given up."

I fell silent, reluctant to admit that she was right. I had stopped fighting.

But why? What was holding me back?

Was it fear of change? Was I afraid to face the future like Darlene had said?

Elise began noisily sorting through equipment, and we didn't talk for the remainder of detention. But I felt like a wall between us had cracked open today, and I could only hope it would make room for some kind of positive change.

The rest of the week was a nightmare so much worse than the mild ridicule I'd endured for kissing Owen. Because this time, beneath all the stares and hushed voices was something else, a quiet menace born of fear and ignorance. Amber and Chelsea seemed to have designated themselves head of the bigot brigade and were doing their best to fuel suspicions and gossip about who Jess's lover was. Of course, given my friendship with Jess, I became a prime suspect. Girls kept whispering and speculating, but Jess wasn't talking. Not even to me.

She began cutting a lot of classes, refusing to respond to my calls and texts, and generally trying to disappear. I knew what this was like. I gave her a few days' space, but by Wednesday, I was tired of waiting. I refused to let her shut me out the way Michelle had.

After classes, I went to Jess's room and knocked. It was all I could do not to pummel Chelsea when she opened the door, smiling sweetly.

"I'm looking for Jess," I said through gritted teeth.

"Who is it?" someone said from behind her. Chelsea opened the door to reveal Amber, picture-perfect in pink leggings and an ombré sweater.

"Oh, are you looking for your girlfriend?" Amber said, lounging on Jess's bed.

"Your wit astounds me," I said. "Can you just tell me where she is?"

"Like we would know," Chelsea said.

"She does live here, doesn't she?" I said.

"Not for long," Amber said.

"What do you mean?"

"I mean, Chelsea went to Overbrook and requested a roommate change," Amber said. "She's not going to sleep next to a dyke."

There was nothing I could say because any response would be giving Amber exactly what she wanted. I rolled my eyes in disgust and tried to slam the door, but it had one of those springs that made it whine slowly closed.

Infuriated, I went back to my room, empty as usual. My go-to form of therapy had become running, so I changed into my gear and set out across the quad, rage and adrenaline driving every muscle. The school buildings rushed past in a blur and then suddenly, I was across the log bridge and inside the protection of the forest.

I was so angry I could barely think straight. But the air was dry and cold here, and it cleared my head. I ran along the stream's edge in a daze, not really sure where I was going, but feeling my feet move of their own accord. It felt good to get off campus, to shut my mind to everything that was going on and just live in the moment.

Pretty soon, I felt that blissful euphoria—a sort of bubble that made everything around me foggy and dim.

And then I came to that familiar place upstream where the boulders piled up toward the sky. I could feel myself growing numb around the edges—my fingers and toes tingling like I was losing circulation. And then the forest grew very still, and the sun burst through a gap in the trees, casting me in a spotlight.

Slowly, I looked around, sensing I was no longer alone. Sure enough, Hester was standing outside her cottage, staring into the distance. She had changed dramatically since I'd seen her last. Her face bore lines drawn by years of strife and sorrow. Her long and lustrous hair had been cut off, and with it her vibrancy and passion.

The lighting around her seemed to echo her transformation—she stood in shadow, like a sullen planet had eclipsed her share of the sun.

When she heard footfalls beside her, she turned to look at me, showing no surprise at my presence.

"I wondered if I would ever see you again," she said. "I had begun to think you were a dream."

"Me too," I said.

"Perhaps I am the dream," she said.

"That doesn't make you any less real to me," I said. Darlene's words echoed through my head. If Hester was a dream, then none of this was real. And yet, I was so deep in the fantasy already that I couldn't pull myself away.

"Last time I saw you," Hester said, "I thought Pearl had conjured you along with her other imaginary playmates. But you are real enough. She will be glad to see you again."

She called out to Pearl, and an elfin voice rang out from below. "I am here, Mother."

I looked down to see Pearl dancing along the stream's edge like a fairy. The sunlight seemed to follow her as she did. At her mother's insistence, she scrabbled up the hillside to meet me.

"Look who is here," Hester said. "Your friend, Emma."

Pearl looked around, her eyes passing over me as if I were a ghost. "I do not see her, Mother."

"But she is right in front of you. I can see her plainly."

Pearl blinked twice, as if trying to clear her eyes. "Mother, all I see is the sunlight on the rocks."

Hester gave me an apologetic frown. "She is such a contrary child. I do believe she is being willful."

But Pearl continued her line of thought. "Mother, the sunshine does not love you. It runs away and hides itself, because it is afraid of something on your bosom. See? There it is, playing, a good way off. Stand you here, and let me run and catch it. It will not flee from me, for I wear nothing on my bosom yet."

"Nor ever will, my child, I hope," said Hester. "Do you know, Pearl, what this letter means which your mother is doomed to wear?"

"Yes, Mother," said the child. "It is the letter *A*."

Hester looked into her little face and frowned. "But do you know, child, why your mother wears this letter?"

"I do," Pearl said, looking into her mother's face. "It is for the same reason that the minister keeps his hand over his heart."

"And what reason is that?" asked Hester, turning pale as she realized how keen her child's perception was. "What has the letter to do with any heart, save mine?"

But Pearl only gave her mother a knowing look far too wise for her age.

"Run away from here, child," said Hester, "and catch the sunshine. It will soon be gone."

So Pearl scampered away, taking the sunshine with her. Hester pressed her hand to the letter—her constant companion and reminder.

"You are far too bound to that letter," I said. "Why not tear it off?"

Hester clutched her heart. "It is too deeply branded. I cannot take it off."

"But it seems to cause you such pain," I said.

"The letter is my penance and my salvation," she said, "for it has endowed me with a new sense."

"What do you mean?"

"It has given me a sympathetic knowledge of the hidden sin in other hearts."

"A sympathetic knowledge?"

"The ability to see inside another's soul," she said. "To inhabit another person in order to understand her secret joys, fears, and sins."

"Oh, I get it," I said. "My stepmother always says, '*You'll never understand someone until you've walked a mile in their shoes.*' "

Hester smiled in acknowledgment, and then her form grew hazy and ethereal, like she was being absorbed into the air. She took my hands into her own and leaned in as if to hug me, but when she touched me, my body went cold all over. I tried to push her off, but my hands met with no resistance. And then after another second, Hester was gone.

Spinning around in search of her, I saw thick skirts twirling around at my ankles. My eyes roved up from black pointy-toed shoes to a drab skirt cinched at the waist to a thick bodice, finally landing on the scarlet letter on my chest, which blazed up at me as if on fire.

I tried to scream, but no sound came out.

Was I in some sort of possession trance? Had Hester or some other spirit inhabited my body? And did I have any control over my own actions?

Terrified, I ran down to the stream to look for Pearl, but she was gone, too. And then two apparitions in black materialized before me, both faceless and terrifying.

One pointed at me and said, "Behold, there is the woman of the scarlet letter. Come, let us fling mud at her!"

They stooped down to gather the earth and began approaching me with closed fists. Instinctively, I ran, but the hillside was rocky and uneven, and I stumbled on my way down. Once on my feet again, I glanced behind at the two amorphous creatures chasing me, panicked that they were steadily closing the gap between us.

Fear and adrenaline surged through me as I ran through the forest, hearing their haunting voices behind me and feeling the pelts of mud at my back. I'd never felt more vulnerable, but I got the sense that someone wanted me to walk literally, or in this case, run, a mile in Hester's shoes.

I scrambled through the underbrush, looking for a place to hide. But then I thought, maybe I shouldn't stop. Maybe I should keep going.

A random memory surfaced. Dolphins never stopped swimming, even when they were sleeping. They had to keep moving to avoid predators.

That's what I would do, too. Keep moving.

But I realized if I was truly asleep, then none of this was real. This was a dream. Somehow I had lost myself inside *The Scarlet Letter* again. But I didn't have to stay here. Like Darlene had said, I could control it.

Just the awareness that this world was fictional dispelled the figures chasing me, and I suddenly found myself alone, running in silence. My body felt lighter, faster, like some weight had lifted, like Hester's spirit had left me. Or that my revelation had forced her out.

When I got back to the bridge, I paused briefly to look at the rosebush. The enchantment had worn off it as well. It boasted no flowers now, only thorns.

As I walked across the bridge to the other side, I glanced down at my sweatshirt and leggings and sighed with relief. The nightmare was over. I was Emma once again.

Only I was becoming less and less certain who Emma really was.

CHAPTER 14

It was dark when I got back to the dorm. I glanced at the clock and saw that I'd been gone for three hours this time. My excursions seemed to be getting longer, and I was beginning to worry about the toll they were taking on my health.

The next morning, I had to force myself to get up for class. In Bio, I sat next to Jess at our usual lab table, but every time I tried to talk to her, she shielded her head in her hands and pretended to be reading the textbook. When Elise strode in, I assumed things were going to get worse. But she came over to us, leaned her forearms on the table, and said, "What's the big deal, Jess? You're gay. So is, like, ten percent of the population."

While this wasn't exactly how I would have chosen to open up the conversation, I admired Elise for her directness. And this approach seemed to work with Jess. At least she looked up from her book and spoke. "Don't start with me, Elise."

"What, I'm not allowed to talk to you?" Elise said.

Jess scowled. "You just want a chance to say *I told you so*. You love that you turned out to be right."

"That's not true," Elise said. "I'm not as evil as everybody thinks I am."

Not as evil. The same words Michelle had said about Elise. I was beginning to think maybe they might be true after all.

"Look," Elise said, "even though you think we're enemies, we're not. I used to be your friend, and I still want to be. You look like you could use a friend right now."

"Or two friends," I said.

Jess softened a touch, but then Brewster was at the front of the classroom handing out quizzes on vertebrate evolution. Any reconciliations would have to wait.

Somehow I endured History and AP English and ate alone at the cafeteria since Jess never showed. But by French class, I'd had enough waiting. Jess had taken to sitting by herself in the back of the classroom where she could shield herself from the worst of the gossip. But I wasn't going to stand back and let her turn me away anymore. I had to make the first move.

I recalled that day months ago when I'd broken down about my mom and Jess had offered me a green apple Jolly Rancher. It had been such a simple gesture, but it had opened the lines of communication. Determined to repay the favor, I rifled through my book bag, finding a tin of Altoids.

I sat down next to her, opened the tin, and said, "Curiously strong mint?" I hoped she would take the bait, but she didn't. "So that's how it's going to be?"

"Look, Emma, I know you're just trying to help, but I'd really appreciate it if you'd leave me alone."

She was doing the whole push-everyone-away-and-be-self-reliant routine that I knew so well. No offense to dear old Ralph Waldo, but the thing about self-reliance is that sometimes, it's entirely unnecessary. Not when you have friends who are willing to back you up.

"Actually, no. I'm not going to leave you alone," I said.

She rolled her eyes, and I remembered the scowling Jess I'd first encountered at the beginning of the year. The one whose external appearance said *hands off,* but whose soul was desperately seeking a friend.

"While I can't imagine what you're going through right now, I do know what it's like to feel completely alone. And as much as I hate to admit it, Elise was right about one thing." I paused for dramatic effect. "You do have friends. And you don't have to do this alone."

Jess didn't say anything, but she did let me sit next to her as we read *Candide*. After class, I waited for her, but she seemed intent on sitting in the room until everyone else had cleared out. But she couldn't hide in the classroom all day.

She chuckled a little when she found me in the hall waiting for her. I began walking with her to Phys. Ed.

"You still have those mints?" she said.

I stopped walking, found the tin in my bag, and handed them to her. "Thank God," I said. "Your breath is rancid."

I dared a smile and saw the hint of one in return. "Sorry," she said. "I've been indulging in a little self-pity."

"You're entitled," I said. "There are a lot of idiots at this school. But you can't shut out the people who aren't idiots, the ones who want to help you."

"Yeah, I know," she said. "I just wasn't sure who they were yet."

"Well, you know you've got me," I said. I slung my arm around her shoulder.

"You sure you want to be seen with me?" she said. "You know I'm contagious."

"Absolutely," I said.

"But people will talk."

I cracked a smile. "So let them talk."

And talk they did.

Over the next few days, Amber and Chelsea continued with their homophobic mission to humiliate Jess. I knew I had to do something to get her away from their toxic abuse. The least I could do was get her out of Chelsea's room.

After class on Tuesday, I went back to my room hoping to talk Michelle into letting Jess crash with us for a while. As usual, she was MIA. Seeing how much time she spent with Elise lately, I went to Elise's room, praying that Amber wouldn't be there. If she was, I might not have been responsible for my actions.

Fortunately, Elise was alone. And despite everything that had happened, she still scowled when she saw me.

"What do you want?" she said.

"Is Michelle here?"

"No." Hostile stare.

I peeked over her shoulder to see if she was lying. "Do you know where she is?" She focused her steely gaze on me, skeptical. "Please, Elise. I really need to see her. It's important."

"She's at the equestrian center."

"The equestrian center?"

"Yeah," she said with attitude. "That's where she goes when she's depressed. I thought you would know that already." Then she closed the door in my face.

Last year, both Michelle and I went to the stables when we were depressed, but when the old barn burned down, I stopped going. Somehow I'd assumed Michelle had stopped going, too. But I'd never bothered to ask.

I ran down the hill toward the equestrian center and let myself in the main doors of the barn. The new facility had endless rows of clinical-looking enclosures, most of which were empty. A few horses stood looking bored, chomping hay from their feeders.

I turned the corner that led to the indoor riding ring and was surprised to see Michelle riding Odin. Odin was Elise's horse, and he had a reputation for being cruel and unpredictable. I walked into the arena and rested my arms on the slats of the gate, waiting for Michelle to circle around and see me. I was half anticipating some crazed scene that involved my face meeting with bloody hooves. But when Michelle spotted me, she barely reacted. I was suddenly worried this had been a very bad idea.

Michelle brought Odin to a halt and dismounted, then grabbed his bridle and began walking him into the barn.

"How did you know where I was?" she said coolly.

"Elise told me."

"Traitor," she muttered. "What do you want?"

"I want to talk to you," I said.

She raised an eyebrow as she put Odin back in his stall and locked the latch. "Why now?"

"I know we haven't spoken in a while, and part of that is my fault. But I have something important to ask you." She turned to face me, but her eyes looked right past me. "Chelsea asked Overbrook to find her a new roommate. And Overbrook wants to put Jess in a single room, but there isn't one available. So I was thinking, maybe Jess could move in with—"

"No," Michelle said abruptly.

Startled, I drew back. "Okay . . . why not?" I said. "Chelsea and Amber are torturing her."

"I know, Emma, and I'm sorry, but Jess can't move in with us."

"I don't understand," I said. "It would only be temporary until Overbrook can figure out where to put her."

"Emma, no." She turned around and began heading toward the double doors.

"Michelle, wait. Are you doing this to spite me? Because if you are, think about it from Jess's point of view. This isn't about you and me."

"I know," Michelle said.

"So why are you so opposed to the idea? Are you buying into all this crap Amber and Chelsea are saying?"

She turned and gave me a look that chilled me. "Emma, you have no idea what you're talking about."

"Then fill me in. How am I supposed to know what you're thinking when you won't talk to me? When you shut me out of your life? Why are you so intent on scaring me away?"

But her defenses had kicked in, and she was moving again, attempting to leave. "Oh, that's right," I shouted at her back.

"Go ahead, walk away. Look, I know I screwed up this year, and I'm sorry for everything that's happened. I'm sorry for kissing Owen. I'm sorry for not being a good friend when you needed one. And I'm sorry I didn't try harder. But are you going to punish me forever?"

She shook her head and turned to go. This was the moment I was sorely tempted to give up, to let her walk away again. But Elise's words haunted me. I had to fight.

"Wait!" I said, grabbing her arm. "You haven't spoken to me in over two months. Please don't walk away from me now. I know you only come here when you're depressed. I want to know why you're here riding Elise's horse. Talk to me. Please. Tell me what's going on."

"You really want to know?"

"Yes, Michelle, I really do."

"Okay." Her hands were on her hips, and her chin jutted out defiantly. "I haven't talked to you in two months because I couldn't face you! Do you understand?"

"Why? Because of Owen?"

"No, not because of Owen."

"Then why? What is it?"

She wiped some hair off her forehead and sighed. "Emma, I couldn't face you because I didn't want you to know the truth. I didn't think you could handle it. Actually, I didn't think I could handle you knowing."

"Knowing what?" I said. She turned away, but I forced her to look at me. "Michelle, what didn't you want me to know?"

And then she began to cry. It was like seeing my father cry—deeply disturbing but also rare and private, a tiny miracle.

"Emma," she said, her voice cracking. She hugged her arms to her chest like she was caving in on herself. "Haven't you figured it out yet?"

I stared at her in wonder, feeling helpless. "No, Michelle," I said softly. "I haven't."

And then suddenly I did.

Michelle's secret romance this summer. The "dark place" Darlene had alluded to. And the way Michelle had just reacted when I asked if Jess could move in with us.

A few seconds passed as I recalibrated everything I thought I knew to fit this new truth.

Michelle finally looked at me, her face weighted with fear and uncertainty. She was waiting for me to say something, and I knew it had to be the right thing. I had spent far too much of my year saying and doing the wrong thing.

But tears came to my eyes, and my throat closed in a lump. And I realized no words would do right now. So I flung my arms around her, hugging her whether she liked it or not. Slowly, her arms dropped, and she let me hug her. And in that moment, it was like every twisted and leaden thing I'd ever allowed myself to feel suddenly dissolved.

When we pulled away, she looked down at the ground, still afraid to see my reaction. "Why didn't you want me to know?" I said.

She sighed, visibly relieved and wiping tears from her eyes. "Emma, I could barely face it myself."

We sat down on a bench in front of the horse stalls. Even though this equestrian center was brand new, it felt like the first time I'd found Michelle up in the hayloft of the old stables, crying over how cruel girls could be.

She bit her lip, embarrassed. "Early this summer, I was spending a lot of time with Owen and the band, and I was really surprised that Jess and I got along. She told me a little about her falling-out with Elise, and I told her all about you, and she seemed anxious to get to know you. It started off as friendship. And then one night, Flynn got wasted, and Owen had to drive him home, so Jess and I were alone at the Depot.

We were listening to music, laughing and talking, and the next thing I knew, she was kissing me. And . . . I kissed back. It wasn't like I planned it. It just happened. I felt so guilty about it later, like I'd done something wrong. But we couldn't stay away from each other."

"So Jess was the summer fling you told me about."

"Yeah," she said. "But then everything got so complicated. I mean, I still had feelings for Owen, and I didn't want to hurt him. And when I told you about it, you got so judgmental."

"Michelle, I didn't know the whole story. I didn't understand."

"Hell, Emma, I don't understand it myself. I still don't know what it all means. And now Jess is dealing with all of this alone. I wish I could be there for her, but I'm just not ready to . . ." She let her head fall to her chest. "I mean, I don't know if I'm gay or if I was just experimenting or what. I'm still working things out. But, Emma, promise you won't tell anyone. I'm not ready for anyone to know."

"Of course not," I said. "I would never tell anyone. I just feel bad that you've been dealing with this by yourself. Does anyone know? Elise? Darlene?"

"No," she said. "Only you and Owen."

"You told Owen?" I said.

"Well, I felt like he deserved an explanation."

"Yeah, I guess," I said. "God, Michelle, I can't believe I was so in the dark on this."

"Well, I was pretty intent on keeping you there," she said. "I'm sorry I pushed you away. And I'm sorry about the whole scene the night of the cast party. I don't know why it bothered me so much when I saw you kissing Owen."

"You had every right to be upset."

"No, I overreacted. I was just so confused, and everything seemed like it was spiraling out of control. I didn't want things to change."

"I am quite in touch with that emotion," I said, and Michelle laughed.

As we started walking up the hill back toward the dorms, for the first time in a long time, I felt like Michelle and I were finally ready to face the future. Because now we had each other.

CHAPTER 15

It was such a relief to be able to talk to my roommate again, to no longer feel as if an electrified fence divided our room down the center. The hardest part was balancing my friendship with Michelle and my friendship with Jess without revealing that I knew their connection. Michelle made it perfectly clear she wasn't ready to deal with what had happened this summer. But I felt sorry for Jess, who was being forced to wait helplessly while Michelle figured out what she wanted. I could relate. Gray had forced me into the same position when he went off to find himself in the Coast Guard, leaving me alone to deal with my broken heart.

The most awkward part of this balancing act was going to the dining hall. Jess and I would be walking to our table, and I'd see Michelle and Elise sitting at theirs. But instead of being able to go over and say hi, I'd wave sheepishly at Michelle, and she'd nod to me like we were barely friends. It was frustrating.

At least Jess seemed to be doing a little better. In fact, since she had been outed, there was a new lightness about her, like an enormous weight had been lifted. She wasn't wearing as much black clothing or as much eye makeup, and her hair wasn't always covering her face. She seemed happy. Optimistic.

One afternoon in French, I was thrilled to be chatting with

her about ordinary, everyday teen stuff instead of life-and-death, monumental teen stuff. Jess was telling me that Ice-9 was playing at the Depot's open-mic night in a few weeks.

"Look, I know you like to be lame and stay home, pining away for your ex-boyfriend, but you're coming, right?" she said.

"Of course I am. I wouldn't miss it."

"And you're going to wear that hot dress we found at Vintage with those ruby heels, and you're going to forget all about Gray and dance with some hot, sweaty stranger."

"Okay," I said, "but does he have to be sweaty?"

Jess burst out laughing, and Madame began walking toward our desk with a scowl. I was expecting her usual owlish reprimand, but she merely slid an envelope in front of me, smiled, and walked away.

Jess looked at me curiously. "Love letter?" she said.

"Ha ha. Very funny."

I slit the envelope open and pulled out a typed letter that began: "Je suis heureux de vous informer"—perhaps the six best words to begin any letter—*I am pleased to inform you . . .*

I had won the scholarship to Paris.

Elation and disbelief swept through me. I was going to spend my senior year at Lycée Saint-Antoine, a boarding school that stood on the grounds of the old Bastille prison!

Jess regarded me quizzically, and I grabbed her shoulders and shook her. It was all I could do not to sweep her across the classroom floor in a waltz.

"You got it?" she said. "Oh my God, Emma, you got the scholarship! I knew you would get it!"

She hugged me, and we did do a little celebratory dance. Madame didn't seem to mind the distraction. Class was almost over.

As we walked to gym together afterward, Jess said, "I'm really happy for you, Em, but I'm bummed, too. I can't believe you're abandoning me!"

"Aw, Jess, I'm sorry."

"How am I ever going to deal with this place on my own?"

"Owen and Flynn will be around, won't they?"

"No, didn't they tell you? They're taking a year off after graduation. They're going to backpack through Europe and try to get some gigs for the band."

"Without their star drummer?"

"I know," she said. "I'm being replaced by a drum machine."

"The nerve!"

"And then there's the little matter of Elise. If you got your letter of acceptance, surely Elise has gotten her rejection."

"Oh God, I hadn't thought of that."

"Don't sweat it," she said. "Elise can go to Paris whenever she wants."

"I know, really. I can't understand why she even wanted the scholarship. Probably just so I wouldn't get it."

"No, that's not it," Jess said. "Mostly it's to get away from her mom."

"What do you mean?"

"Her parents are getting a divorce, and Elise's mom is gunning for custody. And she'll probably get it, too. Her lawyer's a pit bull. But Elise wants to stay with her dad."

I didn't blame her. Last year after Michelle beat Elise in the equestrian championship, Mr. Fairchild gave Michelle a bouquet of flowers and congratulated her on the win. And Mrs. Fairchild slapped her daughter in the face for losing. As tense as things sometimes got between my dad and me, I couldn't imagine him ever slapping me.

"How do you know this?" I said.

She looked at me and grinned sheepishly. "Elise and I have been talking again," she said. "In fact, she told me I could move into her room if I wanted. Amber and I can switch places, and then I won't have to deal with Chelsea's bullshit anymore."

"That was nice of her," I said. But I was still skeptical. "Do you trust her?"

"Yeah, I actually do. She's been really supportive. And I realized she was right. I wasn't fair to her last summer. I pushed her away because I couldn't deal with her knowing the truth. But she's kept my secret all these months, which wasn't easy for her to do. So I'm giving her a second chance, and she's giving me one. Everyone deserves a second chance, don't you think?"

I nodded. But as sure as Jess seemed, I still anticipated some kind of scene over the scholarship in gym class. I nearly fell over when Elise congratulated me in the locker room. I didn't even detect any sarcasm in her voice. And as we played volleyball that afternoon, she didn't try to spike the ball in my face, and I didn't gloat when we beat her team three out of five sets.

Life seemed to be looking up. Not only had I reconciled with two of my friends, but Elise and I had reached détente, and I felt like I was finally moving on from Gray, getting close to a semblance of happiness with the new status quo.

When I got back to the room, I called my dad to tell him about the scholarship. That brought me down a few pegs.

"I'm happy for you, Emma," he said, "but we're going to have to discuss this further. I don't know anything about this school, what kind of programs they offer, how it might affect your college admissions prospects."

"Dad, it will look great to colleges," I said. "How many high school kids get a chance to study abroad?"

Even with all my persuasive tactics, he was still skeptical. And like my grandma had said, at the root of his reluctance was the fact that he didn't want me to grow up. I knew this was partly because I was an only child, and it terrified him to think of me leaving. But if he didn't stop seeing me as his little girl, I'd never be able to become the woman I wanted to be.

I glanced out my window at the steely winter sky. I hadn't

gone running much lately because of all the ice and snow, but I decided a brisk circuit around campus might do wonders for my mood. I'd forgotten how good it felt to lose myself in a run, to let the world flash by in a blur while I tore through air and space.

But I hadn't counted on being so out of shape. When I reached the woods by the stables, I paused at the fateful log bridge to catch my breath. I thought about the last time I'd crossed here, how terrifying it had been to step into Hester's shoes. But if Darlene was right, traveling into her story was forcing me to reconcile the two halves of myself, something I'd been reluctant to do until now. Something I needed to do.

I wasn't sure if the transformation had to occur spontaneously, or if I could in some way make it happen, so I crossed the bridge now and stared into the water, half expecting to see Pearl's reflection on top of my own. But Hester was the one I needed now. If I was ever going to face my future, I had to face the truth about who I was becoming.

Of course now that I wanted it to happen, Hester's world resisted me. It seemed I couldn't force the connection.

I stared wistfully at the rosebush on the other side of the bridge. In another month or two, it would be a riot of red blooms. I remembered plucking that rose back in October—the way the flower had crumpled in my pocket and died trapped in glass.

And that quickly, I was thinking of Gray. The force of my longing hit me like a sucker punch to the gut. Why did grief do this—lull us into thinking we were fine only to wallop us with a fresh dose of misery when we least expected it?

Maybe Gray had known it wasn't the right time for us. Maybe he'd known that by clinging too tightly, we might smother something beautiful and fragile before it had the chance to grow.

I could only hope he was right and that someday, we might get another chance.

CHAPTER 16

Just as I had tried to put my feelings for Gray on hold, Michelle tried to put her feelings for Jess on hold. But it wasn't working. When Valentine's Day rolled around, Michelle told me that Jess had texted her just to say she missed her.

"Did you text her back?" I said. Michelle frowned, looking disappointed in herself. "Why not?"

"I didn't want to encourage her."

"But don't you still have feelings for her?"

"Of course I do. But my emotions are all over the place right now. I can't act on anything yet. Especially not here at school."

"Well, what if we got you away from school?" I said.

"What do you mean?"

"Jess, Owen, and Flynn are playing open-mic night at the Depot this weekend. It would be the perfect time for you and Jess to reconnect. Come with me!"

"I don't know, Em," she said.

"Why not?"

"Because Jess and Owen are both going to be there. Can you say *awkward?*"

"Look, now that you and I are friends again, you're going to be running into Jess and Owen a lot. I'm tired of having to keep all my friendships compartmentalized. It's getting ridiculous. We're all mature grown-ups, right? So come with me to the club. We'll be far away from Lockwood, from all the prying eyes and gossip. Don't you want to try and figure out what's going on with you and Jess?"

She shook her head. "It's too much pressure. I can't deal with a relationship right now."

"Who said anything about a relationship? You and Jess were friends first. Why not start there?"

She told me she'd think about it.

Which is why I felt like quite the matchmaker when she agreed to go with me on Friday night. Michelle seemed excited for the first time in months. She pulled her hair into a chic ponytail and put on a stretchy black dress with a twenties vibe. I wore the blue dress I'd bought at the thrift store with the Dorothy heels, and Michelle did my makeup—eyes lined in smoky plum, lips the color of wine.

I stood at the mirror examining myself. My hair had grown in a bit so it grazed my shoulders, and the blue stretchy fabric of my dress clung to me, giving the illusion of curves. My red streak had faded a little, but I liked the effect of that shock of red amplified by the ruby glimmer of my shoes.

When we arrived at the Depot, it looked so different than it had that afternoon in October when I'd first watched the band rehearse. Then it had simply been a warehouse with the smell of sawdust in the air. Now it smelled of perfume and cologne and sweat. A neo-punk band was playing onstage, and the lead singer—a tiny girl dressed all in black except for a rainbow-striped scarf—was screaming indecipherable lyrics into the microphone. The rest of the club was dimly lit with red track lights creating glowing pools of pink that gave the whole club a bordello vibe. Red velvet benches and glossy low tables lined the perimeter, and the rest of the space was devoted to the dance floor.

Owen, Jess, and Flynn must have been backstage getting

ready for their set, so Michelle and I got some Cokes at the bar and watched throngs of kids dancing and grinding, their animal energy palpable. After a short break, Ice-9 came on-stage and Flynn introduced the members of the band.

"And on drums, we have the incomparable Jess Barrister," he said as Jess waved her drumsticks in the air.

Michelle leaned over to me, looking a little sick. "This was a mistake," she said.

"What do you mean?"

"I shouldn't have come."

But I couldn't find out why because a second later, Jess was clicking her drumsticks together, and then the band launched into their first song. It was a new one, full of sweeping guitar chords and gorgeous harmonies. The song after that was faster and edgier, with Owen's guitar solo providing a dynamic punch at the end. Michelle looked more nauseous with every chord.

As their finale, the band played the song they had played for me back in October. Although the performance had lost a little of its manic intensity, their sound was so much tighter and more polished. Owen's pitch-perfect harmony brought the song sailing to its chorus, and I lost myself in Flynn's voice, surprised once again by how heartbreakingly raw and beautiful it was. My brain latched onto those lyrics again: "In my dreams we are more than friends; the reason I never want my dreams to end. Broken and battered is my heart, but it cannot be ripped apart. It will beat on, like this song. Like a boat against the throng."

When they finished their set to hoots and hollers and thunderous applause, Flynn bounded off the stage and headed straight for the bar. Michelle nearly toppled from her stool, mumbling something about going to the bathroom.

Flynn quipped, "Was it me?" and proceeded to bend over and shake his shaggy black hair like a dog coming in from the rain. Sweat flew everywhere.

"Gross!" I shouted.

"This is the cleanest sweat you're ever going to touch. Smell it!" he said, sticking his head toward my nose. I laughed in spite of myself because he was right. His head smelled of mint shampoo and cloves.

Owen and Jess appeared shortly thereafter. "You guys were great!" I said, hugging them both.

"Really?" Jess scrunched up her nose.

"Jess, you've improved so much. And Owen, the guitar solo? Gave me chills." His face went two shades of pink. "Really, you guys have come a long way."

"Did you tell Emma about the tour?" Flynn asked. "Owen set up some gigs for next summer and fall while we're backpacking through Europe."

"Yeah, Jess told me," I said, looking at Owen. "That's great. Did your dad have a conniption?" Owen's father was his complete opposite—conservative, cold, and relentlessly ambitious. I couldn't imagine him letting Owen shirk college to go prowl around Europe.

"Well, he can't really object seeing as I saved enough money to go on my own. Plus, how can I go to college when I have no idea what I want to do with my life?"

"I'm pissed at the whole lot of you," Jess said. "You're all leaving me behind, and I'm going to be—" She stopped in mid-sentence, staring at something behind me. I turned around and saw Michelle, who looked a little less green but still peaked.

No one spoke for several seconds until Flynn said, "Whoa, did someone just suck all the oxygen out of the room?"

Owen shoved him and said, "Flynn, why don't you get us some drinks or something. Maybe hit on a freshman or two?"

"Whatever, man," Flynn said, going off in search of his next conquest.

Owen and I stayed there feeling superfluous as Jess stood immobile, waiting for Michelle to say something. The next band started playing, slowing things down with a cover of a Snow Patrol song.

"Emma, do you want to dance?" Owen asked.

"Love to." I blinked my eyes gratefully.

He took my hand and led me into the crowd, and we found a little corner to ourselves. I had only danced with Owen once before, last year at the Snow Ball. I was ashamed to admit that I'd spent the entire time looking over his shoulder for Gray. Owen had been tentative with me then, barely touching my body, but now he pulled me close, not timid at all. I could smell his cologne, a fresh green scent, like pine needles.

"So that was pretty intense, huh?" I said.

"Was this your idea?" he asked. "To try and get them back together?"

"Not exactly," I said. "Well, maybe."

He gave me a crooked smile. "I didn't peg you as the matchmaker type."

"Well, my name is Emma," I said, making him smile. It was a welcome sight.

"So what's been going on with you?" he said. "I haven't heard from you lately."

"I've been busy with school. But did I tell you? I got the scholarship to France! I'm going to Paris next year."

His eyes lit up. "Emma, that's amazing." He squeezed my waist as we danced. "You know, Flynn and I will be coming to Paris in the fall. Picture it. You and me walking by the Seine, eating baguettes and Brie, visiting museums and cathedrals."

"Going to the opera?" I added.

"You like opera?" he said.

"I don't know. I've never been to one."

"Well, Emma," he said, offering me his pinkie. "I promise to take you to your first opera. Deal?"

I laughed and wrapped my pinkie around his.

Owen nodded at something behind me. "Look." I turned and saw Jess and Michelle sitting on one of those red velvet benches. Their heads were close, and the moment seemed intimate. "Maybe you've found a new calling," he said. "Fairy godmother to alienated couples."

I smiled and leaned into his shoulder. It felt nice to dance with Owen. Comforting. But as the song's momentum built, Owen bent his head down lower, so I could feel the dampness of his neck on mine. A rush of heat spread through me at this unexpected contact.

And then the lyrics of the song registered. The singer was saying good-bye to the girl he loved, assuring her he'd stay by her side in spirit. His voice broke a little as he sang the chorus, which implored the girl to run away with him so they wouldn't have to be separated. This painful and familiar circumstance jolted me out of my blissful fog. I pulled away from Owen, tears starting at the corners of my eyes.

"Are you okay?" he asked.

"I'm just a little warm," I said. "Do you mind if we take a break?" I stumbled off the dance floor, with Owen's hand at the small of my back.

"I'll get you some water," he said when we reached the bar.

"I just need fresh air."

"I'll go with you."

"No, thanks," I said. I needed to be alone. "I'll just be a second."

I burst out the side door and onto the rooftop of the neighboring building that served as a makeshift balcony. No rails protected the sides, but someone had run chicken wire around the perimeter, I guess to remind people there was an edge. This didn't seem like nearly enough protection for the drunken teenagers who were out there, plus there was an inch of snow

covering the roof. I tottered on my heels, hugging the wall
and wrapping my arms around myself against the cold.

Shivering, I watched some couples talking, smoking, making out. I wondered why it was so impossible for me to move
on. That dance with Owen had been lovely. It should have
felt right to be with Owen, my supremely loyal and patient
friend, but it had felt all wrong. Like I was teasing Owen and
being unfaithful to Gray. I knew this was ridiculous, but I
also knew no one could come close to filling Gray's shoes.

I was standing with my hands cupped around my mouth,
trying to warm myself, when someone sidled up next to me.
Flynn. I laughed and threw my head back against the wall.

"Watch it, girl. You'll give yourself a concussion," he said.
"Here, take this. It'll make you feel better." He pushed his
flask at me.

"No, thanks."

He frowned and slumped a little against the wall. "So
what did you think of our set?"

"I told you, I loved it."

"Yeah, you told Jess she had improved so much and that
Owen's solo gave you chills"—he rolled his eyes—"but what
about me?"

I looked at him in surprise. It was kind of cute to see Flynn
seeking my approval. "You know I love your voice."

"No, I don't."

"I thought I told you."

"Well, you didn't."

"Well, I do." I blushed a little. He took another long sip
from his flask and handed it to me again. "Why is it so important that I drink with you?" I said.

"Nobody likes to drink alone. Makes us feel like alcoholics."

"If the shoe fits . . ."

He rolled his eyes, and for a second, he looked about ten

years old. Behind the goth makeup and the shaggy bangs was this too-pretty boy with eyelashes so long they caught the snowflakes. "Speaking of shoes," he said, "those red sequined heels are hot. You're like Dorothy to my heartless Tin Man. In fact, the shoes, the dress, the hair, the whole ensemble's hot." I arched an eyebrow at him. "What, I'm not allowed to give you a compliment?"

"It's a little alarming, actually. Well, that and the fact that you used the word *ensemble*."

"Why is it alarming that I gave you a compliment?"

"I'm just suspicious," I said. "You hate me."

He pulled his head back, like a dog who's just been scolded. "I don't hate you."

"Oh, really?"

Flynn paused to flick a damp streak of hair off his forehead and take another swig of rum. "I just can't get too close, or your ex-boyfriend might have me pulverized." I grinned. "Where is Captain America these days?"

"Clearwater, Florida," I said, "learning how to drop out of a helicopter from fifty feet, or something like that."

He whistled. "Man, I can't compete with that."

"Are you trying?"

"Maybe."

"Boy, you must be *really* drunk."

He smiled, and I smiled back, surprised by this unlikely truce we'd formed. I shivered again, and Flynn took off his jacket and drew it over my shoulders. "Here, take this," he said.

"Thanks," I said.

As he was pulling away, I noticed the tattoo on the inside of his right arm. "What is that?" I asked, examining the design, which looked like a series of letters or numbers.

"Oh, it's Sanskrit for *fearlessness*."

"When did you get it?"

"About a year ago when all this shit started going down at my house," he said. "I thought it might make me feel a little less powerless."

"And did it work?"

"Not really. But it did prompt a fight with my dad that ended with him leaving the house. So that was a win." He laughed bitterly.

"I wish I could be more fearless," I said. And for some reason, I leaned over and traced his tattoo with my finger. "It kind of looks like pi."

"What?" he said.

"You know, 3.14—"

And then he was leaning in. I didn't know what was happening until his lips were on mine. Dazed, I didn't retreat right away. His mouth tasted earthy and sweet, like smoke and sage. And then I surrendered to the kiss, allowing him to draw me in, one hand on the back of my neck, the other making its way down to my waist. Even then, I clung on, allowing the warm and dreamy haze of his kiss to creep from my flushed cheeks to my shoulders and into my gut, the only part of me that knew this was wrong.

His exit, like his approach, was abrupt, and I drew back, feeling dizzy.

"What the hell?" A familiar voice managed to infiltrate the static of my brain.

"Owen?" I said, backing away from Flynn and watching Owen, whose eyes were full of hurt.

Flynn was gripping his head tightly like he was afraid it was going to start coming apart in his hands.

"What the hell, man?" Owen said. But he was looking at me. I glanced down, unable to meet the accusation in his eyes. "Am I too nice, Emma? Is that it?" he said, his voice gruff and resonant. "You want me to treat you like shit? You want me to act all doomed and tortured like Flynn here? Or

Gray? 'Cause I can do that. You're not the only one hurting, you know. I've got problems of my own, and if you have some twisted desire for me to take them out on you, I can do that."

"Owen, I'm such a fuckup," Flynn said. He tried to put a hand on Owen's shoulder, but Owen flinched away. He was still glaring at me.

"Owen, please don't be angry," I said desperately. But he just gave me a disgusted look before he turned and went back inside the club.

"What is wrong with you?" I shouted at Flynn.

Flynn shook his head, all his bravado gone. "I'm sorry," he muttered. And then he went inside after Owen, leaving me alone on the balcony.

But the question I should have asked was, *What is wrong with me?* This wasn't entirely Flynn's fault. And it wasn't the first time I'd done something stupid like this under the guise of being daring. Why couldn't I stop screwing up?

I stayed outside for a few minutes longer, cursing the heels, the dress, the red streak that had made me feel bold and invincible earlier in the night. Fearlessness without common sense was just plain stupidity.

Once my fingers and nose were entirely numb, I went inside with a knot of dread in my stomach. I didn't know what I was going to do or say, only that I had to try and make things right.

But Flynn and Owen were nowhere to be found, and Jess sat crying on the bench where I'd last seen her. "What happened?" I said.

"Nothing," she spat at me through her tears.

"Well, obviously something happened."

She glared at me with reddened eyes. "Why did you bring her here? Were you trying to prove something?"

"No, I wanted you guys to have a chance to talk. To work things out."

"You shouldn't have gotten involved," she said.

"Why? Jess, what happened?"

"Go ask your roommate. She obviously told you everything else. My entire love life is like some pathetic tabloid news story."

"Jess, that's not true."

"Yes, it is, Emma. You don't understand because you can do whatever the hell you want, and nobody thinks it's a big deal."

I sighed and leaned back against the wall. "Not true," I said. She looked at me, ready to argue. "I kissed Flynn tonight."

"You what?"

"I don't know what happened. One minute we were out on the balcony talking, and the next . . . well, Owen came out and saw us, and now he hates me."

"I'm sure he does," she said.

"Thanks a lot."

"Well, you've been stringing him along all year—first with the kiss at the cast party and then making him listen to all your whining about Gray. And all this time you've known he's had a thing for you."

"I thought we were friends."

"Friends?" she said. "Emma, didn't you listen to the lyrics of our song?"

"What song?"

" 'Capsized Heart.' Owen wrote it about you."

"He did not."

"He did."

"I thought Flynn wrote the songs."

She was shaking her head. "They're collaborations, but that one was all Owen."

"Oh God. I'm such an idiot."

"Yeah, you are," she said. "You and Michelle deserve each other. Neither of you can figure out what the hell she wants."

And then she got up from the bench and started walking away.

"Jess, wait! How are you going to get home?"

"I'll find my way on my own," she said. "I always do."

CHAPTER 17

After texting Michelle and Owen in vain, I walked to the shuttle stop and waited almost an hour for it to come. When I got back to an empty dorm room, I caught a glimpse of myself in the mirror, mascara streaming down my face. I quickly changed out of my clothes and scrubbed my face, wishing I could erase that kiss.

About an hour later, Michelle let herself in the room.

"Michelle, are you okay?" I said.

"I'm fine."

"What happened tonight?"

"I don't want to talk about it," she said. "Right now, I just want to go to bed."

Even though I couldn't stand the fact that no one would talk to me, I respected her wishes and let her crawl into bed without pestering her. I had done enough damage already. In my zeal to play matchmaker, I had screwed everything up. Now Owen and Jess hated me, Michelle resented me, and God knows what Flynn thought of me.

I tossed and turned all night and finally got out of bed around five A.M., knowing it was hopeless to try to sleep anymore. After getting dressed, I took the shuttle into town to get some Dunkin' Donuts, hoping to entice Michelle with sweet coffee, Boston Kremes, and French crullers. On the shuttle back to school, I watched flurries twirl and drift as they made their way to the ground. When I got back to the dorm, Michelle was sitting up in bed, looking like a freight train had smacked into her. She didn't say anything at first, so I handed her a cup of coffee and set a doughnut on her nightstand. "Doughnuts," I said. "Making people happy since 1950."

"Emma, I'm not in the mood for doughnuts right now."

"Sorry," I said. "And I'm really sorry about last night."

"It's not your fault," she said. "I told you it was a bad idea, and I should have listened to my instincts. But I was excited about seeing Jess. I really was. And then I got to the club, and I saw her onstage, and it got . . . real. I freaked out."

"What do you mean?"

"I thought I was ready to take the next step. I thought I was a bigger person than I am. But suddenly I was thinking about what it would mean if Jess and I started dating. I don't want to have some secretive relationship again. But I'm not sure I'm ready to have an open one. I can't be like Jess and come out in front of the entire student body. I'm not strong enough for that. You guys all think I'm so tough, but I'm not."

"Michelle, you're tougher than you—"

"Emma, stop and listen to me. So much of last year, I spent being an outsider, feeling like I had to work so hard just to fit in. And now, I'm finally feeling normal. I just don't know if I can put myself through that again. Look at what Jess has gone through since she came out. If that's what comes from being honest, it's a hell of a lot easier to live with a lie."

I studied her face. "You don't really believe that, do you?"

"Sort of. Has anything good come out of this for Jess? All it's done is make her miserable."

"I thought things were getting better."

"Emma, you have no idea what this is like for her. Or for me." She sounded so defensive and hostile all of a sudden, like I was the enemy.

Not knowing what to say, I went out to the lounge and called Owen and Jess, but neither of them answered my calls. I tried in vain to do some schoolwork, but all I could think about was how I kept screwing up my relationships. Did I have some personal malfunction that made me incapable of maintaining friendships, that destined me for a life of solitude? Maybe everyone would be better off when I went to France next year.

As the hours trudged by, I watched the snow falling in larger, fatter flakes and drifting up against the side of the building. I felt like we were all trapped in our own personal snow globes, imprisoned by what we feared most.

By late afternoon, I had to get out of the room, come blizzard or flood. Michelle was sleeping again, so I changed into sweats, wrapping Michelle's red scarf around my neck for warmth, and slipped out of the room quietly.

I almost fell a few times as I ran down the slick, snow-covered pathway. When I reached the stables, I figured running in the woods might be easier with the forest floor to provide some traction. Through a haze of white, I ran to the stream, treading carefully across the log bridge to the other side.

Even though the trail to Braeburn was obscured by snow, I cut a new path with my footsteps. The sky seemed to muffle and darken as I ran, and the air took on that chemical tinge of snow. When I finally reached Braeburn's campus, the lawn was covered in a blanket of white, sparkling under the half-moon that hovered overhead.

How long did I run? Can it be night already?

The snow shimmered like sequins as I trudged across the field to the hillside where the bleachers should have been. Once again, they were gone, and I knew then that I'd made the passage into that other world. Feeling a keen and familiar sense of anxiety, I ascended the hill, expecting to hear the voices of the townspeople crowded around the scaffold like I'd heard that day back in November.

But when I reached the top, all was silent. Reverend Dimmesdale stood atop the platform alone, and Pearl and Hester stood off in the distance, staring at him.

"Pearl! Little Pearl," Dimmesdale said. Then he whispered, "Hester? Hester Prynne? Are you there?"

"Mother, look," said Pearl when she saw the minister. She grabbed her mother's hand and dragged her over to the scaffold, their feet crunching through the heavy snow.

"Come up, Hester and little Pearl," said Dimmesdale. "Come up, and we will stand all three together this time."

I stood watching the scene from the outside as Hester ascended the steps and stood on the platform, holding little Pearl by the hand. The minister felt for the child's other hand, and took it. Their bond was so strong it seemed the three of them formed an electric chain. And I felt like a voyeur who had no place there, hovering above them like a ghost.

"Minister," whispered Pearl.

"What is it?" said Dimmesdale.

"Will you stand here in the town square with Mother and me tomorrow?"

Dimmesdale glanced at Hester first, then down at Pearl. "I cannot," he said. "One day, I will, but not tomorrow." Pearl tried to pull her hand away angrily, but Dimmesdale held her tight.

"Promise," she said, "to take my hand and Mother's tomorrow!"

"Not then," he said. "Another time."

"What other time?" Pearl persisted. "Why can you not meet us tomorrow?"

"The daylight of this world shall not see our meeting," Dimmesdale said sadly. And I knew what he meant, even if

Pearl did not. Hester and Dimmesdale would not meet again until after death.

Before he could go on, a light gleamed across the sky, like a meteor burning itself out in the atmosphere. It illuminated the cloud cover and brightened the sky as if it were daytime again.

I watched the three of them—Dimmesdale with his hand over his heart, Hester with her letter gleaming, and Pearl watching the sky—all of them showered by this brilliance as if it were the light to reveal all secrets. And then the darkness returned, and red lines streaked across the clouds. I gazed up, astonished, as they took the shape of a letter *A*.

We stood in awed silence until a sound startled us from below. I turned to see Chillingworth's hunched form ambling toward us. "That's him," gasped Dimmesdale, terror-stricken. "The man who haunts my steps. Who is he, truly?"

My stomach clenched as I remembered the oath Hester had made not to reveal Chillingworth's identity. Chillingworth's arrival had broken the spell that had briefly united father, mother, and child. He came and stood behind Dimmesdale.

"Master Dimmesdale! Can this be you?" he said in an oily voice. "Well, you have been busy this night while I have been preoccupied with my studies." He was holding a bundle of unsightly plants.

I could tell Dimmesdale was unnerved by his presence, but he tried to make friendly conversation. "Where, my kind doctor, did you gather those herbs?"

"In the graveyard," Chillingworth said. "I found them growing on a grave which bore no tombstone, no other memorial of the dead man, save these ugly weeds that have taken upon themselves to keep him in remembrance. They grew out of his heart, no doubt, and typify some hideous secret that was buried with him, which he had done better to confess during his lifetime."

Oh, how I hated Chillingworth at that moment. Why did

men like him and Overbrook derive so much pleasure from the suffering of others?

"Perhaps," Dimmesdale said, "he earnestly desired to confess, but could not."

"Why?" Chillingworth said. "Why not, since all the powers of nature call so earnestly for the confession of sin that these black weeds have sprung up out of a buried heart to make manifest an outspoken crime?"

"That, good sir, is but a fantasy of yours," Dimmesdale said. "The hearts holding such miserable secrets as you speak of will yield them up at that last day with a joy unutterable."

"Then why not reveal them here?" asked Chillingworth, glancing aside at Hester. "Why should not the guilty ones sooner avail themselves of this unutterable solace?"

"They mostly do," said Dimmesdale, gripping hard at his breast as if he, too, wore a scarlet letter.

"And yet some men bury their secrets," Chillingworth said, giving Dimmesdale a knowing scowl. I turned to see Dimmesdale's reaction and nearly stumbled off the scaffold.

I had only seen Dimmesdale one time before—on the day when the townspeople had crowded around Hester on the scaffold. Then, Dimmesdale, like the others, had been shadowy and vague, his features unrecognizable. But now in the moonlight, even with his face shadowed by stubble, I could see him clearly. And his eyes were sad and haunted. Familiar. They were Gray's eyes.

I tried telling myself that my brain was playing tricks on me. I was only dreaming. Hallucinating. If I could take control, I'd be able to pull myself out of the dream, to make this end. And yet my heart went out to Gray as if he were standing right in front of me.

I heard myself saying, "Haven't you tortured him enough?"

Everyone looked at me in surprise, and I was suddenly part of the scene, standing just a few feet from Dimmesdale and Pearl, Chillingworth's presence behind me like a clammy hand on my back. It seemed my voice had triggered a transformation because I suddenly wore Hester's clothes, which hung limply from my frame.

Gray's reaction to me was immediate; he seemed overcome with emotion. But I had to remind myself—we were not Emma and Gray. We were Hester and Dimmesdale. Nevertheless, our connection was palpable, and a current of warmth traveled between us through the cold night. Yet something prevented me from going to him. It was as if an invisible force stood between us, preventing us from touching.

"What say you, Hester?" Chillingworth said. "Do you think men should bury their secrets?"

"I will tell you," I said, "if you leave this man and walk me home." Dimmesdale had already suffered so greatly at Chillingworth's hands. His resemblance to Gray made me all the more anxious to spare him any more pain.

Chillingworth agreed to my terms, and I yielded myself to him, letting him lead me and Pearl away from the scaffold and into the woods. I glanced back briefly at Dimmesdale—Gray—and felt such longing and regret that it nearly knocked the breath from me.

The three of us walked in silence through the forest until we'd reached the cottage. My conscious mind was still lucid, taking all of this in, yet Hester's spirit was controlling me, prompting me to move and speak. Her voice came from my mouth, deep and rich.

"It has been seven years since you returned here and bound yourself to Dimmesdale in this sordid pact," I said. "Since that day, no man is so near to him as you. You tread behind his every footstep. You are beside him, sleeping and waking. You search his thoughts. You burrow and rankle in his heart. Your clutch is on his life, and you cause him to die daily a living death, and still he knows you not. In permitting this, I have surely acted a false part by the only man to whom the power was left me to be true. Has he not paid enough for his sins?"

"No," Chillingworth said. "He has only increased the debt." He placed his hand on Pearl's back and told her to run along. Pearl regarded him with fear and mistrust, then scuttled away at his command. Hester's maternal instinct must have manifested itself in me, as I suddenly wanted Pearl nearby. I felt vulnerable without her.

"I wish to speak plain," he said. "Let us go inside where children's ears cannot hear."

Reluctantly, I found the door to the cottage and we entered into the darkness within. I took a seat by Hester's sewing table and Chillingworth stood over me, pacing. "Do you remember how I was nine years ago?" he said. "Was I not a man thoughtful for others, craving little for himself— only kind, true, and constant affections from my wife? Was I not all this?"

"All this and more," I said, speaking Hester's words.

"And what am I now?" he demanded. "A fiend! But who made me so?"

"I did," I said. "So why have you not avenged yourself on me instead of Dimmesdale?"

"I have left you to your scarlet letter," Chillingworth said. "If that has not avenged me, I can do no more." He laid his finger on the letter with a leer.

I plucked a needle from Hester's sewing basket and stood up, brandishing my weapon. Hester's powerful voice erupted from me. "It has avenged you. And now you must end this torture. Dimmesdale must know your true character. What may be the result, I know not. But I must save him."

"I pity you, Hester Prynne," he said. "You pine for this man, yet he has banished you from society. Why do you weep for him when he does not weep for you?"

Immediately, I thought of Gray, of all the time I had lost pining for him, not knowing if he even returned my affections.

Chillingworth sighed in disgust. "I pity you for the good that has been wasted."

"And I pity you," I shouted, using Hester's words to repel him, "for the hatred that has transformed a wise and just man into a fiend!"

"The minister's destruction is his own doing. As is yours," he said, coming toward me. I backed into the wall, fearful of his power. He seemed suddenly capable of great evil and sorcery. "He chose to hide his sins behind a mask of righteousness. And yet I am reviled as evil, and he is respected. I asked before what you thought of a man who buries his secrets, and you told me you would answer me true."

"We all bury our secrets," I said. "We hide what we don't want people to see, those parts of ourselves we think others may not understand. It is human nature to bury one's secrets."

"It is also human nature to bury the dead," he said.

And then the scene departed from *The Scarlet Letter* entirely, taking on nightmarish qualities. Chillingworth pushed me with great force, pressing me into the confined space of the hearth. I sat, stunned, in a pile of ashes as he poured the contents of his basket over me, which seemed to multiply as they fell. Dead flowers and torrents of earth showered over me until dirt covered my hair, my eyes, my ears, until it entered my mouth, stopping my lungs. He meant to bury me alive.

I recalled the way he had cast Pearl out and left me alone without my ti-bon-ange, my little angel. Pearl was now outside these walls, helpless and vulnerable. He was going to leave me here to die and take her—rob me of my conscience. Make a zombie of me. Terror raked through my body.

After he'd poured the last of the dirt on me, he reached in his basket and pulled out one last red rose, which turned black in his hands. He threw it onto my makeshift grave and laughed. "This is your fate," he said. "Let the black flower blossom as it may."

"No!" I tried to scream, but my throat was filled with dirt

and he was already gone—absorbed into the night like a phantom.

My blood curdled in panic. I couldn't breathe. I couldn't move.

And then a lucid thought saved me. None of this was real. This was only a dream. A nightmare, yes, but still a dream.

And I was not powerless.

As a dream, everything in it could be controlled and changed—the rules, rewritten. I remembered the knitting needle I'd grabbed, and I grasped it firmly now, slicing through my earthen grave with a feverish intensity. Chillingworth's last words echoed in my head: "This is your fate."

"No!" I screamed through the dirt mound covering me. "This is just a dream. We make our own fate. We make our own reality."

I continued clawing until I'd freed my limbs, then brushed myself off and tried to crawl toward the door. But my limbs were weak, my breathing shallow. I didn't think I had the strength to do this on my own.

I knew I had to escape and get back to the bridge if I wanted to be released from the spell. But what would happen if I couldn't get out? Would I be stuck in Hester's world forever? Was I as much a prisoner to my fate as she was?

I felt myself fading, losing strength. And even though I knew it was foolish, I called out to Gray. I said his name again and again, repeating it like mantra.

Once upon a time, Gray had called out to me in his time of need, and I had heard him because of the strength of our connection. I hoped that the link hadn't been severed entirely, that my voice was still strong enough to reach him now. With every fiber of faith I had, I made a wish to keep on moving. I made a wish for a second chance.

CHAPTER 18

Iwoke from my nightmare into a terrifying reality. Darkness. Bitter cold. Isolation.

The inside of my head felt thick and slow like it had been stuffed with cotton, and my temples throbbed painfully. I rolled around, feeling dirt under my hands, feeling a fresh burst of terror. For a moment, I couldn't breathe. Was I still in the hearth? Had I been buried alive?

But I soon realized the dirt was only beneath me; my limbs were free. I could move. Which meant I could leave.

Relief surged through me, only to be replaced with fear again.

Where am I?

It was too dark to see. And despite the gloom, I knew very well that I wasn't in my bed. I shivered and tried to use my other senses, feeling around the dank dirt floor and inhaling the mineral scent of the earth. I said Gray's name aloud just to assure myself it was my voice coming out and not Hester's. His name echoed softly against the walls.

And suddenly I knew exactly where I was.

I was inside one of the witch caves.

Claustrophobic fear sent me groping for the walls.

Calm down, Emma. Just find the exit, and in no time, you'll be back on campus.

I carefully made my way around the cave until I felt cold rock give way to an even colder surface. I rubbed my hand back and forth, and my palm came away wet. It was a layer of ice.

Panic bubbled up inside me. I recalled going for a run during the beginning of a snowstorm. How long had I been out here? My excursions had been lasting longer and longer. What if I had spent the entire night in the cave while it had snowed outside? There could be several feet of snow out there! And I had nothing with me—no coat, no cell phone, no food or water.

Frantic, I crept back to the wall of ice and began digging away at it, trying to get a sense of how deep it was and how densely packed. In less than a minute, my fingertips were burning with cold. I pulled my sweatshirt sleeves down over my fingers and tried again, but the icy water soaked through the cotton, leaving my fingers wet and numb as before.

Despite the cold, I was sweating from the effort and from fear. The frigid air only chilled the sweat, making me even colder. But I knew I couldn't stop moving. I carved away madly at the packed snow, losing feeling in both hands, but persisting, clawing, even shoving against it as if I could physically move the wall of ice by sheer force of will. Foolishly, I began screaming—shrieking really—calling for help, making as much noise as I could, feeling like my lungs might burst from the effort.

I kept yelling for at least ten more minutes, until my throat was raw and I tasted blood. I lay down on the hard ground and pounded my fists, out of desperation and hope that it might get the blood flowing back to my fingertips. But I knew I'd freeze to death if I stopped.

So I kept going. I stood up and made a slow circuit of the cave to get my bearings. When I returned to the icy doorway, I tried another round of digging until my hands stung. Something warm and thick leaked from my knuckles. Lifting a hand to my mouth, I licked the surface and tasted salt and iron. Blood. At least I was alive.

How did people survive in jail cells, or worse, in solitary confinement? How did they not go mad within hours? I estimated that I'd only been awake for about twenty-five minutes or so, and it had already felt like an eternity.

My only hope was finding a sharp stone that I could use as a pickax or shovel. I crawled along the ground, trying to be systematic in my search to make sure I didn't miss a single square inch, a single stray rock. *No stone unturned,* I thought, laughing absurdly. That platitude had never meant so much.

Eventually, I found a jagged rock, about five inches long with a sharp pointed edge. The other side was wide and blunt, perfect for scraping away snow. Scrabbling back to the opening, I resumed my attempt at excavation.

Excavation. What they do to dead bodies. Quasimodo and Esmeralda. Skeletons.

Stop it, Emma. Calm down. Just work.

The panic subsided a little, but only because I kept busy. I must have worked away at that wall for half an hour, my shoulders burning from the repetitive motion. It was hard not to despair when I surveyed the wall with my hands and discovered I'd only eaten away at a few inches of ice at most.

My head throbbed with heat, and my body felt weightless and insubstantial, like when one falls off a cliff in a dream. They say if you die in your dream, you really die. Was that true? Or was it impossible to die in a dream?

I resumed my digging, working and resting for short periods, occasionally crying, sometimes screaming. I kept my mind occupied with every survival story I'd ever heard. *The Shawshank Redemption,* in which a man carves his way out of prison with nothing but a miniature pickax. Mountain climber Aron Ralston, who cut off his own arm to escape being trapped in a canyon.

Eventually I slept, if fitfully, and woke to the sound of

voices. And boots crunching and shovels digging. I thought I must have been imagining things. But the sounds kept getting closer and louder. Once I'd convinced myself I wasn't dreaming, I began shouting, only I'd worn out my vocal cords so hardly any sound came out.

The voices and noises seemed to amplify. Relief and gratitude flooded my body. Someone knew I was here, and they were trying to reach me. I called out again and continued digging, trying to meet them halfway. I shook with adrenaline and joy when the voices sounded like they were right outside the wall, a few feet, maybe inches away from me.

Finally, a crack of light burst through the wall of snow. I saw an eyeball as if through a keyhole. I howled with relief as the hole widened, and then I saw hands, chest, a face, a man. Several men. One burrowed his way through the opening, and I fell into his arms, a heap of rubber limbs and frostbitten extremities.

He dragged me out of the cave and hoisted me up in his arms as I shielded my eyes from the harsh light of day. Bodies crowded around me at the mouth of the cave, voicing concern for my health. The man holding me began to walk, and I felt my body thumping up and down as he carried me to a snowmobile, set me down, and wrapped me in layers of blankets.

"Who are you?" I managed to say.

"Bill Sturgess. Fire chief."

"You're a fireman?"

"Thank God your friend knew where you were."

"My friend?"

I looked up and saw Michelle walking toward me, bundled in a dark blue parka. I wriggled weakly out of my cocoon of blankets to reach for her.

"Nice scarf," she said.

I tried to laugh. "Thanks."

"How did you get stuck here?"

"Long story," I said. "How did you know where to find me?"

She raised an eyebrow. "Equally long story."

I was desperate to hear it, but Chief Sturgess was anxious to get me to the hospital. The rides, first in the snowmobile and then in the ambulance, were a blur as I tried unsuccessfully to stave off sleep. When we reached Hopkins General, an ER nurse helped me into a wheelchair and took me to an examination room. I kept trying to convince everyone I was fine, but they were keen to make sure I had no frostbite, no trauma, no permanent damage.

First they stripped me of my damp clothing and dressed me in a flannel hospital gown and a cap for my head to prevent me from losing any more heat. They applied warm compresses to my chest, neck, and stomach, gave me intravenous fluids, and covered me with blankets until I had stopped shivering and was actually sweating. Then they checked all my vitals: breathing, heartbeat, blood pressure.

Once they had determined I was stable, they moved me to a more permanent room, where I dozed for a while. When I woke, the first thing I saw was Michelle's face.

"Michelle," I said, my voice groggy. I reached out my hand, which she took and squeezed.

"How are you feeling?" she said.

"Stupid."

She laughed. "Yeah, well, I'm not going to argue there. This is a little too familiar, me visiting you in the hospital." Last year, I'd landed in the hospital four times. "I called your dad, by the way."

"Oh, good." Although I was sort of dreading facing my father. How would I explain this to him?

"I also brought you a bag of your stuff, just some clothes and toiletries."

"Thank you, Michelle," I said. I sat up in bed, feeling disoriented and weak. "What time is it?"

"Nine," she said.

"At night?"

"No, in the morning."

"How long was I out there?"

"Well, as far as I can tell, you went for a run yesterday afternoon, and we found you a little before eight this morning, so . . . you were out there all night."

"God, it felt like longer."

She stared at me with a protective, maternal expression I'd never seen before. "How did you end up in that cave, Emma?"

"Remember last year?" I said. "The coma dreams about *Jane Eyre*?"

"Yeah," she said.

"Well, it was kind of like that. Only with *The Scarlet Letter*."

She made a twisted face like she was dealing with someone deranged. "But you weren't asleep. You were running, right?"

"Yeah, but I fell into some kind of trance. It's hard to describe."

"Try," she said.

I did my best to explain what had been happening to me. She listened attentively, her brow growing more furrowed as I continued my story.

"This is serious, Emma," she said. "You could have died out there."

"I know," I said. "But I didn't. You saved me."

"Not exactly," she said.

"What do you mean?"

"You're not going to believe this," she said. "You know how you asked how I knew where to find you?"

"Yeah."

"It was Gray. He called me."

"Gray called you?"

"Well, he called you. Last night when you weren't back by

dinnertime, I got a little worried. But I figured you might have gone to see Owen. Or maybe you got a bite to eat in town. When you hadn't come back by nine o'clock, I started to get really concerned. I was going to call you, but you'd left your phone in our room. So I called everyone else—Owen, Jess, even Flynn. No one knew where you were.

"Eventually, I got into bed, hoping you'd be back soon. I didn't want to overreact and call the police. I must have dozed off because I remember waking to the phone ringing. Your phone. Even though it didn't make sense, I thought it might be you. I looked at the display and saw Gray's name. I didn't answer the first time. But he kept calling.

"Finally, I picked up, and he thought I was you. When I told him you were missing, he got all freaked out and said that's why he had called. He said he'd gotten this strange vision of you trapped in some dark place, and that's when I thought of the witch caves. I called campus security and explained that you were missing. They thought I was being paranoid, said you'd probably just stayed the night in a friend's room. But I had this weird feeling Gray's vision might be real. So I called 911. They connected me to the fire department, and I told them you were an amateur spelunker."

I laughed at that one until my ribs ached.

"It was the only way I could think to get them to believe you might be stuck in a cave. It was a long shot, but the fire department thought it was worth checking out. Secretly I think they just wanted to give those snowmobiles a whirl."

I tried to calm down enough to speak. "Michelle, I don't know what to say. Thank you."

"It's not me you should be thanking," she said. "You and Gray have some freaky mind meld thing going. Like Luke and Leia in Star Wars. God, I hope you're not brother and sister."

"Stop making me laugh," I said. "It hurts."

We hung out a little longer until the doctor came in to do

some more tests. As soon as Michelle left, I fished through the bag she'd brought and found my cell phone. Jess and Owen had texted me, and Gray had left about a dozen text messages and one voice mail. I listened to his voice message first.

"Emma, it's Gray. I don't know why I'm calling, except that I got this strange feeling and I'm worried about you. I know you probably don't want to talk to me right now, but please call me anyway and let me know you're all right."

There was a pause during which I could hear him breathing softly, then a hang-up. After listening to his message three times, I had it memorized.

Impulsively, I called him back. When I got his voice mail, I didn't know what I could say that would possibly acknowledge the enormity of what had taken place last night. So I hung up. I texted him a message instead: **Am okay. Thanks for calling.**

The words looked so cold and inadequate. So I typed in the words **I miss you** and stared at the tiny sentence, my thumb poised over the Send button. Then I watched the letters disappear one by one as I deleted them, leaving only the message that I was okay.

CHAPTER 19

My dad arrived at the hospital just as I was nodding off to sleep.

"Emma, thank God you're okay."

"I'm fine, Dad. Just a little shaken up."

"What happened?"

Sparing him the ridiculous truth, I stuck to the story Michelle had told the police and said I'd been out looking for the witch caves. While exploring one of them, the storm had intensified and I'd gotten snowed in.

"What possessed you to go looking for a cave in the middle of a snowstorm?"

Legitimate question. "We studied them in history class, and I was curious. But it was a dumb thing to do, Dad. I'm sorry I worried you."

"Honey, my job is to worry about you. That's what I do, whether you like it or not. When you're thirty-five and a best-selling poet on the Riviera, I'm still going to worry."

"A best-selling poet, Dad?"

He laughed. "No such thing?"

"Exactly. And I'd prefer Paris to the Riviera."

"Don't start on Paris," he said, laughing.

Even though I tried to convince him to go home, he insisted on staying overnight. The doctor wanted to keep me there so he could reassess me in the morning. But I felt fine. At least physically. But all this deception was starting to weigh on me. I hadn't told my dad about the dreams because I was worried he would assume the worst—that I was becoming sick like my mom. And maybe I was.

Last year, a legion of doctors had not been able to explain how I'd survived a lightning strike with no permanent cognitive damage. But what if they'd gotten it wrong? What if I was brain-damaged, and that explained the hallucinations I was having?

There was this possible medical explanation, and there was Darlene's mystical one, and the truth probably lay somewhere in between. I didn't know what I believed anymore.

When I got back to school on Monday, I really wanted to talk to Owen, but I knew he'd be in class. I took the day off to rest, but ironically, I couldn't seem to sleep when I wanted to.

I waited until the afternoon and called Owen's cell, relieved that he actually picked up. "Emma, are you okay?" he said.

"I'm fine."

"God, you gave everyone a scare. Michelle told me you were out *spelunking?*"

I laughed. "You're not buying that one?"

"I figure it probably had more to do with your narcolepsy. Or whatever you want to call it."

"Yeah. Look, Owen, I know I need to get this under control, but I didn't call to talk about the cave," I said. "I wanted to talk to you about the other night. Can I come over?"

There was a long pause, and then he said, "Okay. When?"

"Are you free now? I could walk there."

"Walk?" he said. "In four feet of snow? After last night? I don't think so. I'll come and pick you up. We can get coffee in town."

For a moment, he sounded like the old Owen—conciliatory, sweet, always ready to make me feel better. But as soon as I got in his car, I felt this terrible tension that made my insides coil and tighten. Things between Owen and me had always been so simple and effortless. But I wondered if maybe they'd only seemed simple and effortless to me. Maybe Owen had been struggling with our friendship for a long time.

"How are you?" I asked as we drove into Waverly, wondering how we were going to sustain a conversation over coffee when we could barely fill the space of a ten-minute car ride.

"I've been better."

"Yeah, I know. I'm so sorry about the other night," I said. "I don't know what I was thinking. I guess I wasn't thinking."

He seemed to swallow whatever he was about to say. Then he muttered through gritted teeth, "You don't need to explain." Every word took so much effort, and his body language seemed cold and distant.

Once we got into Waverly, we went to the coffee shop and sat at a table by the window. Owen bought me a latte and scone even though I insisted on paying, and we sat across from each other, fumbling with our place settings. Owen tapped on his mug, and I played with my spoon.

After the silence grew unbearable, I decided to take the direct approach. "How are things with you and Flynn?"

His eyes widened, like he was surprised I'd broached the topic. "We're cool, I guess," he said. "He was really drunk that night. And he's Flynn, you know?"

So he'd forgiven Flynn almost immediately because Flynn was drunk and basically an idiot anyway? But me, he blamed because he'd expected more. It wasn't fair, but it also wasn't far from the truth.

"Are you guys still going to Europe together?"

"Of course," he said. "We fly to London in July."

"And then Paris in the fall?" He nodded. I remembered

our deal to go to our first opera together. I doubted that would ever happen now.

Owen glanced down at his coffee, and more time ticked away. This was torture. I had to say something to crack through his defenses. "So, you're still so mad at me you can't even look at me?"

His eyes flickered up at mine. "Just the opposite," he said. "I still feel something I know I shouldn't. That's why I can't look at you. But that's my problem, not yours."

He dropped his gaze again, and I struggled to say something. "Owen, do you think we'll ever be able to be friends again?"

"I've never stopped being your friend, Emma. But watching you kiss Flynn that night? I've never felt more like a fool. Not even with Michelle. With her, at least I saw it coming. You blindsided me."

"Owen, I can only say I'm sorry again."

"It's okay. You can't make yourself love someone. Especially when you still have feelings for someone else."

"Owen—"

"No, let me finish. After that night when you kissed me at the cast party, I knew you were rebounding, but I let myself believe that maybe someday, you could love me, too. But seeing you kiss Flynn, I realized neither kiss meant anything to you. Because you're still in love with Gray."

His eyes fluttered closed. When I didn't say anything to deny it, Owen tipped back the last of his coffee and pulled his chair back.

We drove back to school in silence, and when we pulled up to Easty Hall, I put my hand on his arm.

"What can I do to make this right?" I said.

He didn't answer right away. "Nothing," he said. "I'm going to need some time."

"Okay," I said. "I can do that."

I smiled softly, but he kept staring straight ahead at the

steering wheel. When I got out of the car, I bent down and peered in at him. "Owen?" I said.

"Yeah?"

"Thanks for seeing me," I said. "I really appreciate it."

He looked up and smiled a little sadly. "What are friends for?"

Over the next few weeks, life got a little better. And worse. Michelle and I were talking again, which was wonderful. Jess had moved in with Elise, and they had reconciled, too. But everyone had found out about my excursion to the witch caves, so now people were talking about me in not-so-hushed voices, saying I was "a witch," "a drama queen," "a mental case." And Amber and Chelsea continued to torture Jess.

In Bio, Ms. Brewster started her unit on plant sexuality. Girls were snickering before she even started her lecture.

"Up until the nineteenth century," she said, "many people refused to believe plants had sexuality because according to the Bible, plants were created on the third day, and it wasn't until the sixth day that the Bible made any mention of gender. Yet scientists know now that plants have a far more complex sexual cycle than animals."

I had to admit, it was kind of funny to hear Brewster talking about stamens and pistils and sepals and hermaphrodite plants. Even the diagrams she put up on the Smart Board looked kind of dirty.

"In dioecious species," she went on, "each plant has reproductive units that are either male or female. The androecious plants produce male flowers only and the gynoecious plants produce female flowers only. In some populations, all plants are gynoecious, thus they must rely on nonsexual reproduction to create the next generation."

Amber leaned over to Chelsea and said, "What do you know, lesbo plants."

Chelsea threw her head back laughing, and the giggles spread like a contagion. But not everyone was laughing. Elise glared at Amber and told her to grow up, and Michelle looked at me like she was going to lose it.

Ms. Brewster slammed her book down on her desk and shouted, "I don't know who is speaking, but the next person who says anything inappropriate will be spending all Saturday in the dissection closet."

Everyone settled down quickly after that, but I heard Amber whisper, "We all know who's been spending time in the closet this year."

"That's it," Brewster said. "Ms. Fairchild, I've warned you for the last time."

Elise looked up from her notebook. "That wasn't me," she said. "I'm just taking notes and doing my reading."

"Oh really?" Brewster said. "Then maybe you'll be kind enough to identify a species of plant that's dioecious."

"The American holly," Elise said.

"And what percent of angiosperms are dioecious?" she asked.

"A little under ten percent."

Brewster was getting more and more frustrated. "And which researcher wrote a treatise on plant sexuality?"

"Christian Sprengel," Elise said. "But his work was discredited because people didn't understand how complex sexuality was. And that was back in 1793. Here we are over two hundred years later, and not much has changed."

My respect for Elise shot up about a thousand points.

"No editorial comments will be necessary, Ms. Fairchild," Brewster said. But I saw some foreign emotion on her face. She'd just been one-upped by her student, yet she wasn't retaliating with her usual defensive tactic. Maybe she'd gained a little respect for Elise as well.

The day wore on in tedious fashion, with Overbrook starting his lecture on Reconstruction Era America and Gallagher continuing our Emily Dickinson unit. Afterward, Michelle and I left class together a few paces behind Jess and Elise. We were all heading to the dining hall, so I glanced at Michelle imploringly.

"Come on, let's catch up with them," I said. "We can eat lunch together and talk."

"I can't," Michelle said. "Not yet."

"It's just lunch."

"You don't understand—" she started.

"No, you're right," I said. "That's what everyone keeps telling me. And I really want to understand because you're my best friend. But Jess is my friend, too."

"Well, you can go eat with her, then. I'm going back to the dorms."

I felt terrible letting her go back to a lunch of ramen noodles, but I knew that just like with Owen, I had to give her time. And I also had to move on with my life.

In the dining hall, I walked over to Jess and Elise, who were sitting at a quiet table in the back corner of the dining hall.

"Can I join you?" I asked.

"Sure," Jess said, moving her bag over to make room for me. "How are you feeling?" she asked. I hadn't really talked to her since the cave incident.

"Fine," I said. "A little stupid, though."

"For getting snowed inside a cave?" Elise said dryly. "We've all been there."

"Shut up, Elise," Jess said. Elise shrugged and continued eating her salad.

"How are you doing?" I asked.

"I'm okay."

"I'm sorry everything went wrong the other night," I said. "I shouldn't have meddled."

"Meddled in what?" Elise said.

"It's fine," Jess said, ignoring Elise. "It was bound to happen sometime."

"What was bound to happen?" Elise said.

"Yeah, but I overstepped my bounds," I said. "I rushed her."

"No, no, it wasn't your—"

"Excuse me," Elise said loudly, "but does anyone want to fill me in on what's going on?" Jess looked at me, then looked at Elise. When neither of us said anything, Elise's eyes widened. "Oh my God," she said.

"What?" Jess said.

"I'm such an idiot. I can't believe I didn't see it until now. I'm usually so intuitive."

Jess shook her head. "Elise, it's nothing."

"No, it is something," she said, looking at Jess. "And it's so obvious now. It's Michelle, isn't it?"

"Elise, just drop it," I said, knowing that we'd already dug ourselves into a crater-sized hole.

"It's okay," Jess said to me. "She can know."

"Don't worry," Elise said. "I'm not going to say anything. I hope you believe that by now. But Michelle, huh? No wonder she never comes over when you're around."

"Yeah, I seem to have that repulsive effect on people," Jess said.

"It's not that," I said, "and you know it."

"But you guys would look so cute together," Elise said.

"The strongest argument I can think of for getting two people together," I said, rolling my eyes at Jess.

"So what's the deal?" Elise said. "She in denial or something?"

Jess appealed to me for help. "No," I said. "She's just not ready to put herself through the gauntlet Jess has been through. She got enough of that last year." I gave Elise a pointed look, and she bristled. But then her face softened.

"All right, you got me there," she said. "I was a bitch to her last year. No doubt. And I used to play all the games

Amber's playing now. I was just immature. Sheltered. But my cousin Steve came out this summer, and that changed everything."

"Oh, are we telling this story now?" Jess said. "Let me get the popcorn."

"What happened?" I asked.

Elise went on. "Steve's in college now at Tufts, but he just graduated from high school last June, a star athlete, an A student, really good-looking kid. Half my friends were in love with him. Anyway, when he came out to his family, his dad freaked and tried to sign him up for this . . . straightening camp, or something like that. He refused and ended up staying with me and my dad for the summer. The night of my sweet sixteen, he was in the kitchen making my friends a pitcher of margaritas when I accidentally said something about him being gay. I thought my friends would be cool enough to handle it, but Chelsea got all weirded out and Amber flipped because apparently—news to me—she had hooked up with him a few times the summer before. So Amber starts telling me he's going to hell, and Chelsea's agreeing with everything Amber says, and I feel like vomiting, partly from drinking too many margaritas and partly because I've just realized my friends are complete assholes."

"Present company excluded," Jess said.

"Of course," Elise said. "Because you . . . you didn't say a thing. You just sat there the whole time looking pale and scared out of your mind. That's when I started to suspect something."

"And that's when I panicked," Jess said. "And picked a fight with you about God knows what just so I wouldn't have to deal with it."

"And then things really spiraled out of control, and I kicked everyone out of my house, and Steve and I got wasted on that pitcher of margaritas by ourselves."

"Good times, good times," Jess said, making us both laugh.

"So that's the sordid story of the Fall of the Fairchild Empire," Elise said. "And what's sad is that now Amber's become a mini-me. She learned from the best. But if she thinks she can go head-to-head with the master, she's a fool."

Jess shook her head. "Elise, don't do anything. It'll only encourage her."

"What's with all this passive resignation?" she said. "Do you remember standing up to me at the end of last year?" Jess dropped her head in her hands, embarrassed. "No, seriously, Emma, you wouldn't believe how Jess rallied to your defense."

"My defense?" I said. "When was this?"

"After I spread that nasty rumor about Gray and tried to ruin his life."

"Oh, that," I said.

"Yeah, well, your girl here totally called me out on my bullshit. And she was absolutely right. I did a horrible thing to you guys. I was just hurt and jealous, and Jess helped me see that."

"Hello!" Jess said. "I'm right here. You can stop talking about me in the third person."

"Sorry," Elise said. "But that's all in the past. And presently, we need to shut Amber down."

Jess looked skeptical, but I felt oddly comforted knowing we had someone else in our corner. Especially someone like Elise.

Our fledgling alliance was put to the test almost immediately. By gym class, the rumors had morphed once again. Because we had eaten lunch together, all three of us were labeled lesbians now. And as Amber's "public service announcements" posted all over the locker room said, "Dyke fever is catching."

Loughlin took down the posters immediately, but a few days later, Amber and Chelsea told her they were uncomfortable getting changed in the locker room in front of lesbians. When Loughlin told them they were being ridiculous, they took the matter to Overbrook. Now a petition to ban us from gym class was floating around campus.

I wasn't sure how many signatures they had actually acquired, but the fact that Overbrook had approved of this travesty was deeply disturbing. Even while all this drama was going on, I never said a word to Michelle or tried to involve her. Like Darlene had said, we were soul friends, and if she needed time, I'd give it to her. But for now, our differences drove a wedge between us.

When I got back to the dorm one afternoon, I saw something sitting in my slot in the cluster mailbox. I hardly ever got mail, so it was a surprise to pull out a hand-addressed letter and even more of a surprise when I recognized Gray's handwriting—small and neat, a weird combination of lowercase and capital letters that I always made fun of. My heart squeezed like a fist.

I raced upstairs and into the room, relieved that Michelle wasn't there for the moment. I wanted to read the letter alone, in case whatever was in it made me burst into tears or into a rage. Tearing through the flap, I pulled out the letter, the first I'd received from Gray since he'd left for the Coast Guard. I held it in my hands a few seconds before reading.

For now, the letter could be whatever I wanted it to be. There was something appealing about not knowing. But eventually, curiosity took over and I scanned the letter, my eyes dropping to the bottom to look for telltale clues. I spotted the phrases: *survive on my own, no good for anyone, I hope you understand.* This didn't look good.

Unable to bear the suspense any longer, I began reading:

Dear Emma,

I know this letter is far overdue. I'm afraid I'm not very good at letter writing. When I think about all the letters you sent me last fall and how I never even wrote you back, it kills me. I'd do anything to take everything back and start all over. But what's done is done. We can't go back and change the past. We can only move forward and hope things will get better.

I am so sorry for my immature behavior on New Year's Day. I had no right to say those things about you and Owen. What did I expect? That you'd wait for me? I specifically told you not to. Although for the life of me, I can't remember why. I've been thinking about you constantly, even dreaming about you, and the dreams feel so real. It's like I'm there with you, talking to you. And it's like you can hear me, too. But then I wake up, and you're gone, and I regret everything all over again.

I've been trying to find a way to explain why I ended things last October. One of the skills we had to learn in boot camp was treading water. While we were all treading away in an eighty-degree pool, our instructor told us about a time when he had to tread water with a bunch of capsized fishermen for over an hour in the Bering Sea. When the water temperature is below forty and you're trying to get injured people into a tiny basket suspended from a helicopter, it's easy to panic and forget what's most important. And that is keeping yourself alive. So he trained us to tread water for five minutes, then fifteen, then thirty minutes, until we could tread for an hour on our own. He said, "You have to be able to survive on your own before you can have any hope of saving someone else."

I don't know if that makes any sense, but that's how I felt last fall. I had to know my life had meaning before I could give myself to you. I had to be strong enough on my own before I could be strong enough for both of us.

I'm so sorry I hurt you. I hope you understand what I did and that in time, you might be able to forgive me.

Yours always,

Gray

I sat on my bed, rereading the lines to decipher their meaning. Was he saying he regretted breaking up with me? Or was he just explaining why he had? I read the letter again—three times, a fourth.

He said he'd had vivid dreams about me. I'd sort of convinced myself that our psychic connection was a fluke. But something had definitely happened the night of the snowstorm. I had called out to Gray, and he had heard me.

It frustrated me that I still needed him, still loved him after all this time.

But the line that stuck in my head most was: *I had to be strong enough on my own before I could be strong enough for both of us.*

What I'd never realized until now was how true that was for me as well.

CHAPTER 20

I went back to Hull's Cove for spring break with a heavy heart. Fortunately, my dad kept me busy, taking me on college visits to Amherst and Hampshire, two schools that had made it onto the short list of my favorites. My dad let me drive, but kept pressing an imaginary brake pedal the entire way there.

First, we visited Amherst College. An upperclassman took us on a tour, culminating with the church tower, its round deck giving us a bird's-eye view of the entire campus—green quads, stately buildings, students camped out on the lawn, shirtless guys playing lacrosse. We grabbed lunch at a vegetarian café in the quaint and bustling town center, then took a break from college hunting to visit the Emily Dickinson Museum, where we saw Dickinson's headstone, etched with the haunting phrase *Called Back*.

Afterward, we visited Hampshire College and talked to the head of the Arts and Social Action program. She told us that each course of study in the department was customized to align with the student's particular talents and interests. If I wanted, I could merge my interest in writing with social activism, learning how to use my pen to root out political corruption, skewer big business, or shed light on the environmental effects of fossil fuels.

When we got back in the car to head home, my dad asked me what I'd thought of the schools. "Right now, I'm leaning toward Hampshire," I said. "But if I decide to major in French, Amherst has the better language program."

"You're still thinking about majoring in French?" he said. He might as well have said, *You're still thinking about going to clown college?*

"Dad, I don't know. I'm seventeen. That's why I'm going to Paris next year," I said. "I want to figure it all out."

His face collapsed at this reminder that I might be leaving. We'd shared such a nice day, and I didn't want to ruin it, but I also didn't want to hear another lecture on responsibility. "You don't want me to go?" I said.

"No, that's not it," he said. "If you really want to, then I'll support you."

"I really do," I said.

"There's no doubt I'd miss you. I mean, I know you're away at school now, but the thought of you all the way across the Atlantic—it terrifies me. It's hard for me to admit you're growing up, that you might really leave me for good someday, and not just for Paris."

"Dad, you know I'll always come back."

But when I looked at his face, I could tell what he was thinking. People didn't always come back.

"You know," he said, "I was always so scared of you in-heriting your mother's disease. I think I thought that if I kept you home all the time, I could somehow keep you safe. But look at you. You're all grown up, driving my car. You're vis-iting colleges and making plans to go to Paris on your own. I never would have had the courage to do that when I was your age. In fact, the farthest I've ever strayed from home is Georges Bank during fishing season."

"That's why you're going to come visit me in Paris," I said.

He smiled. "You're so much like your mother. And not just your looks—I know you're tired of hearing that, even though she was beautiful. But she was beautiful inside as well. You inherited her strength and passion, her kind and generous spirit. She'd be so proud of you right now." I was trying to remain stoic and not cry. "I'm proud of you, too. And I know you won't need it next year because you're going to be in Paris"—he rolled his eyes—"but I want you to take the Volvo back to school with you."

"Really?" I said. "But what are you going to drive?"

"Jim Deikman's giving me his old Ford. A truck's better for deliveries anyway. The station wagon just holds all the smells. As you're well aware."

"Dad, I don't care about the smell," I said. "Thank you. This is amazing!"

As a way of thanking my dad for being so understanding, I offered to cook everyone a French dinner. Not being the world's best chef, I made quiche and a Niçoise salad, and Barbara picked up a chocolate mousse cake at the bakery for dessert.

On Sunday, we all went to Easter services together. I hadn't been to church since Christmas, and I felt a little guilty about it. It wasn't that I didn't believe in God, more that I questioned what kind of God he was. Anyone who's lost a parent must go through this crisis of faith, asking, *How could a merciful God take my mother away?*

Michelle and I had talked about this last year, since she'd lost her mother, too. Michelle claimed to be an atheist, with science her only religion. She often scoffed at Darlene's voodoo beliefs, but deep down, I think Michelle had some faith of her own, even if it didn't conform to any church or institution's view of the cosmos.

I wasn't quite sure what I believed. I was still working it all out. It had been a long time since I'd prayed, but church seemed as good a place as any to try. So I closed my eyes and asked for guidance, for someone to show me the way through these next few harrowing months at school.

There was no greater feeling than driving back to school myself on Monday, cruising along those winding roads with the windows down, the sun streaming in, and Arcade Fire blasting from the radio.

Michelle couldn't believe it when I brought her to the parking lot to show her my new wheels. Later that night hanging out in our room, I told her about my spring break—the college visits and my dad's support of me going to Paris. Then she told me some revelations of her own. Over spring break, she had told Darlene about her relationship with Jess.

"It was so funny watching her face," Michelle said. "At first, she thought I was going to tell her I was pregnant." I put a hand over my mouth and tried not to laugh. "But when I told her, she was so cool about it. She got all serious and sat me down and said"—Michelle went into her best Darlene impression—" 'Baby child, love is love. And hurt is hurt. It makes no difference to me who you give your heart to, girl or boy, so long as they give it back to you.' "

"Darlene said that?"

"Yeah. She told me the most important thing in life is to be happy. And I haven't been very happy lately."

"I can't disagree with you there," I said. "So what are you going to do?"

"I don't know. Darlene helped me open the door a little. I'm not ready to burst through it, guns blazing, but I might be ready to take a look and see what's on the other side."

She gave a shy smile, one full of tempered excitement and hope.

It was a beginning.

CHAPTER 21

In Biology, Ms. Brewster told us we were starting our final and most dreaded lab of the year: the cat dissection. Amber and Chelsea had opted out of the dissection due to "ethical reasons" and were doing a related research project at the library instead. It was nice having at least one period of the day that was cruelty-free.

"I'm afraid we don't have enough cats for each set of lab partners," Ms. Brewster said, "so you're going to have to pair up with another group. Just join the people at the lab table next to yours."

Jess and I watched as pairs made alliances, leaving us to partner with . . . who else? Michelle and Elise. Jess looked annoyed and defensive, and Michelle looked cagey and uncomfortable. A noxious odor pervaded the classroom as we all released our formaldehyde-soaked felines from their bags and laid them in their trays. Even though it was pretty lame of Chelsea and Amber to wimp out on the lab, I had to admit it was pretty gruesome to stare down at a dead, wet cat that seemed to be baring his teeth at us.

"Is it bad luck to skin a black cat?" Elise said.

"Only if it gets up out of the tray and crosses your path," I said.

Elise gave me a look of mock amusement, then said, "Who wants to take the first slice?"

All of us were silent.

"I'll do it." We looked up, startled that Michelle had spoken. She was staring down at the lab instructions with this very intense expression on her face. "Scalpel, please," she said, holding her hand out like a surgeon.

"Yes, Doctor, right away," joked Elise, handing Michelle the scalpel.

Tensions were running high, but Michelle calmly turned the cat over onto its stomach and made a one-inch incision in its neck.

"You're supposed to switch to scissors now," Jess said, reading the instructions.

"I know," Michelle said irritably.

"Okay, okay," Jess said, "I didn't realize you already had them memorized."

Elise and I raised an eyebrow at each other, and then Elise passed Michelle the scissors.

"That's a fine incision there, Michelle," Elise said. "Isn't that a fine incision, Jess?"

"It's just lovely," Jess said. "Perfection itself."

I glanced at Michelle, whose mouth was curling up ever so slightly. Once she had reached the tail, Jess told her to stop cutting.

"What?" Michelle said.

"It clearly states that the skin should not be removed from the anus," Jess said. "I bet you didn't know that."

Michelle looked straight at Jess, and with a deadpan expression, said, "I wouldn't touch this cat's anus with a ten-foot pole."

Elise and I couldn't help but giggle, and once we'd started, it grew contagious. Now Jess was laughing, too, but Michelle was doing her best to play it straight. She continued cutting the skin on all four legs down to the ankles. "Okay," Michelle said. "Now you've all got to help me pull off the skin."

Jess continued reading the instructions, which advised us to grasp a section of skin and pull it slowly away from the muscle, using our fingers to break through connective tissue fibers and cutaneous nerves. "This is so gross," Elise said as she peeled off a layer.

The poor cat lay there prostate and half-naked until we turned him over and peeled the skin off the other side. Jess continued reading. "Now inspect your skinned cat, being sure to remove as much fat as possible from the muscles to facilitate identification."

"That is one ugly cat," Elise said.

"You'd be pretty ugly without skin too," I said.

Jess laughed under her breath. "Okay, now we're supposed to wrap the cat back up in its skin to help keep the muscles preserved."

"Oh, nasty," Elise said.

We put the skin back on the cat like a coat and placed him faceup in the pan. With those little fangs protruding and the black skin hanging off him like a cape, he looked like a tiny vampire.

"Let's call him Edward," Elise said.

This time, even Michelle laughed. By the time class was over, we were all punchy on fumes, making sick dead cat jokes. Unwittingly, poor Edward had brought us all together.

Amber and Chelsea were on their best behavior in History and English, probably because Overbrook and Gallagher had gone into high gear to try to finish the curricula in time for the AP exams in mid-May. It was nice for the four of us—Jess, Michelle, Elise, and me—to be able to walk to the dining hall together without worrying about high school politics for once.

When we walked in, a few senior girls from student council were sitting at a long table by the entrance selling prom tickets. Since Lockwood was such a small school, junior and senior proms were combined so the school had justification to rent out a fancy country club for the night. This year's theme, painted on a banner that hung above the table, was "Star-Crossed Lovers."

"Oh God, is it that time of year already?" Elise asked.

"Unfortunately," I said.

Michelle scoffed in that aloof way that only made it more apparent how much she wanted to go. "The prom was created as an excuse for a bunch of debutantes to march around a room flaunting their assets so some rich guys might agree to marry them. It's antifeminist and elitist."

"It doesn't have to be that way," I said. "I mean, we could subvert the system. Wear Converse with our cocktail dresses."

"Listen to you, Miss Rebel," Michelle said.

Then Jess shocked us all into silence, saying, "I think we should go."

That's when we heard Amber clear her throat behind us. "You can't be serious, Jess." Chelsea stood by her side, laughing nervously. "I'm not paying two hundred dollars for a lobster dinner only to hurl it all up on prom night when I see two girls dancing together."

"Oh, like it would be your money anyway," Elise said.

"Besides, what difference could it possibly make to you who dances with who?" I said.

"It's disgusting," Amber said.

"Why is it disgusting?" Jess said.

"Yes, what exactly is disgusting about it?" Michelle added.

Amber made an exaggerated gagging noise. "If I have to explain it to you, then you must be a lesbian yourself."

Michelle stiffened for a moment. Then she said, "So what if I am?"

We all turned to look at Michelle. "Then it would explain your terrible fashion sense," Amber said.

Michelle didn't back down. "See, I can buy new clothes," she said. "But you can't buy yourself a new personality. You can't buy intelligence or integrity. And you can't buy your friendships back once you've lost them." I was beginning to think this seemingly spontaneous speech had been months in the making.

Amber looked offended. "You'll never have enough money to buy your way into being cool."

"No," Michelle said. "But I have enough money to buy a prom ticket." She got her wallet out of her purse and began pulling out twenties.

"You can't just buy a ticket," Amber said. "The theme is star-crossed lovers. You need to go with a date."

The senior at the table nodded and said, "She's right. It's a couples dance. You need to enter which star-crossed couple you're coming as so we don't get three dozen Romeo and Juliets."

"See?" Amber said.

But then the senior added, "There's nothing that says the couple can't be two girls." And she gave Amber a victorious smirk.

Michelle started laughing, then she looked at Jess, her face utterly resolute. "Jess, do you want to go? Together?"

Jess looked at the ground, suddenly shy. "Are you sure?"

"Yeah, I am."

Jess smiled and blushed. "I'd love to."

"Oh, gag," Amber said.

But Elise and I couldn't stop smiling.

Elise turned to me and said, "Emma, as much as I want to make a statement in front of these morons, I can't go to the prom with you."

I laughed. "For once in my life, Elise, I'm in complete agreement with you."

Jess and Michelle began brainstorming about which couple they would go as. "Oh, this is too much," Amber said.

"We'll see what Overbrook has to say about this. We're already working on getting him to ban lesbians from taking gym class with us. I'm sure he would do the same for prom." Then she blinked three times with those chemically enhanced eyelashes and walked away, tugging Chelsea behind her.

My stomach clenched at the thought of Overbrook getting involved. Elise felt pretty confident that even Overbrook wouldn't go so far as to ban Jess and Michelle from the prom. But I wasn't so sure. Michelle and I didn't have a great track record when it came to him. The thought of him interfering with prom put a damper on our enthusiasm, and we left the dining hall without buying any tickets.

The next day, the news about Michelle and Jess going to prom together was all over campus. By week's end, Amber and Chelsea were perpetuating the rumor that Overbrook was indeed planning to put the ban into effect. The four of us decided to meet in the lounge after school to come up with a game plan.

"I can't believe the bastard went through with it," Jess said.

"I know why," Elise said. "A few influential students got their mommies and daddies involved. Some have threatened to pull their daughters from Lockwood if the ban isn't put in place."

"But it's discrimination," I said.

Elise nodded. "My dad told me that since this is a private school, Overbrook can do whatever he likes. A private school doesn't have to obey the state's antidiscrimination laws."

"So basically we're screwed," Michelle said.

"You know, Overbrook probably wants to sweep this under the rug, keep it hush-hush. Maybe that's our secret weapon," I said. "Publicity. We could call the ACLU. I heard in Alabama, a principal was sued for trying to ban interracial couples from attending the prom. Elise, isn't your dad a lawyer?"

"Well, yeah, but he does mostly consulting now. And he

works in corporate law. I doubt he's had a lot of experience with this kind of thing."

"But maybe he knows someone who does," I said.

"Emma, my dad's on the school board here," Elise said. "It's kind of a conflict of interest."

I remembered that day in detention when Elise had said that Brewster hated her because she was a spoiled "daddy's girl." And from what she'd just said about other girls calling their parents to fight their battles for them, I knew she had a chip on her shoulder about asking her dad for help.

"You know, Amber and Chelsea don't speak for everyone," Jess said. "A lot of girls on campus have come up to me and told me they think Michelle and I are brave for doing this."

"Yeah," Michelle said. "I had one girl tell me she's going to come out to her parents this summer. She was too scared to do it before."

"Then maybe we should organize some kind of protest," I said.

Jess was nodding. "I was reading online about this event called the National Day of Silence. You get students at your school to take a vow of silence for the day to protest bullying and harassment of gay teens. You don't speak all day, not to each other and not even in classes, until six o'clock, when you break the silence publicly."

"That sounds pretty cool," I said.

"I don't know how Elise would make it through the day without talking, though," Michelle said, and Elise stuck her tongue out.

"Why don't we see how many girls might be willing to participate?" I said.

"Yeah," Michelle agreed. "There's no sense getting all worked up about something if it's only going to be the four of us."

"But we better work quickly," Jess said. "The event is next Monday. We only have a week to get organized."

"I'll start asking around," I said. "If we get enough people, we could even send a press release to the local media."

"The media?" Michelle said.

"Yeah, so when we break the silence, they can cover the story. It might get us the publicity we're looking for."

Michelle looked uneasy at the thought of going public. But I was energized by the prospect. It felt good to be a part of something larger than myself, to do something completely unrelated to my own petty troubles.

The four of us set out to get as many supporters as possible, and by the end of the week, we had amassed almost seventy signatures of girls willing to participate in the Day of Silence. Given the enthusiastic reaction, I called the local news station, who agreed to send a small news crew to interview us at the end of the day.

I was walking out of History feeling pretty proud of what we'd done when Overbrook asked me to come see him after school. Again. As soon as I entered his office, I knew that somehow he had gotten wind of our plans and that he saw me as the instigator of our rabble-rousing band.

"Ms. Townsend," he said as I sat down across from him, "it seems you are creating quite the disturbance on our quiet little campus with your . . . silent protest." He touched his finger to the base of his snow globe.

"I'd hardly call a silent protest a disturbance," I said. "It's just a form of civil disobedience. See, we read Thoreau in AP English class, and well, a few of us got to talking, and we think your decision to ban single-sex couples from attending prom is discriminatory."

"A few of you?" he said, his eyes narrowing. "And how many would that be?"

"I have about seventy names," I said, pulling out the sign-up sheet. "And we all—"

"Ms. Townsend," he said, cutting me off. "Before you launch into a well-intentioned but misguided defense of your position, my decision to ban same-sex couples had nothing whatsoever to do with the girls in question being gay. It is simply a matter of wanting to keep the prom an event in which girls from an all-girls school can meet boys in a social scenario. If girls were able to bring other girls, then every girl who had trouble finding a date would do so. We want to encourage a coeducational experience and create an atmosphere in which boys from other schools feel welcome."

"But you're creating an atmosphere in which some of your own students feel unwelcome," I said.

Dr. Overbrook drew his head back and studied me. "I cannot imagine why two girls would want to attend prom together anyway. It will only invite abuse and bullying. The prom is a Lockwood tradition going on one hundred years. It is always elegant, refined, respectable. I would hate for that tradition to be sullied by any kind of . . . ugliness."

"But it's the discrimination that's ugly," I said. "If you're so worried about ugliness, why not ban the bullies instead of the same-sex couples?"

"Ms. Townsend, I have never been a fan of outspoken students. In your case, I had thought the Paris scholarship had been given to a worthy candidate, but I must say you surprise me with this defiant attitude. Perhaps you take your education for granted. Perhaps you fail to see that if this school does not maintain a certain reputation and standing in the community, then scholarships such as yours will cease to exist. Parents will remove their students from our school, and our endowment will dry up. I cannot risk the future of all my girls for the sake of one or two."

"There are more who are afraid to speak up."

He eyed me skeptically. "Lockwood has existed for a hundred and fifty years," he said. "Your friends will survive this minor disappointment, but if Lockwood loses the support of its parents and stakeholders . . . I cannot say the same for it. I commend you on your desire to stand up for your friends, but this matter must be treated delicately. And I'm afraid my decision is final. No sort of protest is going to change that, so I urge you to drop this pointless exercise. Please don't force my hand."

I was so livid I wanted to smash his precious snow globe against the wall. I tried to think of what might convince him, but what could I say to a man like that? Like he'd told me, his decision was final. So I stood up, my chair scraping loudly against the floor.

I was about to leave when Overbrook called me back in. "Ms. Townsend, I would like to have the list, if you please." He held forth his hand, gesturing for me to pass the list of signatures to him. For some reason, I clung to it.

"Why? What difference does it make if you've already made up your mind?"

"A headmaster ought to know his students."

"If it's all the same, sir, I'd rather keep it."

"Ms. Townsend, I did not take you for an insubordinate. As I've said before, my final recommendation is required if you want to go to Paris next year. I urge you to think carefully before refusing a direct request from me."

My stomach dropped. Was he blackmailing me? And if I gave him the list of names, what would he do with it?

"I'm not trying to be insubordinate," I said. "But these girls signed their names in good faith that nothing would happen to them as a result of their opinion."

"And nothing will happen."

"Are you sure?" I said.

"I promise you."

Reluctantly and with my heart in my throat, I handed him the list, feeling like I'd just sold my soul to the devil.

CHAPTER 22

O n Monday morning, the PA system announced an un-scheduled assembly. Everyone else seemed excited be-cause an assembly meant shortened class periods. But my stomach roiled as we walked to the Commons Building. Once we had all assembled in the auditorium, Overbrook approached the microphone and cleared his throat.

"It has come to my attention," he said, "that several among you have conspired to hijack the educational process by refusing to speak in class today, I assume in protest of my recent decision about prom. I have consulted with my lawyer, and the right to freedom of speech includes a right *not* to speak. However, a school has the right to restrict a student's freedom of speech when it deems that such speech, or in this case non-speech, would be detrimental to the learning envi-ronment. Therefore, I am going to insist that all students re-spond to any questions asked of them today in class and continue to participate meaningfully in the learning process. Anyone failing to comply with these instructions will face disciplinary action. Those on this list might want to think very carefully about how much a senseless act of civil disobe-dience will cost them." He held up the list I'd given him and brandished it above the podium.

My heart sank. Overbrook had done it again. Somehow he

had sabotaged our peaceful protest by using our silence against us. I didn't care what his "disciplinary action" would be; I was going to keep quiet today regardless of the consequences. But I knew some of the younger, more impressionable girls would succumb to his scare tactics. And he knew it, too. He left the room with a smug smile on his face.

That morning as Brewster began her lesson, she could barely hide her gleeful smile as she directed questions at me, Michelle, Jess, and Elise, checking off our names on the list when we refused to answer. As expected, many of the other girls capitulated under the pressure, and our Day of Silence, which we'd intended to start a massive wave of protest on campus, made little more than a ripple.

Overbrook added insult to injury by having an unannounced oral exam in AP History. He told us that during the course of class, each student would be asked five questions about the Nixon administration, and every correct answer would garner ten points. The bastard was hitting us where it hurt. The few staunch participants who hadn't caved under pressure thus far now did so with the threat of a failed exam grade looming over them. By six o'clock, only ten of us had maintained silence for the entire day.

We beleaguered few met in front of Easty Hall, where we had told the news crew to meet us. But Overbrook seemed to have anticipated this as well. It was pretty clear that Amber was his secret weapon, spying on us and reporting back what she'd learned. Before the reporter could even make her way over to us, Overbrook and two Lockwood security guards began turning them away, telling them they had no right to trespass on private property. The reporter was stubborn, asking Overbrook why he was opposed to letting her interview us. What was he trying to hide? But Overbrook's security guards did an effective job of steering the cameraman back toward the van.

Once the news crew had left, Overbrook stood on the

steps of Easty Hall and announced that we were all to go immediately back to our rooms and that he would decide how to deal with our insubordination tomorrow. Some of the girls apologized to Overbrook and begged him to be lenient. Others glared at me for selling them out. I felt like I'd let them down. Betrayed them. How could we simply walk back to our dorm rooms and go quietly about business as usual?

"I'd like to take a scalpel to his middle-aged gut and watch his intestines spill out," Elise said.

"I just wish there was something we could do that would hurt him like he's hurting you," I said, gesturing to Michelle and Jess.

"We have to let it go," Michelle said. "Overbrook wins; we lose. It's not like it's the first time."

"How can we just give up after all the work we've done?" I said, turning to face Michelle.

But Jess agreed with Michelle, saying, "We're always going to have to deal with the Overbrooks and Ambers of the world. We might as well get used to it."

However, not everyone was satisfied with all this acceptance and resignation.

After our demoralizing defeat, Elise finally agreed to contact her father, and he was only too anxious to help. Elise told him it would win him points during custody proceedings, but I think he would have helped us anyway. Mr. Fairchild seemed like one of the good guys.

And when Michelle called Darlene to tell her what had happened, Darlene insisted on coming down to the school to try and talk some sense into Overbrook. Against Michelle's wishes, she closed the bakery for the day and took the train to Waverly, where I picked her up and drove her to campus. Michelle warned her it was pointless to argue with Overbrook, but Darlene wouldn't hear of backing down. We waited for her in our room while she met in Overbrook's office for over an hour.

When she came back to the dorm, even Darlene—ever cool and ever wise—looked frazzled and beaten down. "Oh, that man," she said. "That condescending weasel of a man! I'm so angry right now I could spit." Fortunately she didn't.

"What happened?" Michelle asked.

"He told me it was your fault for making this such a public spectacle and then he had the gall to tell me I wasn't a very good guardian if I couldn't control my niece's *impulses.*"

"Ugh!" I said, getting angrier by the minute. "What did you say?"

"I told him he was an intolerant, rigid man, and I threatened him with a voodoo hex."

"You didn't!" Michelle said.

"I did!"

I officially loved this woman.

"What did he do?" Michelle asked.

"He kicked me out of his office."

"Oh, Darlene." Michelle was shaking her head, mortified.

"Well, I wasn't serious about the hex," she said. "I was only trying to make him hear reason. Of course, I did swipe a picture of him from off his desk." She pulled a framed photo of Overbrook out from under her coat.

"Darlene!" Michelle said.

"Stop saying my name like that," she said.

"What's a voodoo hex?' I asked.

"Emma, don't encourage her," Michelle said.

"It's a spell I sometimes use to get rid of someone."

"Get rid of someone?" I said, my eyes flaring.

"Oh, not in that way. We're not talking murder here. It's just a spell that takes a person who's standing in your way and ever so gently . . . nudges them out of it."

"It's black magic," Michelle said.

"It's murky, at best," Darlene said.

But I was curious. "How does it work?"

"Emma!" Michelle said, glaring at me.

Darlene sat down next to me with the photo in her hands. "You write down the person's name on a piece of paper, wrap it inside a photograph, and place the scroll inside a bottle of Four Thieves vinegar and throw it into a moving body of water. Then you call on Papa Legba to remove the obstacle from your path, and you visualize the person moving away from you, repeating the word *good-bye* three times."

"It sounds pretty easy," I said.

"Emma, you're supposed to be on my side," Michelle said.

"I am on your side. That's why I'm considering it. Overbook needs to go."

"But this isn't the way."

"Well, nothing else has worked."

Darlene could sense the tension churning between us. She set the photo of Overbrook on my nightstand and put on her coat. "We better get going, child. I want to make the last train before dark."

Darlene hugged Michelle, but Michelle's body stayed rigid. I got my keys and told her I'd be right back, but Michelle just lay down on her bed and turned onto her side to face the wall. This whole situation had blown up far beyond our expectations.

But still, I couldn't let it go. As I drove Darlene into Waverly Falls, I asked her more about the spell.

"So, is a voodoo hex dangerous?"

"No, not really," she said.

"Can anybody do it? Or do you have to be a voodoo practitioner?"

"Darling, a hex is just a formal way of putting a wish into the universe. The universe likes a balance. And where injustice exists, the spirits like to restore it."

"So, it's sort of like karma?"

"Exactly. But karma takes too long." I laughed. "I'll send you the ingredients," she said. "In case you change your mind. And I've got other spells, too. Even a spell to reunite lovers.

You know, for later." She winked at me, and I smiled. Our little secret.

I watched Darlene board the train, which chugged slowly out of sight, then I drove back to campus, anxious to talk to Michelle. When I got back to the room, she was still in a foul mood. She would barely answer me when I asked her questions, and she looked like she'd been crying. Finally, I asked her what was wrong. At first she said nothing, just put her headphones on, an old tactic that wasn't going to work anymore.

"Come on, Michelle," I said, sitting on the edge of her bed and taking the headphones off her ears. "Tell me what's bothering you."

She rolled over to face me. "I don't know," she said, sighing. "Everything's gotten so out of control. And I feel like it's all my fault."

"Your fault? It's Overbrook's fault. He's the jerk. And he needs to be taught a lesson."

"Stop it, Emma!" she said, sitting up.

"Stop what?"

"Everything you're doing. This isn't your fight."

"Yes, it is. It's everyone's fight."

"No, actually, it's not. You're going off to Paris next year, and I'm going to be stuck here to deal with this by myself. So if you don't mind, it's my fight. And I choose to throw in the towel."

"Michelle, this is your life we're talking about. Darlene said that the most important thing is for you to be happy. How can you be happy the way things are? How can you not want to fight?"

"But that's just it," Michelle said. "Now that everything is this huge spectacle, I'm not happy at all. I'm miserable. Suddenly everyone wants me to be the poster child for coming out in America. I don't want to be an activist. I just want to be able to hang out with my friends and not be reminded every five seconds how I'm different. I want to be able to dance with my girlfriend on prom night like everyone else, you know?"

I did know, but somehow I'd forgotten. I'd allowed myself to get so swept up in this cause that I had stopped thinking about the individuals behind it.

"I'm sorry," I said, trying to comfort her. "I didn't mean for this to get out of hand."

"I know," she said.

"What can I do?"

But she was already off the bed and moving toward the door. "Emma, I don't want you to do anything, understand?" I nodded, holding back tears. "I know you mean well, but you've got to let me handle things on my own, okay?"

"Okay," I said glumly, watching her put on her red scarf, the one I'd borrowed so many times before. "Where are you going?"

"I'm going to see if Jess wants to take a walk with me. I need to get out of here. No offense."

And then she left our room, and I felt like I'd lost her all over again.

CHAPTER 23

Our punishment for insubordination was that we were barred from all school-sponsored activities for the rest of the year, including prom. Not that we cared; none of us were planning to go to prom anyway out of solidarity with Jess and Michelle. But it also meant we were going to miss the school trip, a weekend in Washington DC to visit the memorials. We were supposed to stay at a hotel with a giant swimming pool and a rooftop deck with views of the National Mall. Michelle had been looking forward to it, especially as the trip was scheduled for her birthday weekend.

Amber and Chelsea, of course, reveled in our defeat. I'd become almost immune to their abuse, but a few of their insults still stung. And the disappointed looks from girls who had trusted me were by far the most painful.

Two weeks passed, and Michelle and Jess were spending all their time together. And while I was happy they had grown so comfortable with each other, I felt almost as lonely as I had at the beginning of the year. So I began running again.

One spring afternoon, I burst out the door and took off like a shot toward the woods, running like I was trying to outrun my own shadow. I waited for the endorphins to flood my brain, hoping to achieve some sort of mental escape, even if it was only temporary.

By the time I reached the log bridge, I was winded. Out of shape. I slowed my pace, pressing on toward Old Campus, hoping to feel that runner's high as I made my way uphill. The late April weather had infused the campus with the smell of grass and rain and green things. I felt good but for the stitch in my side. I tried to ignore it, but by the time I reached the Commons Building, my lungs were burning and a cramp was stabbing my abdomen. I doubled over under the scorched tree and tried to catch my breath, inhaling the scent of roses coming from the garden beyond.

Feeling a sudden rush from the heady scent, I wandered past the building and into the garden, expecting to see the burnt-out husks that had shrouded this place in gloom all winter. But everything was pink and green, trees bursting with tiny buds, plants springing their tendrils out of the ground like the first weeds of hope. The recent warm spell had awakened hordes of tiny snowdrops and crocuses and swaths of sunny daffodils. I let my fingers trail along a cluster of lamb's ears, then ducked my way under the forsythia that had grown over the arbor.

Feeling a surge of optimism, I headed back toward the trail and resumed my run, stopping short when I got back to the dorm. Someone was standing in front of the entrance. My brain wouldn't let me accept who it was, but I knew it in my bones and in my blood and in every other part of my body.

Seeing Gray had the effect of a cyclone ripping through campus with me at its center. I simultaneously wanted to run away and run toward him, slap him and kiss him. Even after all the pain he'd caused me, there was something so comforting about his presence—the familiar planes of his face, the soulfulness of his eyes, the white of his oxford-cloth shirt against his tan skin—all of these filled me with longing and joy and that old familiar ache. I had the inappropriate notion that he was still mine, and I wanted to be his too, forever, no matter what happened. I wanted to blot out the past like erasing a giant black cloud from the sky.

When he saw me, some emotion bloomed on his face—happiness? Ridiculously, I pictured him running to me, whisking me up in his arms and twirling me around, like in a scene from a romantic movie. But neither of us moved. His gaze lingered, both familiar and strange—familiar, because this was the boy who had kissed me on summer nights until my lips burned from his stubble, strange because he'd been away for far too long and I wasn't sure if he was ever going to touch me again.

What is he doing here? Not just here in front of my dorm, but here in Massachusetts?

Soon, anger and resentment replaced my euphoria. My hands went defiantly to my hips as I took a few steps toward him. I'd thought about this moment forever. What would I say to him now that he was standing right in front of me?

"Emma," he said, speaking first, his voice so soft it was almost a whisper.

"What are you doing here?" I asked, sounding more flustered than angry.

"I have two weeks' leave before I start 'A' School."

I turned his response over in my mind. "No, I mean what are you doing *here?*"

He bit the inside of his cheek. "I had to see you."

"Why? What's wrong?"

"Nothing," he said, his eyes squinting in confusion. "Nothing's wrong. I *wanted* to see you."

"Oh, so now you want to see me?" I said, feeling an internal collision between the person speaking these harsh words and the girl inside me who was fighting the urge to hug him.

"Don't do this, Emma," he said, his face pained. "Don't be like this, or it'll kill me." He moved slowly toward me, bending his head to study me, to see if I could really be as cold and indifferent as I appeared.

"What do you want me to say?"

He reached out as if to grab my hands. "I just want to talk. I don't expect anything. Can we go just somewhere and talk, you and me?"

No. He couldn't just show up here unannounced and expect me to drop everything. Not with me standing here in my leggings and oversized Lockwood sweatshirt, a sheen of sweat covering my face.

"I don't know," I said, unable to come up with a viable excuse.

"Please."

I could feel my resolve melting. "Let me take a quick shower first," I said. "But you'll have to wait out here. Some of the girls in my dorm would be only too happy to turn me in for having a guy in my room."

"No problem," he said.

I ran up the stairs to my room and showered at light speed, spending far too long choosing what to wear and finally deciding on a pale pink cotton shirt with jeans. When I went back downstairs, Gray was standing in the parking lot leaning against his Jeep. My heart catapulted over several cars.

"Hi!" he said, like he was seeing me for the first time. "You look great."

"Thanks."

"I figured we could go into Waverly Falls, grab a bite to eat. How does that sound?" He was being tentative with me, like he feared at any moment I might dash away.

"Okay," I said as he came around to open the passenger door. I was suddenly emboldened by a desire to show him that I'd changed, that I wasn't the same passive little girl he'd left in October. "Can I drive?" I asked.

"I don't know, can you?" he said, a tease in his voice.

"Of course."

He tossed the keys to me, and I hopped into the driver's seat. Once he'd fastened his seat belt, I let the clutch out and backed out of the parking space, then navigated us smoothly off campus and onto the tree-lined road that skirted Lockwood.

"Wow, you've gotten really good," he said.

"Thanks. My dad gave me the Volvo."

"He did? That's great, Emma. How is your dad doing?"

"He's okay," I said. "Freaking out about next year."

"Why?"

"Oh. I'm leaving. I got a scholarship to study in Paris my senior year."

"Paris?" he said. "Wow, that's incredible." There was a twinge of disappointment in his voice. "You always wanted to go to Paris."

An upbeat song was playing on his iPod, the male vocalist singing about shadows and light, kisses and scars. The driving rhythms gave me a false sense of daring and confidence. This was all too strange. Me driving Gray's Jeep on a beautiful April day. Too much expectation, too much emotion. I was overloading myself, flooding the engines, setting myself up for a crash.

When we got to Waverly, we walked the shops for a while and talked about nothing of importance. Everything felt so raw and new. Gray kept sneaking nervous glances at me. Our hands were so close I could have easily reached out and grabbed his, held it to my lips like I used to.

It was hard to fight the feeling that we were on a first date, fighting against butterflies and hormones instead of our pasts. Because everything here held some significance—the sushi restaurant where we'd gone on our first date, the dress shop where Gray had asked me to the prom, the coffee shop where we'd had our first fight, the bridge where he'd confessed his deepest secret, and of course, the waterfall where Gray had thought about killing himself.

Now I searched for somewhere neutral for us to go, somewhere those old ghosts couldn't follow us. We decided on

Monarch Gardens, the butterfly conservatory, which had walking trails through gardens and koi ponds. We meandered along the path through the gardens as Gray talked about his airman's training, which had been grueling but was supposed to be a breeze compared to the Coast Guard training that came next. We stopped between two rows of butterfly shrubs that made for a private little alleyway. Gray asked how school was going, and I told him about some of the drama that had been going on with Overbrook and our recent punishment barring us from all school activities.

"So you can't go to your prom?" Gray said.

"Well, I wasn't going to anyway because of Michelle and Jess. But yeah, we've all been put on a blacklist."

"That's too bad," Gray said. And then he laughed.

"Is something funny?"

"No, I was just thinking . . ."

"What?"

He was blushing a little, biting his cheek. "It's just, I had this crazy idea that I might be able to take you to your prom while I was home, since you never got to go to my prom last year."

I wanted to fall into his arms just then, forgive him everything, tell him I loved him still. Some shred of self-preservation kept me from doing so. Because what was really going on here? It had taken me so long to get over Gray. And now he'd been back for less than twenty-four hours, and I was already acting like a love-struck idiot.

"You wanted to take me to my prom?" I said.

"I wasn't naïve enough to think you'd say yes. To be honest, I wasn't even sure you'd talk to me. And it's kind of hard to dance with someone who wants you dead." I laughed a little, and his face lit up.

But then I realized playing off my emotions as a joke wasn't fair to me. I'd been devastated by our breakup; I wasn't going to let him off so easy. "Gray, I never wanted you dead, but I did want you to feel as much pain as I did. And I'm sorry if I hurt you. I don't know why I can't seem to get over you, no matter how much time passes. But I know that I was finally doing okay, and now suddenly you're back, and I don't know what to think about any of this."

He took a step toward me. "I'm confused, too," he said, "Well, not confused. I know what I want. I'm just not sure it's fair to ask you."

"Ask me what?"

He took a deep breath and moved closer. "In the letter I wrote, I left something out. Last fall in boot camp, I kept thinking about us, about how young you were and how much of your life you had ahead of you. And I was just this screwup trying to prove something to himself. When I thought about how hard it would be to stay together over the years and distance, I got scared. I told myself I didn't deserve you and that you'd be better off without me. But it's harder to stay away from you than I thought. In all this time, you've never left my mind. You're in my dreams, in every waking thought. What I left out of the letter, Emma, is that I'm in love with you. I have been for a long time. I don't know if I've damaged our relationship too much for you to consider giving me another chance. But I know we belong together. We always have."

I stopped breathing. A brilliant blue and black butterfly suddenly alighted on Gray's shoulder. "Hold still," I said. I leaned in to get a closer look, my face inches from his shoulder, close enough to feel the heat radiating from his chest.

Gray slowly turned his head. "I'm afraid if I move, it's going to fly away."

And then it did. The butterfly fluttered away and disappeared into the blue. And there in that moment, something broke free inside me and soared as well. I leaned in and inhaled Gray's familiar scent, like the ocean at nighttime. Steadying myself with my hands on his chest, I touched the Virgo angel around his neck.

"I thought you only wore this when you went away," I said. "You can take it off now. You're home."

His face softened, and he ran a finger slowly along my cheek. Closing his eyes, he stood still and waited, just as patiently as he had with the butterfly. I wasn't going to fly away. I had no defenses left. Standing on tiptoe, I leaned in and pressed my lips to his. He opened his eyes, surprised. And then he gave in to the kiss, wrapping his arms around me and pulling me close. Kissing Gray was a coming together of opposites, like taking off and landing all at once. It was a sweet kiss, tentative and slow, and I felt like everything—the air, the grass, the earth on its axis—slowed to match us.

Until a little boy came running by with a giant butterfly balloon, screaming, "Eww. Mommy, people are kissing!"

Gray and I laughed and left the garden, but he grabbed my hand and held it the entire way back into town. We spent several hours at the coffee shop, telling each other about all that had happened while he was away. Later, we stood beside his Jeep for another hour, neither of us wanting to leave.

It was especially hard to say good-bye when a time limit was looming over our heads. From that Sunday morning to the following Friday, the days raced by like we were on some planet set to crash and burn within days. I skipped several classes so we could spend our afternoons together, and Gray made feeble attempts to spend time with his family, only to show up back at my dorm every night. We couldn't stay away from each other.

On Saturday afternoon, we drove to Oak Lane Park and walked the trails. The sky was a mind-blowing blue, and the air was heady with pollen. We laid a picnic blanket out in a sunny clearing and unpacked a bag Gray had filled with white wine, raspberries, smoked cheese, dark chocolate. Lying next to each other, we let the sun beat warm on our faces and lost ourselves in the moment.

At one point, Gray was feeding me raspberries, comically. Laughter welled up inside me, my feelings for him so deep and wide they knocked the breath out of me. "If someone were to make a movie of us, it would be nauseating," I said.

He leaned up on his elbow and smiled. "Who cares? No one else matters." I lay on my back again, and Gray began running his fingers very lightly, teasingly, along my chest. "I can't stop touching your skin. I'm in love with these little freckles right here. It looks like someone sprinkled cinnamon over you." He leaned over and licked the spot just below the base of my throat.

I could feel us falling, toppling headlong into some mad tumult together. For now, it seemed like we were floating, but I knew it wouldn't be long before we came crashing back to earth.

CHAPTER 24

I made myself get out of bed on Monday and go to class, knowing I could only milk my excuse of the flu for two or three days at most without arousing suspicion. So I wasn't that surprised when Madame Favier asked to see me after class, figuring she probably just wanted to give me my makeup work. As Jess left the room without me, she made a slashing gesture at her neck. I tried to stifle my laughter as I went up to Madame's desk.

"Emma, assayez voice, s'il vous plaît," Madame said. She sounded like she meant business. I took a chair across from her desk and studied her face, which had gone grim. "Emma," she began again. "Je suis désolé, mais . . ." In the end, she decided to go with English. "Emma, I'm so sorry, but I'm afraid something terrible has happened. As a result of your slipping grades and your recent truancy issues—"

"Truancy issues?" I said. "Madame, I've only missed three days."

"Regardless, Dr. Overbrook has informed me that he's rescinding your letter of recommendation for the Paris program. I'm very sorry, Emma, but he decided to give the scholarship to Elise."

"Elise?" Madame nodded regretfully. "But . . . he already gave it to me. How can he do that?" She shook her head.

"Isn't there anything you can do? You're the French teacher. Can't you talk to him? Change his mind?"

"I don't think so," she said. "The final decision rests with him. I'm very sorry, Emma."

I didn't know what to say, but I knew I had to get out of the room; I didn't want to burst into tears in front of Madame.

Quickly, I made my way from Exeter back to the dorms, hoping not to run into anyone. When I got into my room, I had to resist the urge to flop on the bed crying. I knew one person who'd be happy about this news, but right now I couldn't bear the thought of hearing my dad try to hide his glee over the telephone. I'd call him later when I wasn't feeling so fragile.

For now, I called Gray instead. When I told him what had happened, he hopped in his car and was in front of my dorm in less than forty minutes. I thought he was going to walk into Overbrook's office and threaten him to a duel.

"It's okay," I said as we walked around campus. "But I'm disappointed. No matter what I do, I'm stifled at every turn. I can't seem to make anything work."

"You make *us* work," he said. He curled his arm around me with a reassuring squeeze. "Emma," he said, "if you're not going to Paris, then maybe . . ."

"What?" I said after a long pause.

"Maybe I shouldn't go either."

"What are you talking about?" I said, pulling out from his arm.

"What if I didn't leave this time?" he said. "What if I stayed here? With you."

"But you have to go back. It's the Coast Guard."

"I don't *have* to do anything," he said. "I get to decide. And maybe I don't have anything to prove now except to you. Maybe I could stay here and be with you, for real this time. You know, take some courses at the community college, figure out what to do with my life."

"Are you serious?"

"I don't know, maybe I am. Now that I'm back here with you, I don't know if I'm strong enough to leave."

"But Gray, the Coast Guard was your dream. It's what you've wanted for so long."

"I've wanted you for longer. I mean, what if they send me to Alaska? And you're in France, and we don't see each other for an entire year. Would you want that?"

"I wouldn't want that, but I would handle it."

"But what if you didn't have to?" he said. I could feel my heart soaring, doing cartwheels and triple axels. But my brain was still talking sense.

"Gray, don't do this," I said. "Don't make promises you can't keep. I've spent enough of this year pining away for you to let you play with my heart."

"I'm not playing with your heart," he said, grabbing my hands. "Emma, I love you. I want us to be together."

I couldn't help but be won over by his enthusiasm. "I love you, too," I said shyly. "But are you sure?"

"I've never been more sure," he said. "I want to be a part of your life, to go out on dates, take you to school dances. Well, we might have to wait until next year for the school dances."

"Oh, I don't know," I said. "Last year, I brought the prom to you, remember?"

He laughed. "Okay, Emma. This year, I'll bring the prom to you."

"And how are you going to do that?" I said. "You're not even allowed in my dorm."

"That doesn't matter. I can still buy you a corsage, and we can get dressed up and go to some fancy restaurant that plays violin music, and we can slow dance all night. If you want, we could even invite your friends. Make it more like a real prom."

I smiled. "I always pictured riding to prom in a big limo with all of my friends."

"Okay, so we'll rent a limo and you'll wear a beautiful dress, and I'll wear a tux and we'll do whatever you always dreamed you'd do on your prom night."

I drew his hand to my mouth and kissed his knuckles. "You know, you are the sweetest guy ever."

"Aw, you're making me blush."

We continued walking past the dining hall, and I remembered the day Jess and Michelle had tried to buy prom tickets during lunch. I found myself getting angry all over again. "Hey, were you serious about me inviting my friends if I want?" I said.

"Of course. Why?"

"I don't know," I said. "I was just thinking. What if we really did make our own prom?"

"Yeah, that's what we're talking about."

"No, I mean bigger than that. Like, what if we organized an alternative prom for all the kids who got banned from the other one? Actually, anyone who wanted could come, and they could bring whoever they wanted. Or come alone. The whole point would be there are no rules, no restrictions."

Gray shrugged his shoulders. "It sounds fun to me if you think you could pull it off."

"I think we could. I already know the perfect venue."

I told him about the Depot, and we discussed the possibilities as we walked around campus. And when we said good-bye beside his Jeep, it didn't really feel like good-bye.

Because this time, Gray was staying.

I was so excited to tell everyone my prom idea that I'd forgotten all about my disappointment over the lost scholarship. But as I walked back to my room, I ran into Elise in the hallway. She stopped me with her hand and got this serious look on her face. "Emma, I am so sorry about Paris," she said. "I had no idea this was going to happen."

"It's okay, Elise," I said. "Really, don't worry about it."

"No, it's not okay; it's bullshit, and you know it. I don't want the scholarship this way. I'm going to turn it down."

"No, you're not," I said. "You want to get away from this place as much as I do, and you deserve it. Take the scholarship."

"I don't need the money," she said. "If I turn it down, maybe Overbrook will reconsider."

"Are you kidding? He'll just find someone else to give it to. He's getting back at me for the whole Day of Silence debacle, for daring to tarnish his school's precious reputation."

Jess and Michelle must have heard us talking because they both came out of Elise's room to see what was going on. "Emma, we heard," Michelle said. "I'm so sorry."

"Me too," Jess said.

"You know what I think?" Elise said. "I think Overbrook's afraid my dad's going to stop giving money to the school if I don't get the scholarship. He's trying to protect his assets."

"I'll tell you what he can do with his assets," I said, and they all laughed. But then their sympathetic frowns returned. "Seriously, guys, it might turn out to be a good thing after all."

"How could it be a good thing?" Michelle asked.

I couldn't conceal the smile creeping over my face. "Well, Gray's home on leave and . . . we've been seeing a lot of each other. Actually . . ." Suddenly I was afraid to tell them about our decision.

"Actually what?" Jess asked.

"He's staying." I paused a moment to watch their faces.

"What do you mean he's staying?" Michelle said.

"I mean, he decided not to go back to the Coast Guard. Since I lost the Paris scholarship and I'm going to be stuck here next year, we decided that . . . we want to be together. Not long distance this time, but really together."

All of them were struck silent until Elise finally said, "Wow. He must really love you to give all that up."

"Yeah," I said, nodding.

They smiled and congratulated me and said all the right things, but something about their reactions seemed forced. Wary. To lighten the mood, I told them our idea for holding an alternative prom at the Depot. At first they seemed skeptical, but as I outlined the plans Gray and I had come up with, they started to warm up to it.

Jess was the first to soften. "It's not the worst idea I've ever heard."

But then Michelle said, "How are we going to put a prom together? It's only five weeks until graduation."

"Well, let's map out the basics," I said. "We already have a venue."

"We'll need music," Jess said. "Maybe Ice-9 could play."

"I don't want you guys to have to play all night," I said. "I want you to enjoy yourselves."

"We could hire a DJ," Elise said.

"I happen to know a good one," Jess said, referring to Flynn.

"What about food?" Michelle asked.

"Maybe I could get Gray's parents to donate some trays from All Naturals," I said.

"This is actually starting to seem doable," Jess said.

We decided we should have a follow-up meeting with the guys so we could coordinate our efforts. Owen and Flynn got on board immediately and began spreading the word at Braeburn. On Wednesday night, we met in the garden behind the Commons Building to start working out the details. Gray was going to meet us later after dinner with his family.

When we got to the garden, the guys were already camped out on the steps. Jess and Michelle joined them there, Jess on the step above Michelle, with her arms draped around Michelle's shoulders. Like Elise had predicted, they did look quite cute together.

When Flynn saw Elise standing beside me, he stood up, gave me a brief apologetic nod, then shifted his focus to Elise. He sidled up next to her and tried to flirt. "First thing's first," he said. "Have you kissed or slept with anyone here? It's kind of a requirement of admission in our incestuous little group."

His eyes flickered with a mischievous glint, and I couldn't help but smile. Elise snorted and said no, she most certainly hadn't. But I realized as soon as Gray got here, that would no longer be true.

"The night is young," Flynn said, winking at her.

Elise just rolled her eyes and blew him off, and I laughed in spite of everything. There was something so inherently "high school" about the whole situation—all the tangled webs of relationships, the hurt and the angst—and of course, the inevitable focus on prom.

When I caught Owen's eye and tried to smile, he immediately looked down, his expression like a wounded puppy's. And then Gray turned the corner of the building, and my gut wrenched as I remembered the last time he and Owen had seen each other. Boxer shorts at breakfast, bad blood. I prepared myself for the worst.

But Gray simply came over and shook Owen's hand like nothing had happened. Then I introduced him to Jess and Flynn. Flynn stood up to shake his hand, and I was surprised by how small and deferential he seemed next to Gray.

"Hey, man, I've heard great things about you," he said. That was the most cordial I'd ever seen Flynn. I wondered if he was worried that I'd told Gray about our kiss. I hadn't yet.

Flynn stood there cracking his knuckles and looking uncomfortable. As if things weren't awkward enough already, Elise popped up and came over to talk to us. Gray's jaw went rigid, and his shoulders tensed.

"Hi, Gray," she said.

"Elise."

"Look, before things get all weird between us, I wanted to apologize for last year," she said. "I've already apologized to Emma, but I never got a chance to say I'm sorry to you. And I am really, really sorry." Gray looked wary and defensive, but he let her finish. "If I could take everything back, I would, but it's done. It's part of my past I'm not proud of. But I hope you can forgive me and we can all be friends. Or if not friends, at least not enemies."

Gray cocked an eyebrow and looked at me. I was pinching my lips together trying not to smile because when it came down to it, Elise could be pretty charming when she wanted to be.

"Okay," Gray said. "Apology accepted."

With all these awkward formalities out of the way, we joined the others, who were talking about food and party favors and decorations. It felt so normal to be hanging out with my friends and my boyfriend, talking about prom—a rare preview of what life could be like now that Gray and I were staying together. I grabbed Gray's hand and squeezed.

"So Gray's on food detail, right?" Michelle said. "And Flynn, you're okay with DJing?"

"Aw, man, we have to listen to his music?" Jess said, teasing. "I get to help make the playlist."

"I refuse to listen to My Chemical Romance at the prom," Flynn said, teasing her.

"Hey, we should rent a karaoke machine," Owen said.

"Are you insane?" Michelle said. "Karaoke? At a prom?"

"I thought the whole point of this prom was that it's unconventional. Unexpected," he said. "I think karaoke could be fun."

"Yeah, because you can actually sing," I said. "What about those of us who are vocally challenged?"

"The whole point of karaoke is to hear people singing badly," Elise said.

"Says the girl with the voice of an angel," Jess said.

"Well, I like the idea, Owen," Elise said. Then she gave him one of her sweet-sexy smiles, and Owen beamed back at her. My heart wilted a little.

We all argued the pros and cons of karaoke, and Flynn decided it might be amusing to hear people botch bad pop songs all night. The rest of us finally agreed.

"So we've got food, venue, and music taken care of, now what about the date?" Michelle said, serving as our taskmaster.

"Well, the other prom's on May nineteenth, so we can't have it then," Jess said.

"Why not?" I said. "If we do some creative marketing, we might even be able to lure people away from a boring country club event in favor of our no-holds-barred karaoke prom."

"Yeah," Michelle said. "We could emphasize that unlike *some* proms, ours is going to be all-inclusive, come-as-you-are. Wear whatever you like; bring whoever you like!"

"Do whoever you like," Flynn said, and we all groaned.

"Oh my God," Jess said. "Can you imagine how pissed Overbrook would be if nobody showed up to his prom?"

"And what about Amber and Chelsea?" I said. "I can totally see them out on the dance floor with their dates and three other sad-looking couples, just fuming at the ears ready to murder us."

"That's incentive enough for me," Elise said.

Once we'd delegated responsibilities, it began drizzling, so we decided to disband for the night and continue our coordinated efforts tomorrow. Everyone said good-bye, and we went our separate ways.

On the way back to the parking lot, the drizzle turned into a soft, warm rain. Gray and I stood outside his Jeep, getting wet but not wanting to leave. I felt so happy, and yet I had this tiny stone of guilt lodged in my chest. If Gray was going to stay and become a part of my daily life, I had to tell him about my kiss with Flynn. I was a little worried, especially considering Gray's reaction to finding Owen at my house on New Year's, but I didn't want us to hide things from each other anymore.

I looked down at the ground, swallowed, and told him.

"You kissed *that* guy?" he said. "The one with the eyeliner?"

"Yeah, I know. It was stupid. A mistake. But I thought you should know."

"When was this?" he said, sounding angry.

"A few months ago," I said. "It didn't mean anything. I was just feeling so—"

"Wait a minute, wait a minute," he said, his voice softening. Then he took both of my hands in his. "Emma, you don't owe me any explanations. I broke things off between us. I have no right to get upset. I mean, it kills me to think of you doing . . . that"—he brushed a finger softly over my bottom lip—"with someone else. But you were free to do whatever you wanted. And you still are."

"I know," I said. "But I don't want to kiss anyone else."

"Good. Me neither." He leaned down and brushed his lips softly against mine. The rain was falling steadier now, making Gray's shirt thin and transparent. I ran my hands along the back of his head and his neck. He whispered in my ear, "You drive me crazy. Let's get in the car and go to the park. We're getting soaked."

But I knew exactly what would happen if we went to the park. And it wasn't a game of Frisbee. "I think we should take a night off," I said. "There's no rush anymore. We have all the time in the world."

He smiled. "I don't think I can take a night off. I'm addicted to you."

"Gray, I have school tomorrow. And I can't miss any more classes."

"You won't," he said. "I promise I'll call and make sure you get up." He kissed me on the lips, deeply this time, and I felt my will weakening.

"No," I said, pulling away from him. "As much as I want to, I can't."

"Fine," he said, pouting a little. "Then how about we get off campus this weekend, just the two of us. We'll get a hotel room."

"A hotel room?" I said, feeling my face flush. It would be the perfect weekend to do it, since most of our class would be in DC until Sunday. But still, a hotel room carried certain . . . expectations.

"Friday night," he said. "I'll come pick you up and take you to dinner, then we'll stay at the Waverly Inn. They've got balcony rooms that overlook the falls."

"I can't do Friday night," I said. "That's Michelle's birthday."

"Saturday, then," he said.

"All right," I agreed. "Saturday." And the smile on his face fooled me into thinking I was happy, too.

CHAPTER 25

Of all the things Michelle could have chosen to do for her birthday, she wanted to have a sleepover party. With most of the junior and senior class in DC there were only about a dozen of us left in the upperclassmen dorm. So Jess, Michelle, Elise, and I got into our pajamas, dragged our sleeping bags into the lounge, made a giant vat of microwave popcorn, and sat around in a circle playing corny campfire games.

We started with Truth or Dare, which quickly devolved into Dare after Elise kept asking too many personal questions about our sex lives. On one dare, Elise made me do Bloody Mary, which requires the victim to stand in front of a mirror in a darkened room and spin around three times while saying, "Bloody Mary." The legend says that when you open your eyes, you'll see the face of the man you will marry alongside the ghostly apparition of Bloody Mary.

"But if you see a skull," Elise said gleefully, "that means you're going to *die* before you ever get married. Heh heh heh."

"God, Elise, I never knew you were so morbid," I said.

"Remind me why we're playing this again," Jess said.

"Because it's a slumber party," Elise said. "That's what you do. Scare the crap out of each other."

Now that I had been sufficiently terrified, I walked into the bathroom, followed by the girls, Elise holding a candle. They stood me in front of one of the mirrors and told me to shut my eyes, then they spun me around three times while we all chanted, "Bloody Mary, Bloody Mary, Bloody Mary."

"Now open!" Elise said.

So I did.

Reflected in the mirror was Gray's face, flickering in the candlelight. At least it looked like Gray, although my eyes were swimming with dancing lights. Behind him was a faint aura of red, almost like Hester's ghost was standing behind him.

I nearly fell over from shock, and somebody behind me screamed. Then we all burst out of the bathroom and into the brightly lit hallway, giggling like a bunch of ten-year-old girls.

"You saw something, didn't you?" Jess said.

"Will you guys think I'm crazy if I say yes?"

"We already think you're crazy," Michelle said.

"But seriously, what'd you see?"

When I told them, Jess and Elise shrieked. Ever the skeptic, Michelle said, "There's a logical reason why this works."

Elise pouted. "Are you going to take all the fun out of this?"

"Probably," Michelle said. "But fear or any heightened emotion can put you in a trancelike state. The spinning makes you dizzy, and then the darkness disorients you further, so all your perceptions get distorted. Then you add the power of suggestion, and people end up seeing what they're expected to see."

"It's still freaking me out," I said.

Then Jess added, "What if it is real? I mean, what if the mirror is actually a conduit to the spirit world?"

Elise followed this up with a ghostly "Oooooh."

"Don't waste your breath," I said. "Michelle doesn't believe in anything supernatural. Everything has to be proven with empirical evidence, or it doesn't exist."

"It comes from living with my voodoo-loving aunt," Michelle said.

"I love Aunt Darlene," I said. "And she's a very wise woman. I still think we should have done that spell she gave us."

Elise's eyes lit up. "What spell?"

Michelle shot daggers at me from across the room. "Just this bogus spell she must have bought in one of the voodoo shops in her neighborhood."

"But what kind of spell is it?" Jess asked. "What's it supposed to do?"

When Michelle didn't answer, I said, "It's a spell to get rid of somebody." Elise's eyes went large and eager.

"Like who?" Jess said.

"Like Overbrook, of course," Elise said.

"Guys, it's just a superstition," Michelle said. "We're not going to do some stupid voodoo spell."

"Why not?" Elise said.

"Yeah," Jess said, tugging on Michelle's sleeve and making big doe eyes. "It sounds like fun. And if you don't believe in it anyway, what's the harm?"

Michelle grumbled and sighed. "We can't just do it here," she said. "We need vinegar and a moving body of water and—"

"Darlene sent me the vinegar," I said.

"And we have a stream right on campus," Elise said. "Hey, we should go to the woods to do the spell, and then . . . I dare us all to spend the night in the witch caves."

We all snickered, thinking she was joking.

"Been there, done that," I said. "No thanks."

But now it was Michelle's turn to get back at me. "Why, Emma? Too scared to go back?"

"Come on!" Elise said. "This time you won't be alone. You'll have us with you. What could possibly happen?"

"Let me see. Some actual Salem witches could haunt us, we could be ravaged by wild animals, a serial killer could have staked his claim on Lockwood—"

"Okay, but seriously, what could happen?" she said.

"I'm in," Jess said. "So long as Emma is." Then she batted her eyes at me. "Pretty please, Emma. Pretty, pretty, pretty please with a giant cherry on top?"

"Okay, okay," I said. "You guys are relentless."

We gathered up our sleeping bags and flashlights and other important provisions I hadn't had with me the last time, like cell phones and snacks. Then I packed the spell, the vinegar, and the photo of Overbrook, and we sneaked out of the dorm and walked down the path toward the woods.

When we got to the log bridge, we went halfway across and sat down, letting our feet dangle as we listened to the water rush below us. I opened my backpack and took out a piece of paper and wrote Dr. Overbrook's name, then placed it in the center of his photo, rolling them up together and stuffing them inside the bottle of Four Thieves vinegar. Then I stopped the lid with the cork.

"What do we do now?" Elise said.

"We call to Papa Legba," I said.

"Papa who?" Elise said.

"Papa Legba," Michelle said. "The guardian of the spirit world."

"Is she for real?" Elise said to Jess, who just shrugged.

"If you don't believe, it's not going to work," I said. "Now we all have to say this together." I fed them the lines Darlene had written down, and we chanted them in unison.

"Papa Legba, hear our plea. Remove this obstacle from our path."

I told them to visualize Dr. Overbrook's face—his beady eyes, his oily lips, his purple birthmark—as I tossed the bottle into the stream. Then we all repeated *good-bye* three times as we watched the bottle get swept out of sight.

Afterward, we sat for a minute, stunned and a little scared by what we'd done. But then Elise roused us all with a bottle of rum she'd smuggled, and we began the trek up to the witch caves, with me walking point.

"I didn't know it was all uphill," Elise said. "I would have worn my hiking boots."

"We're almost there," I said.

We ascended upon that now-familiar knoll, studded with rocks and shrubs. "Welcome to Casa Emma," I said, beckoning them to follow me inside.

Aiming our flashlights into the entrance, we crawled through the overgrowth and into the cave. "Sorry about the décor," I said as four flashlight beams arced against the bare walls.

We pulled out our sleeping bags and arranged them in a circle, with Michelle's Coleman lantern perched in the center like some ancient totem.

"We bow down to you, oh god of the cave," Jess said, erupting into hysterics.

"And she hasn't had any rum yet," Elise said.

"Speaking of which," I said, "I think a toast is in order."

Elise pulled some Dixie cups from her bag and poured us each a shot. "To Michelle," I said as we raised our cups up to meet. "The best roommate a girl could have."

"And the best lab partner," Elise said.

"And the best girlfriend," Jess said.

Michelle leaned over and kissed Jess, and the two of them got all gooey-eyed.

"Aw," Elise said. "This is so damn cute. Let's sing!"

We treated Michelle to a very loud version of the birthday song that echoed off the cave walls. After a few ill-advised ghost stories and some more gratuitous female bonding, we were all laughing hysterically, succumbing to the rum. But as the night wore on and we grew tired, Michelle and Jess curled up together in their sleeping bag. Elise was attempting to sleep upright since she couldn't stand the tiny rocks jutting into her back. The Princess and the Pea had nothing on her.

I lay on the ground tossing and turning, trying to sleep. But I couldn't banish the image of Gray in the mirror. Was he my soul mate? Were we really destined to get married? Or had I seen what I'd wanted to see?

Was there any real magic in this world? Or was I just crazy?

As I fell into that hazy state between lucidity and sleep, I startled at a shuffling sound outside the cave. Shivering, I recalled all the various scenarios I'd given in answer to Elise's question: *What could possibly go wrong?* I glanced around for my friends on the cave floor and panicked when I saw that I was alone.

Impossible! They wouldn't have left me here by myself, not after what had happened to me in February. That would be the cruelest practical joke ever, and even Elise couldn't be that mean.

Maybe I was still asleep. I lay back down and shut my eyes, trying to conjure some sign that I was dreaming. When I opened them, I was lying on a rug looking at an empty hearth and a table with sewing needles. This was Hester's cottage. Hester and Pearl weren't here, but I had a feeling they were somewhere nearby. And I knew I was supposed to see them one last time.

I'd fallen into this trance so many times before, but this time I wanted to maintain control. I wanted to remain lucid. Like Darlene had warned me, I had to be an active seeker of truth, not a passive victim of controlling spirits.

I tried to remember all of Darlene's advice. Tell your body to stay put, and create a mirror image of yourself to send out into the dream. I imagined myself a dolphin, half of my mind shut down to let me rest; the other half active and alert. It was this second half I sent out wandering.

Feeling like an airy spirit, I crept outside of myself and left the cave, amazed by how bright it was in the forest. The moon, almost full, lit the clearing like a stage set in a play. Standing quietly, I listened for the muffled sounds I'd heard before and jolted when I heard someone say, "Is it you?"

The voice was so familiar that I wasn't frightened. When I spun around, I was no longer wearing my T-shirt and pajama pants, but instead, Hester's gray frock with a red cloak, my head covered in a black cap. From my chest shined the scarlet letter.

When I lifted my gaze, I saw the figure of a man dressed in black with dark hair and dark stubble. Dimmesdale. But when he stepped forward into the light, I saw those sad hazel eyes staring at me.

"Gray?" I whispered.

He came toward me and spoke with a burning regret. "Do you know what a relief it is to look into an eye that recognizes me? When I see you, it's as if I've come home. I see only truth and goodness in your eyes." He was speaking Dimmesdale's lines, and yet every word made sense.

"I am neither true nor good," I said. "I've made so many mistakes. Can you forgive me?"

He came a step closer and took both of my hands in his. With deep sadness in his voice, he said, "Of course I forgive you. I made mistakes, too, the worst of which was leaving you. But I never stopped loving you."

"Nor have I," I said. With desperate tenderness, I threw my arms around him, pressing my head against his chest to hear that familiar heartbeat. He let me stand like that for a long time without speaking.

"Be strong for me," he said. "Advise me what to do."

"There is the broad pathway of the sea," I said. "It brought you here. If you choose, it can take you back again." As I spoke the words, I knew I was repeating Hester's lines to Dimmesdale, but right now I meant them all. "Let's get on a boat and sail far away from this place, go to some rural village in Ireland, or to France or Italy, a place where no one can find us."

"I can't," he said, although his eyes were wistful, longing for the dream. "I have to fulfill the mission I started. Lost as I am, I must do what I can for others who are lost. I can't quit my post, or my punishment might as well be death."

How was it that Gray's mission of saving lives had become tantamount to Dimmesdale's mission of saving souls? They were both so desperate to atone for their pasts that they'd become martyrs to the cause. And yet Gray—the Gray waiting for me back in my real world—was about to give up that cause for me. Could I really let him do that?

"You are still crushed under your guilt," I said, trying to buoy him up with my own energy. "You are paying for the mistakes of your past. But you can leave it all behind and begin again with me."

"Oh, Emma!" he said, and we were no longer Hester and Dimmesdale, only ourselves. "I'm so sorry. I was a fool to leave you once. I can't do it again."

"Let's not look back," I said. "The past is gone. This is the beginning of our future." And with that, I undid the clasp fastening the scarlet letter and tossed it to the ground. Then I took off my cloak and cap, too, letting my hair fly loose from its bindings. At that moment, I knew I was in a dream, yet I didn't want the dream to end.

Gray removed his jacket, and I approached him slowly, a feverish heat rising to my face. I gently pulled his shirt open to reveal his broad chest, bare except for his dog tags, which appeared to be burning his skin. I moved the pendants aside and laid my finger on the scar left there, tracing its shape. Gray's gaze lingered on me as I touched his skin, so hot I thought it might burn me, too. I leaned in and tenderly kissed the scar, my lips brushing softly across each line. When I pulled away the mark was gone, as if I'd somehow erased his pain.

Gray took my hand and led me down to a log by the stream. "I have a strange feeling that this brook is the boundary between two worlds," he said, "and that if I leave now, I will never be able to cross it again."

"Then stay with me," I said, turning to kiss him. Our lips met gently at first, and then his mouth pressed hard against mine. For a moment, I lost all sense.

But the stench of rotting leaves and decaying matter brought me out of my fog. We both pulled away, gasping for breath, as we watched Chillingworth limp toward us with Pearl in tow.

The last time I was here, Chillingworth had tried to bury me alive, and he'd taken Pearl with him. Now she pointed at me with her forefinger, and a frown gathered on her brow. In the stream below us was her reflected form with the same condemning gesture. Then she burst into a fit of passion, gesticulating violently and shrieking so loudly that the woods reverberated on all sides.

I knew what the problem was. I had taken off Hester's scarlet letter, and Pearl couldn't bear the sight of her mother without it. Just seconds ago, I had flung the letter recklessly into space, had felt one moment's peace at the thought of Gray and me running away together. Like Hester and Dimmesdale, we had foolishly let ourselves believe we could escape our responsibilities. But here it was again—the scarlet letter, symbol of the burdens we all carried. All my passion and optimism seemed to wither in an instant as the moon disappeared behind a cloud.

Chillingworth held a skeletal hand out to Gray, who let himself be led away as if by his executioner. *Wait! How can he just leave? Why doesn't he fight?*

But then I understood. He was facing up to his obligations. Just as Hester couldn't shed her scarlet letter, neither could Dimmesdale shed his past or run from his mistakes. And neither could Gray and I. We all had to face the consequences of our choices.

I got up from the ground and walked to the spot where the scarlet letter lay on the forest floor. When I picked it up, it had the heft of a lead weight. This was the burden Hester had borne for all these years. Reluctantly, I attempted to fulfill Hester's destiny by fastening the letter back onto my chest. But the pin pierced me in the heart, and I doubled over, feeling an intense pain rip through me, like someone was tearing off my skin. Some force deep inside me was pushing outward, and the pressure was almost unbearable.

Every nerve felt raw and exposed, like I was suddenly standing naked to the elements, facing the truth for the first time. After what felt like a violent internal combustion, I dropped to the ground, feeling weak and utterly exhausted. And then I looked up and saw them—Hester and Pearl. They were holding hands beside me, and I was standing on the outside, alone.

They gazed at me and held out their free hands. Slowly, I walked to meet them and grasped their hands, so the three of us were linked together—my past, present, and future colliding at this crossroads in the woods.

Pearl said to her mother, "Will we go back, we three together, into the town?"

"Not now," Hester said. "We must face our future. And Emma must face hers." Then she kissed my brow tenderly. "Farewell, Emma," she said.

"Am I not coming with you?"

"No," she said. "I have but one journey to make. But you . . . have many paths to choose."

"How do I know which is the right one?" I said.

"There is no right path," she said. "How would you know the right path if you never chose the wrong one?"

"But . . . I don't know where to go," I said.

"Follow your heart," she said. "It will not steer you wrong." Then she grabbed Pearl's hand and the two of them disappeared into the woods, leaving me on my own.

Hester had said she knew what her journey was. Sadly, I knew it, too. Hester and Pearl would go to the town square tomorrow, where Dimmesdale would deliver his last sermon. There, he would invite Hester and Pearl to stand with him on the scaffold. He would strip away his clothes and reveal the scarlet letter singed onto his chest. Then he would collapse and die, freeing his soul from the tyranny of Chillingworth's revenge.

And Chillingworth, deprived of his only reason to live, would die shortly afterward, leaving his fortune to Pearl, making her the richest heiress of her day. Hester, always stoic and strong, would persevere. She would take Pearl to Europe, and in her absence, her scarlet letter would become woven into legend.

But one day, Hester would return to this place and take up residence in her old cottage. Yet the townspeople would have forgotten all about her former transgressions. In fact, because of her independence and strength, people would speculate that the *A* on her breast stood for *Able,* not *Adultery.* And Hester Prynne, the former outcast and sinner, would become a counselor for all women with nowhere else to turn. In a sense, Hester would reinvent herself.

In a daze, I moved away from the stream and found my way back to Hester's cottage. But I felt like I was returning to myself. I lay down on the floor and closed my eyes, hoping to wake in the morning to find not Hester and Pearl, but my real friends. My real life. My future.

Hester's story was over; mine was just beginning.

CHAPTER 26

I woke inside the cave once again. Only this time, it wasn't pitch dark, and I wasn't alone. My friends were gathered around me, asking me questions like at the end of *The Wizard of Oz*.

Michelle: "Emma, are you okay?"

Jess: "How many fingers am I holding up?"

And this gem from Elise: "Get this girl a toothbrush."

I sat up and checked my feet for mud and leaves, signs of travel. They were clean. Something had kept my body grounded this time. I hadn't gone anywhere except in my mind. Just like Darlene had told me. I wanted to laugh.

"We couldn't wake you," Michelle said. "You were dreaming so hard."

"Yeah," Elise said. "You were running in your sleep like a dog."

"Did you have a nightmare?" Jess asked.

"Yeah," I said, sitting up. "And you were there. And you. And you—"

"Oh, shut up," Michelle said. "We're just glad you're alive."

"Me too," I said.

And the strange thing was, I felt really alive—more rested

and energetic than I had in a long time. Whatever metaphorical scarlet letter had been burdening my soul had been lifted, and I felt lighter. Stronger. Ready to face whatever lay ahead of me.

As we gathered up our belongings and headed back to campus, Hester's last words repeated in my head: "You have many paths to choose . . . follow your heart." An uneasiness swept over me as I contemplated its meaning.

I spent the day getting ready for my big night with Gray, showering and shaving, packing a bag with clothes and sexy underwear, perfume and candles. But I was feeling anything but romantic. Was I really ready for this?

Gray came and picked me up at school around six, and we had dinner at the sushi restaurant where we'd had our first date. I was trying to loosen up and have a good time, but the hotel above the waterfall kept looming over me like a giant warning sign. After dinner, we walked up to the falls, where the air was ten degrees cooler and smelled of ozone. I shivered remembering Gray standing at the crest last year, me standing on the rocks below calling out to him, begging him not to jump. He had been so haunted by his past, and I had tried my hardest to heal his wounds and make him feel worthy and complete. And now he had returned the favor by coming back and promising to stay.

So why did I feel so conflicted? Maybe it was because in choosing to stay with me, Gray was relinquishing his dream of joining the Coast Guard. The instructors at "A" School would be expecting him in North Carolina on Wednesday morning, but he would never arrive. He hadn't even called to tell them he wasn't coming, which perhaps spoke of some ambivalence on his part.

The events of the past few weeks had been such a whirlwind that we hadn't really paused to think things through, hadn't discussed what his decision might mean for our future. Maybe that was why the future seemed so vague in my mind. I wanted to talk about it now, but we were deaf to anything but the roar of turbines and falling water.

Once the sun began to set, it got cold very quickly, so we went to check into the hotel. The lobby was brightly lit and furnished with antique sofas and chairs, expensive-looking art lining the walls.

The clerk at the front desk eyed us suspiciously as Gray handed over his credit card. I felt like a fraud—far too young and inexperienced to be staying at a hotel with my boyfriend. But Gray just smiled and grabbed my hand as we took the elevator to the top floor.

He had splurged on a honeymoon suite overlooking the falls, and I gasped when I saw the spacious room, the lavish furnishings, and the king-sized bed, perched on a six-inch platform so it hovered over the pale blue carpeting like a giant ark.

I couldn't remember ever feeling so nervous. But then Gray started kissing me—a slow graze along my neck—and my mind went numb. I wanted to slow down, to make us come back to earth, but at that moment with Gray's mouth on my ear, I forgot everything.

His hands roamed down my sides, clutching my waist and nearly lifting me off my feet. That's how I felt . . . both weightless and out of control. He picked me up and carried me to the bed, setting me down gently in a pile of down-filled pillows and comforter.

It was like a scene from a movie. And yet, I felt removed from the moment, like I was watching it from the outside. I was pretty sure this wasn't how I was supposed to feel. I was supposed to be swept away by emotions and lust.

"Gray," I said as he lay down on top of me. I shimmied backward, so I was sitting up against the pillows.

"What is it?" he said, looking concerned. He moved to sit next to me, so we were both leaning against the headboard. How could I tell Gray that I felt like I was suffocating? That as much as I loved him, I didn't want to go through with this?

"I don't think I can do this," I said.

He grabbed my hands and drew them into his chest. "Is it something I did?"

"No, no, it's just . . . I'm not ready."

His arm came around me then, and I leaned into the protective warmth of his chest. "Emma, you know I don't care about sex. Well, that's not entirely true," he said, biting his cheek in this adorable way. "Of course I want to have sex with you, but it's only because I want us to be as close as we can. I want to feel as connected to you as possible."

"I know what you mean," I said. "But sex just makes everything more complicated. And we've been kind of overdosing on complicated lately."

He didn't say anything, just looked at me curiously. "It's strange," he said. "Even though I'm with you right now, I'm still afraid of losing you. Why is that?"

It was like he knew what I was about to say.

Getting up from the bed, I walked to the window and opened the curtains so I could see the view. The falls were one of Gray's favorite places. He told me once that the reason he loved them so much was that he couldn't think amid all that noise and tumult. He could exist only in the moment.

But for some reason, I couldn't.

It was Saturday night. "A" School began on Wednesday. If Gray had any hope of continuing with the Coast Guard and not losing all he'd worked so hard for, he would have to leave for North Carolina tomorrow. Monday at the latest.

This meant doing something almost inconceivable: I had to tell Gray to leave.

Was I crazy? Gray had finally admitted he loved me and agreed to give up everything for me. If I followed through with my decision, it would mean another year of loneliness and the chance that Gray might never return.

But I also knew I could never forgive myself if I let Gray walk away from his dream.

"Gray, why did you join the Coast Guard?" I asked.

"What kind of question is that?" he said.

"Just humor me, will you?"

He sighed and came to stand behind me by the window, placing his hands on my shoulders. "You know why."

"I want to hear you tell me."

"Because I wanted to make a difference. I wanted to help people."

"And has that changed?" I said, turning to face him.

"No, it's just . . . I can help people in other ways. I don't have to put my life at risk. Now that I have something to live for, I don't want to lose it." I faltered then, placing my hand on his temple and caressing his face. I didn't want to lose him either. "I had this dream last night," he said. "You and I were going to run away together. But then suddenly, this man was pulling me away from you. And I was suddenly standing on top of some kind of platform, and I looked down and there was only water as far as the eye could see. I knew that if I jumped in, I was going to die. But somehow I knew I had to jump anyway."

"Oh God, Gray," I said, feeling a shiver. "I had a similar dream."

I didn't know by what mechanism we were able to meet in our dreams or call out to each other in the darkness. But I knew that we didn't need to have sex to feel close, just as we didn't need to give up everything else to be connected. Our connection went far deeper than that. "You're scared to leave. Because it's real now. I'm scared, too. But we can't run away from the future. It's going to come all the same. We can either hide from it or face it. And I know you're not one for running away from anything. You're a fighter."

"Why are you telling me this?" he said.

"Because you have to go back."

"What are you talking about?"

"I know we decided you would stay, but we weren't thinking clearly. You can't give up now after everything you've worked for."

"Emma, you don't know what's best for me," he said. "I tried to make that decision for you once, and look where that got us."

"It's not just you I'm thinking about," I said. "It's me too." His face looked stricken. "I've got important decisions to make, decisions about my future, and I'm afraid if you stay, I won't be able to see anything but you. I want you in my future, but you can't *be* my future. I need to stand on my own, too."

He swallowed and looked down at the floor. "Emma, I've never wanted to get in the way of your future."

"I know that, but I lost too much of this year waiting for you to come back to me, missing you. I didn't really live. And I need to live right now."

His face looked crushed, but I could see something else in his eyes—relief maybe. Some deep part of him knew I was right.

Finally, in a voice so sad and quiet it nearly tore me apart, he said, "I was going to ask you this at prom, but it looks like I won't get my chance." He pulled something out of his jeans pocket. "Would you please wear my necklace again? If I'm going away, I want you to have this with you."

"Of course," I said. I leaned in and kissed him, so grateful that he understood, that we had finally turned to the same page of our story. "Will you?" I said, turning around so he could fasten the necklace for me.

He gently pushed my hair aside and secured the chain around my neck. I stood silently for several seconds until his hands rested on my shoulders and he kissed the back of my neck.

"Why are you so smart?" he said.

"Years of tortured introspection."

He laughed, and the sullen mood lifted.

Since the pressure to have sex was off now, we moved back to the bed and stayed up eating ten-dollar candy bars from the mini-fridge and watching *The Powerpuff Girls* on the Cartoon Network. Eventually, we fell asleep curled in each other's arms.

And the next day, Gray drove me back to Lockwood, where we stood beside his Jeep saying good-bye for what seemed like days but could not have been, since the next day he was gone.

The only thing that kept me going during those last few weeks of the school year was the distraction of AP exams. I knew that if I didn't do well, my entire academic year would have been a complete waste. So I buckled down and reread books and studied my notes until my vision blurred.

I almost laughed when I saw the question for the open-ended essay on the English exam: "Choose a character from literature who demonstrates how exile or exclusion can be an enriching or enlightening experience."

I knew exactly which character I was going to write about. Hester Prynne was the ultimate outcast and the fiercest heroine I knew. I even wove in a quote I'd memorized:

> *The scarlet letter was her passport into regions where other women dared not to tread. Shame, Despair, Solitude! These had been her teachers . . . and they had made her strong.*

The Scarlet Letter had been my passport, too.

I saw now that we were all exiled at one point or another, cast aside for our beliefs, our actions, or even something beyond our control. And when we were isolated, we had to learn to tread water on our own. But we didn't have to remain alone forever. Self-reliance was only good if it made us strong enough to help each other.

In the weeks leading up to our prom, I continued to help with preparations even though I wasn't entirely sure I wanted to go. The thought of attending without a date seemed too depressing. But I faithfully took carloads of decorations and other supplies to the Depot in my Volvo, draped violet gossamer fabric on the walls, hung glittering stars from the ceiling until an old warehouse slowly began to transform into a celestial wonderland.

Since Gray's mom had agreed to provide the food, I arranged to pick up the trays at their house that Friday afternoon. Simona gave me a rib-crushing hug and chatted with me about school and gossip. It was clear she had no idea how close her son had come to giving up everything for me.

"So who's taking you to prom?" she asked.

"I'm not going," I said.

"But you have to!"

I wasn't sure how much Gray had told her, so I just said, "I don't have a date."

"It doesn't matter," she said. "In my day, girls who didn't have dates went stag. There was always someone to dance with."

"I'm just not sure I'm up for it," I said.

"It's a shame Gray didn't have a longer leave. He could have taken you."

"Yeah, it is a shame," I said, trying not to tear up.

After packing my car up with the trays, I thanked Simona for all she had done. "Of course, Emma," she said. "You know you're like family to us. In fact, I have something for you."

She went back inside the house and came out with a large plastic clamshell box. "Here," she said. "With your mother not around, I didn't want you to go to prom without one. I couldn't resist."

I opened the lid to reveal a gorgeous wrist corsage, an immense red rose surrounded by greenery. "Oh, Simona, it's beautiful. But—"

"In case you change your mind," she said, gripping both my hands in hers. "Please go to your prom, Emma. If you don't, you might regret it."

Perhaps Simona knew more than she let on. I took the corsage out of the box and slid it over my wrist. The flower looked bold and fearless—a wonder of nature. "Thank you," I said.

I knew this rose would wither and fade, like all flowers must, but I also knew that some relationships overcame the odds, withstood the ravages of time and distance. Some loves were eternal.

CHAPTER 27

All the way to the Depot, I thought about prom, making excuses about how I didn't have a dress and didn't have a date. But I'd just lectured Gray about the need to stand on my own, and now during my first real test, I was going to take the easy way out by staying home? Pathetic.

I double-parked by the train station and ran the trays up to the Depot kitchen, placing them in the large walk-in re-frigerator. As I was heading out, I ran into a few of our prom recruits, who had taken charge of the decorations. One of them was Sophie, valedictorian of the senior class.

She came up to me and said, "This was such a great idea, Emma. I never wanted to go to prom because I didn't have anyone to ask. Plus, proms are usually a disaster—last year, my date got wasted and threw up on my two-hundred-dollar shoes. But this prom's going to be epic. I hope you keep the tradition going next year!"

I smiled and told her we'd try our best. But as I headed back to Lockwood, Sophie's words began to sink in. So what if I didn't have a date or a dress? That was the whole point of alternative prom. The important thing was to have a good time with friends and celebrate the end of this difficult year. We'd earned ourselves a night of fun.

When I got back to the dorm, Michelle and Jess were getting ready in our room. I asked Michelle about borrowing a dress, and she hopped off the bed and grabbed my hands, flailing like a madwoman.

"You're coming?" she said.

"I'm considering."

Jess shook her head. "You have to come. You helped make this happen."

"And of course you can borrow a dress," Michelle said.

"And you can borrow Michelle for a dance, too," Jess said.

"Oh, are you giving away my services now?" Michelle said, swatting Jess's arm. Jess caught her hand, and the two of them leaned in for a kiss that was so tender and adorable, I couldn't help but smile. They seemed so confident together now, so comfortable in their own skins. If anything good had come out of this year, it was this moment right here.

I chose a simple strapless red dress from Michelle's closet to go with the rose corsage and wore my ruby red slippers. I wondered, if I clicked my heels together would it bring Gray back to me?

Elise met us in our room around six o'clock, looking surprisingly understated in a silver sheath dress. Michelle wore a vibrant orange-and-green dress that looked like a Monet watercolor. And Jess, God love her, wore a slinky black dress with black high-top Converse. We all took turns at the mirror, double-checking our outfits, hair, and makeup.

While we were walking out to the parking lot, we saw Amber and Chelsea dressed in their finery and standing in front of a ridiculously long limo. We had opted not to rent a limo to save some money, so I was driving everyone in the Volvo. But Amber couldn't resist making one more cheap shot.

"Going to your ball in a pumpkin carriage?" Amber said. When we all ignored her, she added, "Be sure to be back by midnight, Emma, or you might turn into a lesbian."

Chelsea followed this up with her usual laughter, and Elise shouted, "Hey, Chelsea, be sure not to think for yourself, or you might turn into an actual human being."

Chelsea's mouth dropped, but it was Amber who looked the most insulted. Jess and Michelle high-fived Elise as we walked to the car. But I felt a little sorry for Chelsea. She hadn't figured out who she was yet, and when she did, she was in for a rude awakening.

But this night wasn't about Amber and Chelsea; it was about us.

When we arrived at the Depot, a news van was parked outside. The same anchorwoman who had tried to cover the Day of Silence approached us, flanked by her burly cameraman. Somehow they'd found out about our underground prom and wanted to do a story on us, hoping to expose institutionalized discrimination at Lockwood and make local heroes of Michelle and Jess.

I could tell Michelle and Jess felt sort of trapped under the scrutiny of the camera, which was already filming as the anchorwoman spoke. She was being really pushy, asking a lot of personal questions: *How long have you two been together? What's it like being gay at a conservative prep school? Do you want to say anything to the public that might help your cause?*

"You know what?" I finally said to her. "This is our prom night. We don't want to fight any causes or make any statements tonight. All we want to do is dance."

I walked away as determinedly as I could, and Jess and Michelle followed suit, leaving the anchorwoman and her cameraman standing idly on the sidewalk, bereft of their hot story.

"Thanks, Emma," Michelle said once we got inside. I nodded and smiled, full of gratitude and love for her.

We all stopped short when we saw the interior of the club.

The room was awash in a violet glow, with fake gas lamps set up around the periphery casting silvery pools of light. The mirrored stars we'd hung caught the light, projecting mini-stars onto the ceiling. Everything looked sparkly and ethereal.

We split up to make final preparations for the food, favors, and music, then stood around talking as we waited for the guests to arrive. After about an hour, the place was packed with prom-goers mingling and eating.

"How many people do you think are here?" I asked Michelle.

"At least sixty," she said. "Maybe more." We had definitely siphoned off a good portion of the traditional prom crowd, and for this, I felt immensely gratified.

Around seven o'clock, Flynn took the stage and announced the karaoke machine officially open for business. When no one volunteered, he rounded up Jess and Owen, and they opened with a rousing rendition of the Rolling Stones' "Sympathy for the Devil." Flynn affected his voice to sound British and did the Mick Jagger rooster strut, while Owen and Jess provided the *who-who*s.

Once they finished, to screaming applause, Owen grabbed Elise from the audience, and they stood onstage with Flynn conspiring about something. Michelle looked at me in surprise, and we maneuvered our way through the crowd, getting as close to the stage as we could without getting trampled.

The song began with a catchy drumbeat, and then Owen's crystalline voice sang the first few words of Fun.'s "We Are Young." As soon as everyone recognized the crowd-pleasing song, they began to jump and cheer, and then Elise chimed in on the haunting chorus. Owen and Elise must have been tapping into their stage chemistry from *The Crucible* because they were really working the crowd, building the song to its anthemic crescendo. At the end, Owen hopped from the stage and held out his hand to help Elise down. The crowd went wild. Michelle and I had to pick up our shocked jaws from off the floor.

A group of Braeburn guys got up next and sang the Killers' "When You Were Young," which got the entire crowd on their feet. Before I could argue, Jess ripped my arm out of its socket, thrusting me into a sea of humanity, all of us writhing and jumping and swaying to the music. Michelle and Elise were out there, too, and a few seconds later, Owen and Flynn joined us, Flynn bouncing around in a one-man mosh pit. By the end of the song, we were all drenched and happy and starved for more.

We danced like crazed fiends for another few songs, until some girl requested "Gravity" by Sara Bareilles. I took a breather by the bar and watched people slow dance, feeling just a little bit sorry for myself. And then, Owen and Elise stepped onto the dance floor. At first I thought they were heading to the karaoke booth, but then Owen wrapped his arms around Elise's waist and pulled her close, and Elise curled into the crook of his shoulder like they'd done this many times before. When had this happened?

I was wondering how serious they were when Flynn sidled up next to me. "Wanna dance?" he said.

I raised an eyebrow, and he suddenly looked a little unsure of himself. That brief moment of vulnerability made me say yes.

We walked out onto the dance floor, and he tentatively placed his arms around my waist while I rested my arms around his shoulders.

"So what's wrong?" he said. "You seem depressed. And it's your prom night. You shouldn't be depressed. Is it Gray?"

I nodded. "I wish he was here."

"Yeah, me too," he said, letting one of his hands roam down my lower back toward my butt.

I grabbed his hand and placed it back on my waist. "Seriously, dude?"

"I'm just joking," he said. "But there's something else bothering you, isn't there? I see you watching them. You can't stand the sight of Owen dancing with Elise."

"No, it's not that," I said. *Okay, it is partly that.* "It's our friendship I miss. I don't think Owen's forgiven me yet for . . . kissing you."

"Don't worry," he said. "I'm alcohol-free tonight. I won't be molesting you any time soon."

"Good to know," I said.

"And I am sorry."

"It wasn't your fault," I said. "It was that damn tattoo."

"My tattoo? What, you find it sex-eeee?" he said, wagging his eyebrows up and down.

"No," I said, laughing. "It's just that when you told me what it meant, it made me want to do something fearless, but it turned out to be something colossally stupid instead."

"Thanks a lot," he said.

"You know what I mean."

Then he gave me a mischievous look. "You know what would be really fearless?" he said. "If you got up on stage and dedicated a song to Owen."

"You mean, actually sang him a song?"

"That is what you do in karaoke."

"Flynn, I can't sing."

"That's the point," he said. "If you could sing, it wouldn't be such a sacrifice."

"Yeah, but what song could I possibly choose that could make things right?"

"Let's go over to my booth and take a look."

We strolled over to his karaoke case, and I marveled that Flynn was being so kind without a discernible motive. He flipped through a list of the karaoke selections and said, "How about Akon's 'Sorry, Blame It on Me'?"

"Akon?" I said. "Uh, Flynn, can you see me rapping?" He regarded me for a fraction of a second, then burst out laughing. "Okay, it's not that funny," I said.

"Oh, yes it is," he said. "How about Good Charlotte's 'Say Anything'?"

"Mmm, too emo."

"Okay, let's try a different approach," he said. "What about 'You've Got a Friend in Me'?"

"The song from *Toy Story*?"

"No good?" He kept scanning his list, and then he said, "Bingo."

"What?"

" 'Count on Me' by Bruno Mars. It's a big, melty pile of commercial cheese, but I think it'll do the trick."

"Hey, I like that song!"

"Well, good, because that's what you're singing."

"But I don't know the lyrics," I said.

"No problem. They'll pop up on the screen, and you just have to sing along."

"Are you sure I should do this?' I said, feeling a slow churning in my stomach.

"You *have* to do this," he said. "For Owen. Besides, the song is short. It'll be over before you know it."

Flynn had a point. I had to put myself out there if I was going to redeem myself in Owen's eyes. So reluctantly, I said yes.

But once I'd committed, all I could do was pace around and sweat for the next ten minutes until Flynn called me to the stage. When Michelle and Jess saw me up there, they stopped in their tracks, staring up at me in disbelief. Michelle's awestruck face had me second-guessing my decision. She'd heard me sing in the shower, and it wasn't pretty. But if I was going to win back Owen's friendship, I had to do this.

Somehow, I had pictured myself striding up to the microphone and jauntily announcing, "This one goes out to Owen

Mabry, a good friend who deserved better." I imagined everyone talking and laughing over me, so no one would really pay much attention.

But now the room was eerily silent, and the stage lights were burning down on my face. When I peered out into the crowd, they were staring at me with a perverse sort of fascination. Like watching a naked person walk down the freeway.

When it became clear I wasn't going to be able to speak, Flynn announced, "This song goes out to Owen from Emma. She's really sorry, dude, and so am I."

When Owen heard his name, he made his way to the front of the stage so he was staring straight up at me. I couldn't even look at him. Instead, I focused my attention on the little TV screen. I heard bongos and a guitar, and then the little red ball began bouncing over the words, and I knew I was supposed to start in, but I was frozen. And I could hear a tambourine jangling in the background, making it all the more obvious that I wasn't singing.

Everyone in the audience just stood there, waiting for me to begin, their eyes wide and expectant. Briefly I caught Michelle's eye, and she made a horrified expression like, "Emma, please do something!" It was like one of those nightmares where you have a big wad of gum in your throat and you can't scream. Sweat began pooling at my temples, and I swayed a little, feeling dizzy.

Somewhere in my mind I knew I'd skipped the entire first verse. I glanced at the screen again and saw the red ball poised over the chorus. I had to jump in here. Bobbing my head slightly, I began to sing.

"Louder!" someone shouted from the audience. "We can't hear you!"

Oh my God, someone get me off this stage!

Flynn had said the song was short, but I felt like I'd been up there for three hours. Sweat dripped off my face. My hands shook by my sides. I gulped in some air and wondered if I had enough spit left in my mouth to finish the song. Or maybe I could just run off stage and move to Alaska?

Even though my heart was beating wildly and my mouth was dry as stone, I tried to start in on the second verse, but I couldn't locate my strength or confidence. They had both run screaming out the exits.

And then, like a miracle, someone else's voice broke in, an angelic male voice—and at that moment, the most beautiful voice I'd ever heard.

I whipped around and saw Flynn belting out the words of the song like he'd written them himself. He was standing next to me now, nudging my arm and nodding at the screen. With his voice carrying the tune, I joined him, softly at first, then gaining volume as my fear faded.

By the time the chorus repeated, we were singing together, with Flynn's voice sailing beautifully over the *ooohs* and *yeahs*. When we got to the bridge, we were actually singing in harmony, and I had to admit we sounded okay. Better than okay.

Near the end, some of the audience joined in on the chorus, and when we finished, the crowd went wild, mostly because this cringe-worthy debacle of a song was finally over.

I blinked gratefully at Flynn, then stumbled down the stairs and raced toward the exit, bursting out the door onto the rooftop balcony. The air felt refreshingly cool, and the beads of sweat on my body chilled immediately. Adrenaline still surged through my body.

Owen appeared a few seconds later and began clapping. "This is the best prom ever," he said.

"Oh my God," I said, covering my face with my hands. "If you came out here to mock me, you can go back inside."

"I came to make sure you weren't jumping off the roof," he said, smiling. I felt a fresh burst of humiliation, but then I started laughing. Because it was kind of funny. "Seriously,

Emma," he said, "that was probably the nicest thing anyone's ever done for me."

"The most humiliating, at any rate."

"You know, you weren't as bad as you think. Once you got over your stage fright, you and Flynn sounded pretty good."

"Oh, come on," I said.

"No, seriously, you've been holding out on us."

"Well, if you don't mind, I'm going to continue holding out on you. Please don't ever let me sing in public again."

"Aw, not even on my birthday?" he said. "You promised."

"I didn't promise. I said I'd think about it," I said, smiling. "Besides, you'll be in Paris next year for your birthday, and I'll be stuck here."

"Oh yeah," he said. "Elise told me. Sorry about that. I know how much you wanted to go."

"Yeah, well, maybe Elise can sing to you instead," I said. "You guys looked pretty cozy out there on the dance floor." He just flashed me a shy, dimpled grin that told me nothing.

"Seriously, Emma, thank you for the song."

"You're welcome," I said. "Am I forgiven?"

"Mmm," he said, pretending to consider. "Maybe after one more song." I scoffed and hit him playfully in the chest. "Of course I forgive you," he said.

"Thank God. Because I hated not talking to you."

"Me too," he said. "Now, let's get you back inside. Your fans are waiting."

I smiled as he linked his arm in mine and escorted me back into the club.

Michelle and Jess tried to convince me I wasn't as bad as I thought. But I just kept shaking my head and laughing. Flynn was still up on stage, this time singing a haunting rendition of Joy Division's "Love Will Tear Us Apart."

"Dance with me?" Jess said to Michelle. Michelle beamed and took Jess's hand.

264   *Eve Marie Mont*

Owen and I watched as they took the dance floor, gliding comfortably in each other's arms. "They look happy together," Owen said.

"Yeah, they do."

"This was a great idea, this prom," he said. "You did a good thing here."

I nodded, smiling. "I had a lot of help."

I was about to ask Owen to dance when Elise wandered up behind him, placing her hands on his shoulders. "Hey, you," she said in a flirty voice.

"Hey," Owen said, looking pleased to see her.

"Emma, mind if I steal him?" she said.

"Not at all," I lied. "You kids have fun."

Owen turned and smiled at me in this way that blew my heart wide open, and then they left me on the sidelines.

I sat on a bar stool, watching my friends dance and listening to the melancholy lyrics of the song. Elise was playing with Owen's floppy hair, Jess was resting her head on Michelle's shoulder, and Flynn was hamming it up on the stage.

I shivered a little, knowing Gray wasn't going to come up behind me and ask me to dance. No one was going to rescue me tonight. I was completely on my own.

But it was exactly where I wanted to be.

CHAPTER 28

The Star-Crossed prom had been an unequivocal disaster. At least that's what we heard the next day from a few of the girls who had gone and lived to regret it. Apparently, attendance had been poor, the band they'd hired seemed to be from the 1970s, and the food was overcooked and flavorless. All in all, it sounded like our prom had been way more fun.

We wondered if Overbrook would somehow find a way to blame us for this. But in those next few days, he made no moves to reprimand or punish us for our underground dance. We went through the motions of studying for exams and finishing final projects, just waiting for the hammer to drop. But as the final weeks ticked by, we began to hold out hope that such punishment might never come.

The senior graduation was always held on the Monday of the last week of school, and the entire student body was required to attend. For the first time, I actually listened to the valedictory address. Sophie Hannigan's speech was about how hard it is to be true to yourself, to shut out all the voices telling you what you should do or who you should be.

She ended by saying, "For all of us in high school, it's easy to slip into a role. It almost seems necessary so at least you'll have a place to sit in the lunchroom: with the jocks or the artists or the cool kids or the freaks. But sometimes you come

266 Eve Marie Mont

to identify so much with the group you belong to that you forget who you really are. And the hardest thing of all is to be yourself. It can be lonely and frightening. I'm still learning how to do it. But I'm hoping with time, I might be as brave as some others I know. Deep down in their souls they know who they are, and that makes them heroes to me. So my advice to you today isn't to try to get into the best college or make the most money or be the most popular girl in your class, but to find out who you are and then be the best version of that you can be."

We clapped wildly for her and then settled in for a nap. It was customary for Dr. Overbrook to follow the valedictory speech with his Headmaster's Address, invariably full of tedious inspirational clichés. But this time, no one fell asleep.

After Overbrook greeted the students, parents, and faculty, he began talking about journeys—journeys beginning for the graduates and other journeys ending.

Then he said, "It is with great sadness that I announce my resignation as headmaster of Lockwood Preparatory School."

A collective gasp overtook the room.

Once the murmuring died down, he continued his speech, saying, "I have worked here for thirty-three years, and in all that time, Lockwood has been my home. These girls have been like daughters to me. Though I am loath to leave the place that has given me so many rewarding years, one must recognize when one journey is over and when it is time to start down a new path. But please know that every girl who has walked down these hallways has left an indelible imprint in my heart, and I will hold those memories dear until the day I die."

I was trying not to gag as I watched some of the girls begin to cry. I felt nothing more than a mild pity for him and a deep satisfaction that he would never torment another student. Despite my relief, I felt a slightly guilty conscience. Was it possible the spell we'd done had actually had some effect? Was Overbrook's resignation in any way related to the words we'd recited? Could thoughts and wishes really be so powerful?

I brushed aside my concerns and tried to look appropriately sorrowful. But I began wondering what would happen to Lockwood now that Overbrook wouldn't be here to keep everyone in line. And who would take his place?

I didn't need to wonder long because Overbrook finished his speech by saying that, per the Lockwood charter, the head of the school board would take over running the school temporarily. Elise's father, Mr. Douglas Fairchild, would be interim headmaster until a permanent replacement could be found.

Mr. Fairchild stood up from the first row of chairs and walked onstage, meeting Overbrook at the podium. Then Overbrook invited the graduates to the stage, and he and Mr. Fairchild shared the duty of distributing diplomas.

We were all reeling from this bombshell as we gathered for the after-party in the Commons garden. "So Brewster's going to love me even more now that my dad's interim Headmaster," Elise said.

"Elise, do you know what happened?" I asked. "Did it have something to do with that spell we did?"

Elise looked at Michelle warily. "Think we should tell them?" she said.

"Tell us what?" Jess asked.

Elise gestured for us to follow her, and we all crept around to the side of the building. Elise said in a hushed voice, "All right, you guys, I'm going to tell you what's going on. But you have to promise not to tell anyone."

Jess and I swore a vow of secrecy.

And then she told us how, thirty years ago, Dr. Roger Overbrook had been Mr. Roger Overbrook Hall, a teacher at a private boarding school in London. After three years of service, he had been terminated for having an inappropriate relationship with one of his students.

"Oh my God," I said. "How do you know this?"

"My dad's friend, the ACLU lawyer, dug it up during his investigations."

"Wow," Jess said. "I mean, I always knew Overbrook was creepy, but I didn't know he was a pervert."

"Actually, he was only twenty-five when it happened," Michelle said, "and the student was eighteen." I couldn't believe Michelle was defending him.

"It's still pretty shady," Jess said.

"Just listen," Elise said, continuing. "After the scandal, Overbrook came to America, changed his name slightly, and tried to put his past behind him."

"But it caught up with him," Michelle said.

"Wait a minute," I said. "So Overbrook is resigning because he had inappropriate relations with a student thirty years ago?"

"Not exactly," Elise said. "He's resigning because the school where he taught in London was . . . an all-boys school."

It took me a moment for the implication to register. "Do you mean . . . ?" And suddenly it all made sense. "But then why . . . why would he come down so hard on you and Jess?" I asked Michelle. "Why was he so unsupportive?"

Michelle sighed. "I think because we reminded him of everything he'd tried so hard to forget. He was so scared of people finding out the truth about him that he decided the best thing to do was pretend it didn't exist. Try to keep everything safe and secure inside his little bubble."

"His snow globe," I said.

"What?" Elise said.

"Nothing. Never mind. So, Elise, why didn't your dad go public with this information?" I asked.

"It didn't feel right," she said. "My dad wasn't about to out Overbrook to the world. It's his secret, something he's had to come to terms with on his own. As much of a bastard as he is, my dad wouldn't expose him like that."

Just like Hester wouldn't expose Dimmesdale. And Jess wouldn't expose Michelle. People had to learn to accept themselves on their own terms.

After we'd recovered from the shock, we went back to join the party. Overbrook was walking around saying his good-byes to various girls and their parents, seeming genuinely sad about leaving. I suddenly saw him with new eyes. All his ego and bluster seemed to have deserted him. He looked like a smaller, withered version of himself, much like Chillingworth had after Dimmesdale finally broke free from his control.

It must have been painful for him to bury the truth about himself for so many years. And lonely. I actually felt a little sorry for him.

The final days of school were a breeze. Since I'd already taken AP exams in biology, history, and English, my only final exam was French, and it was a cakewalk. When I turned the test in to my proctor, she told me that Madame Favier had requested to see me in her office.

Curious, I walked over to Easty Hall with a slight bounce in my step, excited that summer break was about to begin. I found Madame sitting at her desk, grading her first round of exams. When she saw me, she jumped up from her chair, beaming.

"Ah, Emma, asseyez-vous s'il vous plaît. J'ai des bonnes nouvelles et bonnes nouvelles!" This, I liked the sound of: She had good news and more good news.

I sat down across from her and listened as she told me that Overbrook's resignation had negated the need for his recommendation for the scholarship to Paris. So long as the acting headmaster gave his approval, our sister school would accept me into the study program.

I knitted my brow in confusion. "So I need Mr. Fairchild's recommendation now?" I said. "But Elise got the scholarship already. Her dad's not going to take it away from his own daughter to give it to me."

"That's the other good news," she said. "I explained to the school's director the unfortunate circumstances of your case and some of the mitigating factors in Overbrook's refusal to write the recommendation. Given the awkwardness of having already awarded the scholarship to someone else, the director agreed to open up two slots for next year. There is still only one scholarship available, but Elise and her father have turned down the money. They are willing to pay the full tuition."

"You're kidding," I said.

"No, Emma, I'm not. So long as your parents consent, you're going to Paris next year!"

I staggered to my feet while Madame hugged me. She seemed genuinely thrilled to be the one to deliver the good news. I was still in shock.

I was a little concerned about telling my father I was going to Paris again. This hadn't been an easy year for him as far as I was concerned. But I had every confidence he'd deal with this just as he dealt everything else in my life: with initial skepticism and eventual acceptance. He really had no choice. This was my life, not his.

I left her room in a bit of a daze and thought about how strange life could be. Despite all the turmoil and drama of this year, certain people had come through for me in the end. And they weren't necessarily the ones I'd expected. Elise. Mr. Fairchild. Even Flynn. I guess people weren't all good or all bad. In *The Scarlet Letter*, Dimmesdale finally owns up to his mistakes and takes Hester's hand in public. Even old Chillingworth leaves his entire fortune to Pearl, ensuring a good life for her. Redemption sometimes comes from unlikely places.

On our final night at Lockwood, the new "Fearsome Four"

met in the lounge to say good-bye before leaving for summer break. Elise had already broken the good news about Paris.

Michelle pouted. "So Owen, Flynn, Elise, and now you are all going to Europe? Is this some kind of conspiracy?"

"I'm not going anywhere," Jess said, grabbing Michelle's hand. "Lockwood's going to be like the island of misfit toys next year. You and I should room together."

"Absolutely," Michelle said.

"Oh, Michelle," Elise said, "I want you to look after Odin for me. I wish I could explain to him where I'm going. He's going to be so lonely."

"I'll take good care of him," Michelle said. "And I'll ride him whenever I can. I've been thinking about getting back into riding."

I smiled at her pronouncement. Because I'd been thinking about getting into writing again, too. It seemed as much as things changed in life, some things remained the same. There was comfort in that.

The next day, Michelle and I emptied our room, packed our suitcases in the Volvo, and drove away for the summer. I dropped Michelle off at her aunt's, and we chatted a bit as Darlene stuffed us with pastries. Then I finished the remainder of the drive on my own.

When I got home, my dad and Barbara and Grandma Mackie were all waiting for me. Barbara had made a big dinner in my honor since I'd somehow finished the year with a 4.4 weighted GPA. Not knowing exactly how to tell them that Paris was on again, I wore my beret to the table.

"Uh-oh, it's the return of the beret," Barbara said when I walked into the dining room.

"Oh no," my dad said. "You didn't get a blue streak in your hair this time, did you?"

"What would you say if I told you it was blue, white, and red?"

"Huh?" my dad said.

"You know, the colors of the French flag?" He eyed me suspiciously, so I told them about getting the scholarship back.

Silence followed until my Grandma Mackie began to clap. Then Barbara followed suit. My dad was outnumbered. He had no choice but to join in.

"Here's the deal," he said after the applause died down. "You're going to Paris in the fall, but before you do, I own you. You're going to get all your college applications in before you leave. You're going to crack open that SAT book once a day. You're going to work for me part-time making deliveries in the Volvo. And you are only going to wear that stupid beret on Bastille Day, got it?"

I laughed and nodded. "Got it."

We finished our meal, and I helped Barbara with the dishes, then we all sat out on the deck and watched the first fireflies emerge from the ground. Grandma and I chatted in the den until I got sleepy, then I said good night and headed up for bed. But I couldn't fall asleep right away. I was too excited about next year.

I sat in bed, flipping through a Parisian travel guide. My fingers swept across a map of the different arrondissements, stopping on sites I wanted to see: the Musée D'Orsay, Sacré-Coeur, the Tuileries, the Opera House. I'd study French literature and Gothic architecture, maybe even French cooking. And the best thing was, I'd learn how to be on my own. But I wouldn't be lonely. Owen and Flynn would come visit, and Elise would be there, too. Even though we weren't exactly best friends, I was pretty sure Elise had my back.

I must have dozed off because at some point I found myself on the beach, walking across the dunes and toward the stretch of water where my mother drowned. Only I wasn't a child this time, and I no longer felt afraid. The ocean was calm and serene, and I walked to the shoreline without diffi-culty.

My mother looked back at me once, her beautiful hair bil-lowing in the moonlight, and then she dove into the water, disappearing peacefully into the silvery waves. I felt no need to go after her. She had broken free. Or maybe I had finally let her go.

I woke a little before dawn. But I knew I'd never get back to sleep. Instead, I threw on running clothes and took a quick glance at myself in the mirror. The red streak was almost gone, grown out and faded. But Hester's influence on me would never be forgotten.

Just like my mother's. Even though she was gone, I knew that whenever I needed her, I could call on her. Sort of like prayer. I wasn't entirely sure if God existed or where to find him if he did. He was part of a universe I couldn't see or touch. But I had to believe in some things even if I couldn't prove their existence. Like God. Magic. Love.

The sun was rising steadily as I ran across the beach, head-ing toward the lighthouse. Once there, I climbed out onto the rocks below it and stood with my back to the sun, my face toward the ocean, which as always, reminded me of Gray.

Were Gray and I destined to be star-crossed lovers, I won-dered, forever separated like Hester and Dimmesdale?

The more I experienced of life, the more I realized that des-tiny was a myth. Hester didn't crumble and fall apart after Dimmesdale died on that scaffold. She summoned her strength, moved with Pearl to Europe, and started life over again. She made a decision to keep on living.

Love itself was a decision. And if Gray and I really loved each other, we would stay together because we wanted to, not because it was written in the stars. Being with Gray wasn't my destiny but my choice.

I glanced up at the lighthouse, its beacon a steady source

of comfort for all those waiting for someone to come home. The sky was pink with sunrise, clouds forming on the horizon. I tried not to think of that old sailor's proverb.

Instead I imagined Gray somewhere boundless and blue. And I stood on that rock and put one more wish out into the universe.

A Touch of Scarlet Playlist

Music is a huge part of both my writing process and the world of my books. In *A Touch of Scarlet,* several of the characters sing, play instruments, even write their own music. And the big finale of the book—the alternative prom that Emma and her friends organize—is a bit unconventional in that the guests provide their own entertainment by singing karaoke!

While I was writing *A Touch of Scarlet,* I created a playlist of songs that either feature specifically in the book or set the mood for a particular scene. If you haven't read the book yet, be wary, as there are a few spoilers ahead. To hear the playlist online, please visit the Links & Extras page of my website: evemariemont.com/extras.html.

"Falling Off the Face of the Earth" by Matt Wertz
The lyrics of this song perfectly echo Emma's and Gray's feelings as they spend their last night together before Gray leaves for the Coast Guard.

"Dream On" by Aerosmith
Michelle plays this song in the dorm on the first day back at school. Not only does Michelle love classic rock, but the lyrics are appropriate, too, as they deal with letting go of the past and moving on—an important theme in the book. The song is also about the power of dreams, which guide Emma on her path to self-discovery.

"They" by Jem
This song captures the hardships of living under peer pressure and making decisions based on an arbitrary set of rules dictated by the popular crowd. I always associate the "they" of the title with Elise and her friends.

"You Will Leave a Mark" by A Silent Film
I have no idea what this song is actually about, but I modeled "Capsized Heart" (the song Owen writes) on this song. I also think Owen would sound just like A Silent Film's lead singer.

"Where I Stood" by Missy Higgins
This song captures the insecurities and doubts that cause Gray to break up with Emma. It also seems to speak of Gray's regret when he sees Emma with Owen on New Year's Day.

"Mr. Suit" by Wire
Both the lyrics and the fast-driving rhythms of this punk song reflect Flynn's rebellious, bad-boy attitude. I imagine him playing this song at the cast party in the garden after *The Crucible*.

"Clubbed to Death" by Rob Dougan
While this song has no lyrics, the music is powerful and dark and would make an excellent soundtrack to Emma's travels in search of the witch caves. I imagine her listening to this song on her iPod as she runs through the woods.

"You Can't Escape Them" by Weaver at the Loom
This song is about living in fear and trying to break through the doors that hem us in. I associate it with Michelle's attempts to face the truth about herself.

"Run" by Snow Patrol
Emma dances with Owen to this song at the Depot, but the lyrics remind her of Gray, thus ruining what could have been a romantic moment.

"Ready to Start" by Arcade Fire
This song plays while Emma drives her dad's Volvo back to school after spring break. Even though the lyrics are some-

what strange and ambiguous, the chorus makes me think of Emma's newfound confidence and independence.

"A Kind of Hope" by Pilot Speed
This song plays after Gray returns to Emma and they drive into Waverly Falls; it has a great energy that mirrors Emma's hopes for a reconciliation.

Songs Sung Karaoke-Style at the Alternative Prom

"Sympathy for the Devil" by the Rolling Stones
I picture Flynn kicking off the karaoke night by singing this song in a British accent and dancing around onstage doing Mick Jagger's rooster strut.

"We Are Young" by fun. and "When You Were Young" by the Killers
These two songs, as their titles suggest, are about being young and living in the moment, but they both have an undercurrent of sadness and regret. Perfect for prom night, right?

"Gravity" by Sara Bareilles
The lyrics of this song speak of wanting to free oneself from another's "gravity." Emma sometimes feels this way about Gray, knowing she should move on but feeling helpless to do so.

"Count on Me" by Bruno Mars
I knew Emma had to get onstage at the prom and sing a karaoke song for Owen, but I struggled with which song to choose. I went through several possibilities, but all the songs about being sorry seemed dated or too melodramatic. So I began looking at friendship songs instead, and this one seemed perfect—sweet but not too sappy.

"Love Will Tear Us Apart" by Joy Division
Flynn sings a haunting version of this song while Emma stands on the sidelines at the prom, watching all her friends dance and realizing she's going to be just fine on her own.

Final Song

"I Will Follow You into the Dark" by Death Cab for Cutie
I imagine this bittersweet song playing "over the credits" as Emma stands beneath the lighthouse thinking about Gray and wondering what the future holds.

The Unbound trilogy comes to a breathtaking finale
in Eve Marie Mont's

A PHANTOM ENCHANTMENT

Read on for a special sneak preview and, like Emma,
get lost in a good book . . . literally!

What struck me first as we left the airport and got onto the highway was how all cities look alike, to a certain extent. Somehow I'd been expecting Paris to beguile me from the moment the plane touched down, but as we followed a trash truck through sluggish traffic, passing railroad tracks and gas stations and graffitied buildings, I began to feel I'd been duped by Hollywood.

Even when we entered the city limits, the landscape still mirrored urban America with its MoneyGram and telecom shops, ethnic takeout places, characterless office buildings, and of course, the omnipresent McDonald's. It was all a bit disheartening.

Until we went below an underpass somewhere around Gare du Nord. Then it was as if some mystical creature had waved her magic wand and commanded that everything from that point on be enchantingly beautiful. Unlike American cities, which were vertical, modern, and masculine, Paris was old, ornate, and sprawling, like a queen on a divan with no other purpose than to delight her own senses. Each corner was bedecked with some sign of the city's history—a church, a statue, an obelisk—and I wanted to stop at them all to find out what they signified.

Elise told me we weren't far from Montmartre. From this

vantage point, I couldn't see anything, but in my mind I envisioned Sacré-Coeur's alabaster domes rising up against the blue sky, saw the painted ladies of Lapin Agile, squinted at the neon lights of Moulin Rouge. I wanted to pinch myself.

Here was quintessential Paris—the ivory stone buildings with wrought-iron balconies and window boxes full of flowers, their mansard rooftops gilded by the sun. We came to a giant circle bustling with people, and then Monsieur Crespeau took one of the narrow avenues that spiderwebbed off it. Each road was tree-lined and flanked by rows of buildings, houses, shops, cafés. One building was so delicate and narrow I wondered how it didn't topple over. Another building in a wedge shape looked like a slice of wedding cake.

For the first time since I'd signed the scholarship forms, I began thinking of this trip as more than just a notch in my résumé.

Paris was going to be an adventure.

We came to yet another circle with a statue of an armed woman in the middle, and then Monsieur Crespeau mumbled something, I think "Tout proche" or "Very near." I glanced up at a street sign and saw we were on Boulevard du Temple, a broad thoroughfare that separated the 3rd and 11th arrondissements. Along this road, we passed dozens of cafés, patisseries, boulangeries, charcuteries—all of them with brightly colored awnings and outdoor tables beckoning you to sit down and relax, have a bite, stay a while. I'd never seen more eating establishments in one city block. My grandma was right—food did seem to make the Parisian world go round.

I could see the July Column of the Bastille up ahead, so I knew we were almost there, and then we turned on Rue Saint-Antoine, and Monsieur Crespeau nodded at a building about three storefronts wide and five stories high, but otherwise resembling every other building we'd seen except for its arched blue doorway.

"Voici," he said.

He pulled the van onto a tiny alleyway off Rue Saint-Antoine and parked in a small space reserved for the school. We got out, and Monsieur Crespeau told us he'd bring our luggage directly to our rooms so we could report directly to Mademoiselle Veilleux, the head of the school, in the administrative building across the quad. When I insisted we could carry our own bags, he waved us off with his enormous hand and sent us on our way.

Elise and I were staring at a stone wall with a massive iron gate, but all we could see through its slats were narrow little trees. But then Monsieur Crespeau opened the gate, and we walked into an immense courtyard with tennis courts, green lawns, cobbled squares, and manicured walking paths. Who would have thought that tucked hidden away in the middle of Paris was this dream of a campus?

Since school wasn't in session until next week, the courtyard was empty, so it seemed more like a church cloister than a schoolyard. We followed the main walkway as instructed and entered the administrative building, then walked down a long hallway, all gleaming floors and domed ceilings. An arched doorway led to a spacious foyer or lobby area with an even higher ceiling and a black-and-white floor tiled in geometric patterns.

A tiny woman came out of a far hallway and began walking toward us, her heels echoing through the cavernous space. "Ah, bienvenue," she said, her voice low and rich. "I am Mademoiselle Veilleux. Monsieur Crespeau just called to tell me you were here. Bienvenue, bienvenue!"

She kissed us both on each cheek and smiled warmly. Her black hair was pulled off her face in a bun, but instead of making her look prim and schoolmarmish, it made her look beautiful in an almost alien way. Her porcelain skin looked like it was lit from within, and a rose-colored scarf only enhanced the effect. As I'd come to expect from French women, she exuded style in a slim black skirt suit with impossibly high black heels.

"I am so glad you were able to come a few days early before the rest of the students arrive," she said with a charming French accent. "It will give you time to get acquainted with the building and its facilities and, of course, your schedules."

She handed us our course schedules, which pretty much had us occupied from eight in the morning until five in the evening most days. Our jaws must have dropped because she explained, "The French academic schedule may be a bit more rigorous than what you're used to. As you know, we had to schedule you at the Lycée Internationale for your Advanced Placement courses, so three days a week, you will be required to take the Metro across town. But the school is right by the Tour Eiffel, and I think you'll enjoy doing some sightseeing after your classes."

If we're not completely exhausted, I thought.

"I'm sure for now you're very tired and would like to get situated in your rooms." She began walking us out the way we'd come. "Elise, your father took the liberty of calling and asking to have your rooms furnished and decorated. I hope you don't mind."

"No, not at all," Elise said, opening her mouth in a big circle and looking at me.

We crossed the courtyard to one of the dormitories, then took the stairwell five flights up. I was glad now that Monsieur Crespeau had been so insistent about bringing our bags, although I wondered how he managed with his limp.

When we reached the top floor, Mademoiselle Veilleux didn't even seem winded. She led us down the hallway and hesitated at a door, then moved to the next room and pulled out two keys attached to velvet ribbons. "There are two adjoining bedrooms with a shared bathroom. The room on the left is a bit smaller and well . . . no, never mind. It's just a tri-fle smaller, so perhaps you could flip a coin to decide?" She looked a bit flustered suddenly, like she'd momentarily for-gotten her manners, but then she composed herself and handed both keys to me. "I'll leave you to your unpacking, but please don't hesitate to call me in the main office if you have any questions. Oh, and since the dining hall is not open yet, lunch is on me," she said. "Most everyone in the neighborhood knows who I am, so just find a place you like and give them my card. I'll take care of the bill."

We thanked her profusely and watched as she glided back down the hallway on those impossible heels.

Elise looked at me and smiled. "Is this amazing or what?"

"Yeah, except for the nine-hour school day."

"I know. What's with that? Quelle douleur."

"So," I said, dangling the keys from my fingers, "heads or tails?"

She leaned her head to the side and gave me her patented pout-smile. "I was hoping you'd take the smaller one. You don't need as much space as I do."

"Is that a jab about my height?"

"No, your wardrobe. I know you didn't pack as many clothes as I did."

I couldn't argue there. I imagined poor Monsieur Crespeau carrying all Elise's suitcases up those narrow stairs.

"Fine," I relented. "I'll take the smaller room."

But believe me, it didn't matter. My room was bigger than the one I'd shared with Michelle by at least double, with a ten-foot ceiling to boot. The walls had been painted lavender with ivory trim, and Mr. Fairchild had bought us comforters to match. A plum-colored settee sat in front of a large, ornate mirror with a Gothic frame. My luggage sat neatly in front of a built-in closet, partially camouflaged by a purple organza drape. But the best part was the immense French windows, which opened out over the alleyway so I could see the rooftops of Rue Saint-Antoine. It was the most beautiful dorm room I had ever seen or was likely ever to see again.

After a few minutes of inspecting and sighing happily, Elise and I met in the bathroom, which was equally impressive with a tub and shower combo, double sink, toilet and bidet (which I'd been warned about), all of them fitted with gleaming brass fixtures.

"Did this place used to be a hotel or something?" Elise asked.

"Actually, it used to be a prison," I said. "Well, not really. The building's nineteenth century, but the school is built on the grounds of the old Bastille."

"How do you know?"

"I read about it online. In fact, Saint-Antoine was sort of ground zero for the revolution. Have you read *A Tale of Two Cities*?" She shook her head. "Dickens describes this neighborhood as a cesspool of humanity with raw sewage pouring through the streets, lots of derelicts and drunks. And revolutionaries, of course. Apparently, the ghosts of the Bastille still haunt these grounds."

"Oooooooh," she said. "Spooky." But her face betrayed the tiniest hint of fear. "Speaking of derelicts and drunks, where do you want to eat? We can drink wine here. Like, legally."

I laughed. "You've been here before. Do you know of a good place?"

"I know of a thousand good places."

We ended up walking toward Place de la Bastille. Across the circle by the July Column was a large round building with a mirrored exterior. It was very modern and seemed out of place here amid all this history.

"What's that ugly building?" I said.

"Oh, that's the Opera House."

I had seen pictures of the Opera House, had watched the

movie version of *The Phantom of the Opera* twice. I knew
that the Opera House was majestic and grand, with white
columns and gold statues and a giant green dome, plus a
grand foyer inside with that famous cascade of stairs. There
was no way this was the Opera House.

Elise saw my confusion. "Paris has two operas now. There's
the Palais Garnier, which is the one you've seen in the movies.
And then there's this new one, Opéra Bastille. These days the
old Opera House is used mostly for ballets, while the operas
are usually performed here. I thought you would have known
that already, Ms. Travel Guide."

I was surprised I didn't. And then I remembered a pact
Owen and I had made to go to our first opera together. I had
imagined us getting all dressed up and taking a cab to the
Opera House, then climbing that giant marble staircase and
taking our seats inside the red-and-gilt theater under an enormous chandelier. I laughed now at my romanticism. He'd
probably take Elise now instead of me.

We turned toward the river onto Rue Henri IV, a street
filled with produce stands and bookstores and flower stalls
and eateries. Vespas and bicycles filled the stands on each
corner. Elise recommended a brasserie just a block from the
river with ample outdoor seating and chalkboards advertis-
ing their specials.

I got shivers as the host seated us at a table with a view of
the small park across the street. The interior looked like
something from the set of *Amélie*—all dark wood and brass
rails with art nouveau lamps and golden décor. It was
thrilling to read a menu entirely in French and then order in
French from a real garçon.

I ordered a croque-madame and a glass of Beaujolais, and
Elise got the salmon tartare with a side salad and a glass of
Chardonnay. When the food arrived, I was literally salivat-
ing. Since we hadn't eaten a decent meal in so long, the wine
went straight to our heads, and we were both feeling a little

giddy. Michelle had been worried about me eating enough here, but if all the food tasted this savory and delicious, my bigger problem would be my cholesterol and fat intake—although conventional wisdom said that the French, despite their rich diet, were far healthier than Americans because they ate sensibly and walked a lot.

We would soon discover the rigors and pleasures of walking around Paris. After a leisurely lunch, we decided to cross the river and check out the Rive Gauche, or the Left Bank—famous as the haunt of bohemian writers and artists during the turn of the century. We paused halfway across the Pont de Sully, and I nearly yelped when I saw Notre Dame in the distance.

"Oh my God, that's it!"

Elise, jaded from years of traveling to Paris, just laughed at me, but it was surreal to see this magnificent place I'd read about and seen in so many movies suddenly here in front of my eyes. Like Dorothy must have felt when she first spied Oz.

"It's kind of a long walk, but we can see it up close if you want. Actually, we should stop at Shakespeare and Company on the way. You are going to love this bookstore!"

Once across the bridge, we walked the Quai de la Tournelle and took a set of stairs down to the cobbled walkway that ran along the Seine. There, I saw the ubiquitous riverboats and had a perverse desire to be an ugly American and hop aboard. I knew Elise would never go for that, so we kept walking under the shade of the trees, chatting idly.

"This looks like a good place to go running," I said.

Elise scoffed. "Emma, Parisian women don't run, unless they're chased. It's a very American thing to do."

"So what?" I said. "I am American after all."

"I'm just saying people might look at you like you're some kind of freak."

"Well-traveled territory," I said.

We continued our stroll on the pedestrian walkway until

we neared the bookshop. The neighborhood where we emerged was swimming with tourists, souvenir shops, and flashy restaurants.

"Wow, it's so different here," I said. "Crowded. I guess because we're near Notre Dame."

"Oh, this is nothing. Paris clears out in August because that's when the French take their holidays. It's actually quiet here compared to what I'm used to."

Despite being so famous, Shakespeare and Company was set back from the main street on a cobbled alley behind a median of trees. We went inside and were bombarded, not surprisingly, by books of every color, genre, and size. Every square inch of wall boasted bookshelves packed to the rim so you actually felt a little overwhelmed by the towering stacks and the dizzying swirls of dust. A soot-speckled cat wandered close my by ankles as we walked past books piled shoulder-high on tables, fine arts prints, ladders perched precariously against shelves, and quirky signs and postcards. This was clearly a place for people who loved the written word.

The smell of must and old books permeated the air, and I inhaled deeply, feeling once again a pang of disbelief and gratitude that I was here. I wandered back toward a cozy nook off the main room and let my fingers graze across the spines of antique books—leather, cloth, and paper. And then I saw an irresistible copy, especially considering where I was: *Le Fantôme de l'Opéra,* Gaston Leroux's gothic masterpiece written in the original French.

Like almost every American, I had seen the Andrew Lloyd Webber musical years ago, but I'd never read the book. This copy was from 1965 and had a red cloth binding with a black-and-white illustration on the front of a skeletal Phantom in top hat clutching the fainting body of a beautiful girl. It was cheesy and over-the-top and wonderful. I snatched the book without a second thought and handed over my ten euros at the front counter. Elise came up a few minutes later to pay for her stack of books, and then we headed with our spoils across the river to visit Notre Dame.

Nothing can really prepare you for the splendor of this cathedral. Yes, it's made of stone and glass like any other church, and you've probably seen its image enough times on postcards to think you've experienced it already. But Notre Dame is truly a wonder of human ingenuity and artistry. The west end is impressive with its Gothic stone towers and rose window glowing under the sun, but it was the east end that floored me with its gravity-defying buttresses and that delicate spire, like an ornament of spun sugar. I couldn't wait to come back and see it at night. But for now, Elise and I were practically the walking dead, so we deferred the full tour for another day and started back toward school and what would be our home for the year.

Everything was quiet as we entered our dormitory and climbed up five staircases, listening to the creaks our feet made on the wooden stairs. Even though it was only a little after six, I was bone weary and ready to fall into that lovely lavender bed. But we'd walked several miles in full sun, so I decided to take a shower first, checking with Princess Elise to make sure she didn't need the bathroom.

Afterward, I wrapped myself up in my fluffy robe and sat on the bed, then called my dad for a brief rundown of the day's events. Then I called Gray, hearing his phone ring four times before the inevitable recording of his voice mail. I left him a message saying that I missed him and wished he were here, not in a trite postcard sort of way, but deeply and truly. Gray would love Paris, and we would love it even more together.

I went to stand by the window and flung open the panes to the Paris sky. The sun hadn't set yet, but it had dipped below the buildings, casting my little rooftop view in glowing silhouette. Rooftops gleamed ochre and patina green. Not a soul ventured through the alleyway, and except for the low rumble of traffic, it seemed for a moment as if I was entirely alone in the city.

My freshman year of high school, I'd had virtually no friends, and I'd struggled mightily over the past two years for the friends I had now. I was no stranger to loneliness. But this feeling tonight was different. Standing at an open window in a virtually empty dormitory in a foreign city, it felt like loneliness was a presence in the room with me, sucking up all the air, making my heart thud against my rib cage, breeding panic. I closed the window and tried to breathe.

Why doesn't Gray call me back? Where is he tonight?

And then I remembered. In California, it was just eleven o'clock in the morning. He was probably right in the middle of his EMT training.

To distract myself, I decided to unpack, slowly filling the closet with my paltry wardrobe, tossing lotions and hairbrushes and perfumes onto my vanity. And that's when I found the gift bag from Darlene.

I riffled through the tissue paper and found a bottle of dried rose petals, a length of red yarn, and a compass. A tiny note was tied to the neck of the bottle that read: *Here are the instructions for the spell to reunite lovers, as promised. But remember, love casts its own spell.*

Even now, Darlene was looking out for me.

I set the ingredients down on the vanity and looked into the antique mirror. It must not have been one of Mr. Fairchild's purchases, as it seemed genuinely old with scuffing along the frame and silver-black marbling on the surface. A shudder ran through me as I watched my reflection warp slightly in the old glass.

There was something sinister about mirrors, especially old ones.

I remembered last spring at Michelle's birthday/slumber party, we had been playing a silly campfire game, the one where you spin around three times in a darkened room chanting

"Bloody Mary" and then open your eyes in front of a mirror. Legend says you're supposed to see the face of your beloved in the mirror.

And I really had. I'd spun around and said the words and opened my eyes to see Gray's ghostly image staring back at me. Of course, I had screamed and we'd all erupted into giggles and written it off as the power of suggestion, but there was something almost supernatural about mirrors and their ability to reflect and distort reality.

Mirrors were also a powerful symbol of the self. Last year, I'd suffered from what I guess you could call waking nightmares, trance-like states in which I'd occasionally wander away from campus, sometimes waking up hours later in the woods, and one time, in a cave.

Darlene had taught me a lucid dreaming technique that had ended my sleepwalking days for good. She told me, "Whenever you get the sense that you're dreaming, create a mirror image of yourself and send that version into the dream so your body stays put."

The first time I'd tried the technique, it had kept me from wandering, and I'd been using it ever since whenever I felt my dream world pulling me too deeply.

Right now, I wished I could somehow send my mirror image out to Gray, wherever he was. I missed him that much. But I wouldn't use the spell. As Darlene warned me, I'd wait until I needed it and hope I never would.

Feeling fatigue and muscle aches overwhelm me, I crawled into bed, luxuriating in the satiny sheets, the plush pillows, the dense comforter. Even though it wasn't cold in the room, I wanted the comfort of thick blankets pulled up tight around me.

As tired as I was, I usually needed to read in order to fall asleep. So I grabbed my copy of *Le Fantôme de l'Opéra* from the nightstand. Reading a book in French took a lot more time and focus than reading in English, so I struggled to get through the first five pages. The book begins with a prologue by the author explaining how he learned of the Opéra ghost's existence by studying interviews, letters, and other documents from the archives of the National Academy of Music. The first chapter launches into his reconstruction of the Phantom's tale.

Rumors about a ghost with death's head on his shoulders are flying though the dressing rooms of the Opera House. An unseen tyrant has been threatening the managers into reserving a private box for him. And then, a scene changer is found dead in a third-floor cellar, hanging from a beam. The police suspect suicide. And yet when they go to cut the man's body down, the rope he'd been hanged on is gone.

I stopped reading and shivered as if a cool breeze had come through the window. Impossible, since I'd closed it earlier.

And then I heard voices, faint and murmuring. They were so quiet I couldn't tell where they were coming from or if they were speaking French or English. Ordinarily, I would have attributed the noises to a television program, but Mr. Fairchild hadn't bought either of us a television. I perked my ears to see if I could discover the source of the sounds. They seemed to be coming from the hallway.

I breathed a sigh of relief. Maybe some students had arrived back to school a few days early. As scared as I was, I crept out of bed and padded to the door, then stood there, heart racing, trying to drum up the courage to open it.

Come on, Emma. Stop being such a coward. It's just the novel taking hold of your imagination or your own stories of the ghosts of the Bastille getting the best of you.

Quickly, before I could wimp out, I sprang the latch and whisked open the door. I looked left and right and even went to stand out in the middle of the hallway. Nothing.

Laughing at my own superstitious nature, I went back inside the room. But the moment I shut the door, the voices resumed, fainter this time, like they were moving away from me.

What if I'm dreaming right now?

I looked around for signs of dreaming, what they call "reality tests." *Do my hands look normal? Can I flip the light switch off and on? Can I tell the time on the digital clock? Can I read a piece of text?*

After trying each, I determined that I was still awake.

And then I remembered another reality test: to look into a mirror. If the image is absent, blurry, misshapen, or doesn't match the objects around you, it could signal that you're dreaming.

Quite honestly, I'd gotten myself so worked up I was afraid to look into the mirror. But I knew I was just being silly.

I went to stand in front of the mirror and, as quickly as I could, I glanced into the surface. Recoiling in fright, I ran to my bed and jumped inside, cowering under the covers. After four successful tests, I was pretty sure I was awake. Which made the truth all the more horrifying.

Because even though I'd only caught a glimpse out of the corner of my eye, the reflection I'd seen in the mirror wasn't my own.